LAST CALL

JAMI GRAY

Cover Art: Deranged Doctor Design, www.derangeddoctordesign.com
Publisher: Celtic Moon Press First edition, 2026
ISBN: 978-1-948884-76-1 (ebook) ISBN: 978-1-948884-77-8 (print)

sign up for free reads from jami!

Join Jami's newsletter to be the first to hear about new releases, free books, special prices and other nifty events.

Sing up at: https://www.subscribepage.com/jami-gray-books

what readers say…

About Arcane Transporter:
"Taking a refreshing approach to fantasy magic, this fast-paced, economical thriller is told from a highly likable perspective." —
Red Adept Editing

About PSY-IV Teams:
"This story is an emotional roller coaster, from betrayal, anger, fear, love…" —InD'tale Magazine

About the Kyn Kronicles:
"…a fantastic paranormal action novel is quite possibly the best book I've read this year. I could not put it down, and had to exercise serious self-control to keep from staying up all night to finish it." —The Romance Reviews

About Fate's Vultures:
"…if you like your characters with a bit more bite, with secrets, with hidden agendas, and all those sorts of things, and your worlds are a far more deadlier place, then this is for you." —
Archaeolibrarian

also by jami gray

Arcane Wonderland

Last Call

Bitter Spirits

Rune & Tonic

ARCANE TRANSPORTER

Ignition Point (*Prequel Novella*)

Grave Cargo

Risky Goods

Lethal Contents

Collision Course

Blind Spot

Terminal Drift

THE KYN KRONICLES

Shadow's Edge

Shadow's Soul

Shadow's Moon

Shadow's Curse

Shadow's Dream

Shadow's Fall

Tangled in Shadows (*Short Story Collection*)

FATE'S VULTURES

Lying in Ruins

Beg for Mercy

Caught in the Aftermath

Fear the Reaper

PSY-IV TEAMS

Hunted by the Past

Touched by Fate

Marked by Obsession

Fractured by Deceit

Linked by Deception

BOX SETS

PSY-IV Teams Box Set I (Books 1-3)

The Collapse: Fate's Vultures (Books 1-4)

The Kyn Kronicles Box Set (Books 1-6)

Arcane Transporter Box Set I (Books 1-3)

Arcane Transporter Box Set II (Books 4-6)

"There is no chance, no destiny, no fate, that can circumvent or hinder or control the firm resolve of a determined soul."

- Ella Wheeler Wilcox

acknowledgments

With every book I write, there is an entire community at my back ensuring I make it to "THE END", and to them I want to give my profound thanks.

To the readers who keep picking up my books, you guys have made this introverted writer's heart quiver with your kind words and endless excitement about what happens next.

To the friends and family who listen to me take off on strange tangents and patiently wander the wildly uncharted paths they take, I love you all.

To the best three men I know, my Knight in Slightly Muddy Armor and my two Prankster Princes, you guys will never understand how much your support and love gets me through. You guys were the best thing Fate could hand me.

I love you all!

Jami

contents

chapter 1

Cass

"I'M GOING TO KILL HIM," Isa said just loud enough to be heard over the blend of casual conversations and the hip-swinging beat drifting through the bar. She set her tray on the bar top's smooth surface and braced her palms on either side as she leaned in. "I'm fairly certain his body will fit in my trunk."

Unfazed by her friend's violent streak, Cass topped a pair of ice-filled highball glasses with lime slices, to complement the dark rum and ginger beer, and snuck another look at the two men sitting at a nearby high-top. While Isa's intended murder victim was a regular, his friend was new to the establishment and kept catching Cass's eye. Lean muscle, messy brown hair, dark eyes, and an attractive scruff—put it all together, and you got a damn hot version of the boy next door.

Man next door, she amended silently as he caught her gaze and gave her a flirty grin. She quickly looked away, feeling heat bloom along her face. Turning back to the fuming woman in front of her, she warned, "You'd be less likely to get caught if you made it look like an accident." She set the two Dark 'n' Stormy cocktails on Isa's tray. "Gives you deniability when the Cordova Family comes around asking questions."

Isa's full lips, painted deep crimson, twisted into a feral smirk. "That, right there, is why we're friends—because you've got all the angles covered." She straightened but did a half turn so she could aim a glare at her nemesis, who lifted his bottle in a mocking toast. "I swear he comes in just to mess with me."

Personally, Cass suspected there was something much more salacious behind Locke's perverse attention, but she wasn't going to share that suspicion with Isa. Not if she wanted to keep her head on her shoulders. When it came to Locke, her bestie wasn't rational. It didn't help that Locke wasn't hurting for female approval, with his alluring ultra-light-blue eyes and hair a mix of browns and blonds in a shaggy cut, all wrapped up in an edgy bad-boy vibe. He was her best friend's version of catnip.

Cass tapped the rune carved into the quartz screen next to the well, bringing up the next drink order. "You know, you could always ignore him," she suggested as her hands moved by rote to set up four rock glasses.

"Yeah, tried that. Didn't work." Isa turned back to her. "Those mine?"

"Yep." Cass made quick work of the jigger as she measured out the needed shots before adding the quartet to Isa's tray. "Booth nine."

"Got it." Isa picked up her tray then wove her way across the floor to drop the drinks off, passing Locke's table on the way.

The male in question followed the sway of Isa's hips as she stalked by. Cass shook her head in amusement. Dear gods— she wished the two would just hop into bed already, but considering that Locke was a Hound for a powerful Arcane Family, it would be a frigid day in hell before Isa allowed that to happen.

A flicker at the back of the bar snagged her attention. It

wasn't much, just a shift of shadow along the back wall, but it left a sliver of unease crawling down her spine. When the movement came again, she narrowed her eyes and tried to see beyond the bar's atmospheric lighting. As she stared, the wisp of shadow took on the shape of a small screech owl.

How the hell did that get inside the bar?

Before the question could finished forming, her mind stalled. Dread sank sharp nails into her heart, which stopped for a beat before it resumed, stronger than before. She locked eyes on the feathered omen as icy claws of foreboding seared through her veins. A burst of laughter from one of the patrons broke the strange staring contest, causing Cass to blink. She sucked in a hard breath, and when she looked back to where the owl had been, nothing but shadows remained.

You're just tired. Her hands shook as she tried to convince herself it was nothing, but the little voice in the back of her mind cackled like a madwoman. As an Oracle, she knew better. Omens like that always meant something to people cursed with glimpses of the future.

"Hi there. Can I get a rum and coke?"

The request broke through her inner turmoil and snapped her back to the present. Cass faked a smile for the perky brunette standing on the other side. "Sure."

She shoved the uncomfortable premonition into a dark corner, determined to keep her feet in the present as she juggled the multiple incoming drink orders. Maybe later she'd brave wandering those darker fields, but for now, there was work. Midweek might not be the most popular night for a downtown bar in Phoenix, but Wonderland was still admirably busy. What had started out as a unique bohemian underground pub with fantastic drinks, great service, and good food had morphed into an eclectic gathering place. At first, the majority of their customers had been the colorful creatives who drifted in at odd times for a break from their artistic muses, but somehow, word had spread to the various Arcane Guild members looking to kick back and relax, bringing in an edgier crowd. Then came the after-business-hours patrons in their tailored corporate best, wanting to hook up with the more exotic element not found in the land of cubicles. Now each night was an adventure waiting to happen.

Cass loved it—and loved even more the steadily increasing profits she, Isa, and Des shared. Working at Wonderland sure as hell beat the earlier years of wondering if they'd made a mistake by taking on the bar. In the beginning, the situation had been touch-and-go, but their little family of three had carved out a niche in the Arcane world, one they protected as fiercely as any Family did its territory. Unlike the powerful players, who relied on blood connections, their family was tied by choice, which in her opinion was massively preferable.

"Hey, Cass." Leon, their part-time waiter and full-time college student, cleared his tray of empties. "The Long Island on table three wants a heavy pour."

She double-checked the ticket number she was working and saw that Leon's timing was spot-on. "Got it." She finished up with the mojito and G&T then made quick work of the Long Island. "Heard anything on your internship yet?"

He shook his head. "Not yet, but it's only been a couple of days."

"I'm sure you nailed it." She tucked the sprig of mint next to the lemon slice.

The drinks in front of her wavered and disappeared, replaced by an image of Leon working his way through the maze of metal and wires above a stage while directing another man to aim it more to the left. She tilted her head and blinked. The empty tray reappeared, and she set the drinks on it before meeting the hint of stress in his normally bright eyes.

"Don't worry—you're going to be fine," she said.

His grin wavered a bit as he picked up his tray. "From your lips..." Then he was off to work the floor.

"How much do we have in our rainy-day fund?" The rumble of Des's question came from her left as he set two long-neck bottles in front of a mismatched pair of Guild mages, who barely looked up from their conversation. He came to stand next to her and braced a hand on the bar, the overhead lights glinting off the silver rings on his thick fingers.

Cass followed the direction of his gaze to see that Locke had caught Isa by the wrist. "Not nearly enough." There was no doubt Isa was a hair's breadth away from committing murder. "I doubt they'd grant bail—not with this many witnesses."

Des folded his arms over his broad chest, the movement turning his intricate ink into a fluid piece of art. "Think we have a chance in hell of convincing a judge it was a group hallucination?"

She gave an amused snort. "Our drinks are good, but not that good. Besides, Kelly's not working tonight." Having a Charmer on staff had its benefits. Especially when trouble broke out.

"Speaking of which... she told me she got a job offer out of state."

"Well, shit," Cass muttered. "I'm not surprised. She's damn good with crowd control." Hiring college students meant dealing with an expiration date, but they were also the ones who tended to apply for server positions. "How long do we have?"

"End of the month."

She sighed. "I'll get a posting up. We'll need to hire two servers."

"Leon?" he asked.

Nodding, she added a couple of cherries to a cherry blossom, pulled a draft beer, and then headed down the bar to set the order in front of a white-haired couple. After a minute of small talk, she did a visual check of the bar-top patrons. When no one signaled, she headed back to where Des stood. Together they watched the drama playing out between Locke and Isa. They weren't the only ones. The sexual tension between the two was enough to leave helpless bystanders with third-degree burns.

Speaking of which...

Unbidden, her gaze drifted to Locke's friend, only to be captured by his dark eyes. As he watched her, a smile curved his lips. He winked and tipped his drink toward the still-arguing couple as if he found them amusing.

A tendril of desire unfurled, taking her by surprise, and in a space she'd ignored for a long time, something shifted. *Am I really considering...?* Caught in that gaze, she admitted, *Oh yeah, I'm definitely considering taking a chance.* Maybe Isa wasn't the only one about to get burned.

What is it about this man that calls to me? Better question: Is it worth finding out?

"You going to flirt all night or do something about it?"

Des's voice tore her attention away from temptation and spun her into embarrassed discomfort. She shot her friend a frown. "I'm not flirting." *Much.* "I'm providing backup for Isa."

Dark eyebrows rose, and he drawled, "Right."

That was the thing about best friends—they could always see through your shit.

The screech of a chair scraping over the floor brought their attention back to the floor. Des straightened, going from amused to intense in a heartbeat. Cass set a hand on his arm in warning. Locke was on his feet, going nose to nose with Isa. The two were so close that if either took a breath, they'd be locking lips.

Locke's friend leaned over the table and said something

that broke through the impending drama and drew the couple's attention to their audience. Those sitting within orbit of the two made no bones about watching them. Color swept up Isa's face, and she yanked her wrist free of Locke's grip. His expression morphed into a stony mask, and his empty hand flexed as if he battled not to grab Isa again. It didn't work. He caught her arm before she could get more than a few steps away.

In full-on protector mode, Des bit out, "Maybe I should interrupt."

"She's got this," Cass said as Isa shoved her tray against Locke's chest, forcing him back a step.

Isa snapped something threatening that had Locke jerking back and letting her go. She spun around, her long ebony ponytail smacking him, before she stormed toward the bar. A couple of customers scooted their chairs out of her path as she blew through.

"And I'm out," Des declared, leaving Cass on her own.

She shook her head and waited for Hurricane Isa to land. It didn't take long.

Isa slammed her tray on the bar top and all but snarled, "I need two longnecks for the asshole."

Torn between laughter and worry, Cass grabbed two bottles from the nearby well, popped the tops, then set them on the tray. She kept hold of both bottles until Isa looked at her, a storm swirling in her normally calm gaze. *Yep, Locke definitely knows what buttons to push.*

"Breathe, babe, before you burn down the place," Cass said.

Isa seethed for a long moment, color riding high along her cheeks, her breath short, her body stiff. Cass continued to hold her gaze, knowing that when her friend was this worked up, it could take a minute for her to step back from the edge. She just needed to wait Isa out.

Finally, Isa dropped her gaze. She drew in a lungful of air, held it, then blew it out as the angry flush slowly ebbed. "I don't know why I let him get to me."

The answer to that would have left Cass wading in a viper's pit of denial. *Thank you, but no.*

Somewhere behind her, a phone rang, but she left it to Des to answer. Since Cass had gotten her ass handed to her the last time she'd proposed that Isa take Locke for a ride between the sheets, she decided to go for a more mature suggestion.

"You know, maybe if you explained—"

"Cass!" Des called. He was holding the wireless handset to the bar's landline. "You've got a call."

Who in the hell would call me at work? The two most important people in her life were right there at the bar.

Cass let go of the bottle and held a finger up to Isa. "Hold that thought." She took a moment to rinse and dry her hands then met Des by the door to the back space, where the office, bathroom, and kitchen were tucked away. "Who is it?"

Des shrugged. "Didn't ask, but you might want to take it in the office, where it's quiet."

She took the phone from him, put it to her ear, and pushed through the door. When Anna, their cook, looked up from the griddle, Cass lifted her chin then took a left and headed to the office. "Hello?"

"Hello," a man said. "Is this Cassandra Alcmene Ambrose?"

A tendril of trepidation unfurled, and she stilled, her hand still poised above the knob of the office door. A low, indistinct rustle of feathers filled the hall. Her gaze instinctively darted around, even though she knew deep down, there would be no owl. It was a warning, one she hadn't heeded earlier. "This is Cassandra Alcmene."

There was the sound of a throat clearing. "My apologies,

Ms. Alcmene. This is Eric Swanson." He gave his name as if she should know it.

"Who?" Cass opened the office door and stepped inside, doing her best to ignore the nauseating pitch of her stomach. She stood between Des's prized hefty desk and the small sofa that Isa tended to sprawl on. Normally, the familiar space would bring her comfort, but at the moment, it felt foreign.

"Eric Swanson," he repeated in the same alarmingly formal tone. "I'm sorry to call so late, but I was unable to reach you on your cell."

Her gaze darted to her bag, which sat on the floor beside the sofa. Her cell was in it, but she didn't grab it. Instead, she braced herself. Whatever was coming was going to be bad.

"I'm at work." It was a stupid comment, since he was talking to her on Wonderland's landline, but a hint of unreality was wrapping clammy arms around her.

"Right." There was a distinct pause. When he spoke again, it was clear he was trying to tread carefully. "Your parents asked me to inform you that your grandmother has passed away."

The words landed like a sucker punch and left her sucking in air so fast she choked. "What?" An eerie shriek echoed through her mind, nearly drowning out his voice.

"Your grandmother, Iris—she passed away."

"No, there must be some kind of mistake." Her sharp denial couldn't deflect the awful truth, and the reality of it sank deep.

"I'm sorry, Ms. Amb... Alcmene." And he genuinely sounded it. "I know this is unexpected."

Unexpected? No, it's... wrong, so wrong. She stumbled back and sank onto the sofa, her grip on the handset tightening as she fought the urge to babble denials. Her voice squeezed past her tight throat, scraping it raw. "What happened?"

"She passed in her sleep last night." Fortunately, he kept

going, obviously familiar with what questions would come next. "She'd come down with some sort of bug earlier in the week but appeared to be getting better. She joined your parents for dinner last night, confirmed she was feeling better, and then went up to rest. This morning, when she didn't join your parents for breakfast, your father went up and found her."

He continued speaking, his explanation joining the wall of white noise filling her head. Hot and cold chills raced over Cass, leaving her off-kilter. A pain in her scalp had her realizing she was pulling at her hair, a mindless outlet for the storm of sorrow swallowing her whole. Her yaya was supposed to live forever. Seventy was too damn young. Cass fought to find her balance, gaining a delicate grip on the here and now. Her brain was slow to put the words together, but when it did, she went back to what Eric Swanson had said earlier.

"Wait. You said, 'this morning'?" she said, cutting him off midsentence.

There was a pause followed by a soft clearing of his throat. "Unfortunately, your parents were unable to call earlier as they were dealing with other things." Discomfort marred his urbane tone.

A familiar hollow ache pierced the grief. *Unable or unwilling?*

It was a useless question since the answer never changed. She squeezed her eyes closed, pulled the phone from her ear, and pressed it against her forehead, fighting back a sob of pained anger as old resentments rose. The emotional overload triggered a creeping numbness, and she pulled the lack of feeling closer, huddling in its dubious protection as she drew in a breath.

When she opened her eyes, she put the phone back to her ear and managed a faint "Of course they were."

His pause, this time, was longer, and when he spoke again,

it was with a curious gentleness. "Ms. Ambrose." He stopped then continued before she could correct him. "Cassandra, your grandmother loved you very much."

His compassion was enough to trigger tears. The pressure rose, demanding release, but she refused to blink and set the tears free. "I know." Taking another ragged breath, she stared at the desk in front of her. "Can I ask, where is she now?"

"She's staying with Desert Willow Funeral Home here in Vegas, until her service on Saturday morning. She'll be laid to rest next to your grandfather."

A man Cass didn't remember but whom her grandmother had remained utterly devoted to in the twenty-odd years since she'd lost him. *At least now they'll be together.*

"The reading of her will is to follow the service, and your presence, of course, is requested. Your parents have asked that the reading take place in the privacy of their home. If you prefer, I can send you the details for the service."

"To my cell, please." Functioning on autopilot, she managed to stumble through the awkward goodbyes before disconnecting.

Cass held the phone to her chest and slowly curled over her knees. Grief tore through her, sending fissures spiderwebbing through the unnatural numbing fog. Memories rushed in. Her grandmother's joyous laugh. Her strong arms that held a broken teenager desperate to make amends. Iris's unflappable strength as she defied her daughter and son-in-law to support a grandchild left in pieces by her parents' machinations. Her unending patience as an angry Cass pushed every limit she could find and then some. Iris's pride when Cass, Isa, and Des had opened Wonderland. If there was one constant in Cass's life, it was her grandmother's love and acceptance. Without her, Cass was well and truly alone. Again.

What do I do now?

The whisper of wings gained strength, turning into a wave

of deafening thunder. She didn't have the strength to fight her way free of the caustic mix of guilt, love, regret, and grief. The snaking cracks turned blindingly hot, searing past bone, leaving her heart bleeding. A harsh sob finally tore free.

"Cass. Cassandra." An arm curled around her shoulders, pulling her into a broad chest that vibrated with Des's worried rumble. "What happened? Who was that?"

She lifted her head and was surprised when Des's hand went to her face. He pulled off her glasses and set them down.

She sniffled a quiet "Thanks," and used the back of the hand holding the phone to wipe at the wetness on her face. She blinked away the blur of tears as she stared at the handset she held.

"Here, let me take that." Des gently pulled the phone from her hand and set it aside. "Talk to me."

"A family lawyer," she said, answering the easiest question first.

He frowned. "Family lawyer?"

She managed a jerky nod.

"Did something happen to your parents?" he asked, a hint of anger creeping under the worry.

A harsh noise escaped her before she could stop it. "Not them. It's Yaya—" She choked, unable to finish and make it real.

Des's face paled, and his arm tightened. "Iris? Is she okay?"

She couldn't watch him as she said it, so she dropped her gaze, absently realizing she was clutching at Des's T-shirt in a white-knuckle grip. "She's gone."

The chest she leaned against stilled, but the arm around her didn't loosen. "Gone?"

She nodded. "This morning," she rasped. "In her sleep."

He finally inhaled sharply and let out a pained "Gods dammit. I'm so sorry, Cass."

There was nothing to say to that, so she didn't try. The

next couple of minutes passed in silence, each of them lost in thought.

"What do you need?" he finally asked.

For this not to be happening.

But since that wasn't an option... she took a breath and straightened her shoulders. Swallowing hard, she looked up. "I need to get to Vegas."

chapter 2

Grayson

GRAYSON SMOTHERED a chuckle as Locke dropped back into his seat and scowled at his empty beer. It wasn't often he got to witness the Hound getting shot down so hard that he should be standing in the middle of a smoldering crater instead of a very cool bar. Based on the clenched jaw, dark glare, and nearly visible steam coming from Locke's ears, the man didn't enjoy the experience. Which made teasing him an easy call.

"You okay over there, Prince Charming?"

"Fuck you, Gray."

"You're not my type." Grin widening, Grayson picked up his beer. "Not sure you're hers either."

Locke blew out a breath, shook his head, and muttered, "Whatever." He sat back, picked up his bottle, took a long draw, and set it back, all without taking his eyes off the raven-haired woman's ass as she leaned into the bar to talk with the very intriguing bartender.

Speaking of types... There was something about the woman holding court behind the bar. She moved gracefully from one spot to another, a fascinating combination of bohemian and rocker chic. Her hands flew in a graceful sweep, like an orchestra director, as she mixed drink after drink. Her wildly colorful hair, pulled back in a half-tamed tail, held browns and blacks with glints of bright gold and streaks of deep red. It twirled and bounced as she moved.

Grayson's hands itched to sink into that wildness. He was too far away to see her eyes, especially since she wore wire-frame glasses, but he could definitely feel the weight of her gaze every time it landed on him. And he sure as hell hadn't missed the flush of color that filled her witchy face when he winked. Or the way she bit her full lip before she looked away.

"You know," Locke said, "Cass is Isa's best friend."

Grayson reluctantly turned his attention from the two talking women to the man across from him, who now wore a shit-eating grin.

"So," Locke continued, "the odds are not in your favor."

Ignoring his friend's opinion, Grayson focused on what was more important. "Cass?"

Locke's grin widened. "That's the name of the woman you've been eyeing all night."

"Whatever."

Locke laughed, his amusement chasing away the last bits of his earlier irritation. "Don't worry. If those looks she was giving you are anything to go by, she's interested."

A rush of anticipation zipped through him then cooled. Unfortunately, he was heading home the next day, so as much as he might like to pursue the beautiful Cass, it wouldn't happen that night. "Wish you'd brought me here earlier, when I didn't have to head out in the morning."

"Well, I appreciate you coming in to help on such short notice." Locke studied him for a moment. "You sure you don't want to consider moving out here? There's a lot of opportunity for a Key like you in the Valley. Hell, I know for a fact the Cordovas would be happy to put you on their payroll."

Grayson couldn't deny that the idea held some appeal, especially since his feet had been getting itchy. Still, he wasn't sure he should upend his life when the offer hinged on being beholden to an Arcane Family, even if it was one of the better ones. He had no problems contracting out with the Western Arcane Guild, which covered southern California, Texas, Colorado, New Mexico, Utah, Arizona, and Nevada, because that gave him the option to pick and choose his jobs, but tying himself to one Family? *Yeah, no thanks.* Still, he wasn't one to burn his bridges, because you never knew where life would take you.

"I appreciate the offer, but I'm happy in Vegas."

"Fine." Locke shifted in his chair and stretched his legs out alongside their table. He tilted his half-filled bottle and absently rolled it back and forth. "At least I can let Zev know I tried."

"How's he doing?"

About a month earlier, Grayson had been called to one of the Vegas hotels by an old business friend and fellow Guild Key, Lena Davis, to help out Zev Aslanov, the right-hand man of the Cordova Family—well, more like to help out Lena's friend, Rory Costas, another intriguing woman who was more than she appeared to be. The Arcane Transporter was slowly gaining an impressive reputation and not because she was Zev's significant other. The whole situation had been an interesting experience to say the least. The modified bane hex that had been set on Zev should have been fatal, but he'd been protected by something, or someone, very powerful, which had provided Grayson the slim opening he needed to counter the highly illegal and complex plague hex.

"Zev is good, actually. He's getting ready to move in with Rory."

"Wait—I thought Rory and Lena were roommates."

Grayson noticed Cass take a phone from the big guy working with her then disappear into the back.

"They are... were." Locke set his bottle down, his gaze drifting to Isa as she went back to working the floor. "From what Zev told me, Lena wanted to move in with her guy, so she offered Zev the option to buy out her half of the condo. He took her up on it."

"If housing prices are anything like they are in Vegas—"

"Worse," Locke said.

"Then good for him," Grayson finished, trying not to smirk when Isa swept by without acknowledging Locke.

Locke's gaze followed her before he shook his head, lost his sprawl, sat up, and leaned forward, his arms folded on the table. "Yeah, I'm glad I got into my place when I did."

"Speaking of, how's the rehabbing going?"

A year before, Locke had bought a fixer-upper and spent what little spare time he had doing endless projects. As stunning as Locke's results were, Grayson preferred to make a phone call and have someone else deal with things like leaky faucets and nonfunctioning appliances. In any case, he wasn't ready to set down roots.

"I got the master bath done, and now I'm working on the kitchen cabinets."

Locke was in the middle of a story involving a sketchy landscaper when the man behind the bar motioned to Isa. She headed over, the two had a short conversation, then Isa set down her tray and slipped behind the bar. The man went through the door and disappeared. Grayson tuned back in to Locke's story but couldn't stop his occasional glances at the bar. He wondered where Cass was, and—even more irritating —why had the other guy followed her to the back. He squashed the flash of unwarranted jealousy before it could become a massive pain in his ass.

Locke turned to follow Grayson's gaze. "What?"

"It's nothing." Grayson idly played with his beer.

Locke gave him a "don't bullshit me" look before turning to eye Isa, who was setting drinks on the tray of one of the younger servers. He gave a soft grunt of amusement. "Where's Cass?" Before Grayson could answer, he frowned and added, "And Des?"

Grayson stilled his restless movements. "Des?"

"Yeah, the other bartender." Locke scanned the room. "He tends to stay on the floor."

Grayson lifted his bottle and tipped it toward the bar. "They both disappeared through that door."

"Huh." Locke drained his beer and stood, his chair sliding back from the table. "Come on."

Not sure what Locke's deal was, Grayson didn't move. "Where?"

"The bar," he answered in a tone that indicated he questioned Grayson's intelligence. "If Isa's covering the bar, something's up." Empty bottle in hand, Locke turned away. He took a couple of steps then stopped and looked back. "You coming?"

Well, shit. Grayson picked up his nearly empty bottle, finished it, and then got to his feet to follow Locke to the bar. They were almost there when the back door swung open and Des walked through, his face strangely blank as he reached out to tag Isa's arm. In the midst of preparing a drink order, the raven-haired woman stopped and turned. Whatever Des said to her had her shoulders going rigid as she tossed aside a bar towel. The two switched places, Des moving to finish up the drink order and Isa rushing through the door to the back.

Locke's casual stroll went predatory even as a curious tension wrapped around Grayson. Something was definitely up. Des caught their arrival and made a gesture for them to wait as he served customers. They set their empties on the bar top.

It didn't take long before Des was standing across from them and picking up the empties. "Need another?"

"Nah, we're good, thanks." Locke lifted his chin to indicate where Isa had gone. "Everything all right?"

Des tossed the bottles into a bin, and the sharp clash of glass against glass rang out. "Nothing you need to worry about."

Undaunted, Locke kept at the man. "That nothing sure lit a fire under Isa's ass."

"Maybe give said ass a break, yeah?" Des folded his thick arms as he glared at Locke. His dark gaze went to Grayson. "No offense, Don Juan, but you might want to try your luck somewhere else tonight."

"Okay, Des, cut the shit," Locke said. "What's going on? Is there something we can help with?"

Des studied the Hound for a long minute, ignoring the flashes of light that burst like fireflies from the order-display rune embedded in the counter. Concluding his internal debate, he eventually exhaled and grimaced. "As much as I appreciate the offer, this isn't something you can help with unless you want to clear tables."

Grayson was as surprised as Des when Locke took the bartender's suggestion seriously. "If that's what you need, I can do that."

A small curve hit Des's mouth, easing some of the hard edges. He turned to Grayson. "That go for you too?"

Since his early twenties had included working the casino bars in Vegas, it was an easy ask. Besides, he was curious. He shrugged. "If you need the help, sure."

"Right. Meet me at the pass. I'll get you set up."

Grayson followed Locke to the end of the bar, while Des took the same path behind the tall counter, stopping here and there to touch base with patrons. At the pass, Des gave them a quick rundown of the floor, handed them aprons and dish bins, then set them loose. The next few hours were spent clearing tables and helping the two servers.

He kept his eyes peeled for Cass, but she never came back. Isa made a couple of appearances to talk to Des before going back, presumably to be with Cass. The first time Isa came out, she did a double take when she spotted Locke out on the floor, but that was the only look she spared the man. The routine of working the floor was interrupted only once, when Des was busy hustling drinks and a well-lubricated guest was intent on creating a scene. Grayson and Locke set aside their aprons to escort him from the premises and into a rideshare, then it was back to the floor.

Eventually, the door closed behind the last customer. The two young servers settled up with Des while Locke and Grayson upended chairs on tables. Grayson laid his apron on the bar as the door to the back swung open and Cass stepped through. Isa was on her heels, speaking. Her voice was low, but he still caught the tail end of their conversation.

"No way you're staying with those vultures, Cass. It's bad enough you're going to have to deal with their crap on your own."

Gone was the vibrant woman from earlier, and in her place stood a wan, red-eyed, and—based on the stubborn angle of her chin—determined female. "Not like I have a choice, Iz. We've got commitments to keep, like the band coming in on Thursday, and then there's that..." She pulled up short when her gaze hit him and Locke. "That other thing you took on," she finished. "Hey."

"Hey," he said, ignoring the strange undercurrents swirling between the two women.

Locke came up beside him and dropped his apron on top of Grayson's.

Cass watched with a small frown. She opened her mouth,

but before she could say anything, Locke got there first. "What's going on?"

Cass looked away, and her shoulders hunched. Behind her, Isa and Des shared a look.

Des finally answered, "Cass's grandmother passed, and she needs to get to Vegas."

Grayson checked his watch, noting that it was closing in on midnight. "Are there flights heading out this late?"

"No, we checked," Isa answered. "The next one leaves at five fifteen in the morning."

Cass rubbed her forehead and, in a weary tone, gritted out, "I can drive."

"No, you can't," Isa shot back. "That thing you call a car is barely functioning."

Cass dropped her hand, folded her arms, and glared at Isa. "But it runs, and if I hit the road in the next hour, I'll make Vegas by seven."

Des waded into the conversation. "It's a crapshoot if it'll make it to the freeway. Not to mention you're in no shape to be driving."

Cass's stiff shoulders slumped as pain washed through her face before she wiped it away. She ran a hand over the back of her neck, the soft clack of beads on her collection of leather bracelets joining her sigh. "Yeah, I know."

Something about her resignation got to Grayson. "I can drive you." The offer escaped him before he could rethink it.

The three barkeepers turned to him, each wearing an expression of surprise. "What?" Cass asked as if not sure she'd heard correctly.

He didn't blame her. Hell, he had no idea why he'd offered, but now that he had... "I can drive you," he repeated. "I was planning on heading back in the morning anyway. No reason I can't leave a few hours early."

Color rose under Cass's skin, the flush easing the shadows in her face. "I appreciate it, but—"

"I can vouch for him." Locke stood at Grayson's side, his hand braced on the bar as he set a boot on the footrail. "I don't know what's going on, but if you need backup, he's not the worst choice."

"Wow, thanks for the vote of confidence," Grayson muttered.

Locke shot him a smug grin. "Just sayin'." He turned back to Cass, his smile fading as he turned serious. "Whatever it is that you're heading up to deal with, neither Des nor Isa is happy about it, so maybe having a friendly face, even one like his, isn't such a bad idea."

When Cass's attention switched to Grayson, he realized her glasses were gone, revealing long lashes and brown and green flecks intertwined with gold. She studied him with wary interest. "You sure you don't mind?"

He tried to ignore the way his body heated under her regard. "Not at all."

She worried her bottom lip before finally giving in. "All right, then. Thank you." She looked around, clearly searching for something. "I can meet you back here in about forty minutes. I just need to pack and book a room." She looked at Isa. "Happy now?"

Isa nodded as Grayson winced.

"What?" Des demanded.

When Cass and Isa turned to Grayson, he shrugged. "Finding a room might be a problem. The annual E-Con is happening this weekend, and that typically spikes room rates and availability."

"He's not wrong," Locke said. "And it's not just them. There's also a scheduled meeting for the heads of the western Arcane Families to discuss quarterly business plans."

Isa snorted. "Is that what they're calling it now?"

Locke shot her a dark look but went on. "You might have more luck with a private rental."

"Maybe." Cass closed her eyes and pinched the bridge of her nose. "I'll figure something out."

Isa's mouth thinned. "Promise me you won't stay with those people."

Cass's eyes flew open as her hand dropped to her side then curled into a fist. "Those people are my parents, Iz." There was a hint of warning in her voice.

Isa remained unmoved. "And they're toxic, so promise."

"Enough." Cass turned from Isa to Grayson. "Forty minutes?"

There was no missing the struggle between anger and tears, so he did what he could to help. "I'll be here," he promised.

She dipped her chin in acknowledgment, gave Des a quick hug, lifted a hand to Isa and Locke, and then went through the door to the back. Weighted silence filled the space for a long moment.

"What do I need to know?" Grayson finally asked.

When Isa and Des visibly relaxed, he figured he'd landed on the right question.

"Her parents are the epitome of assholes," Isa said. "Her father will all but ignore her, and her mother will ride her ass into the dust. I know it's a lot to ask, but can you stick with her until she finds someplace else to stay?"

"I can do that." Since Grayson was between jobs, it was an easy promise to make.

"Good. Iris..." There was a depth of grief in the way Des said that name. "Was a hell of a woman and the only decent member of Cass's family. She's the biggest reason Cass is who she is. Otherwise, she'd have ended up like Sofia."

"Sofia?" Locke asked.

Isa's nose wrinkled. "Her younger sister, aka the golden

child. I'm sure she'll be there too," she said with an edge of mockery.

"Right." There was a story there, but considering how tricky family dynamics could be, it was probably best to get the details from Cass. *Speaking of...* "You mind giving me Cass's number?"

Des rattled it off, and Grayson entered it into his phone with the fleeting thought that this was not how he'd planned on getting Cass's number. Once done, he realized he needed to add a couple more numbers to his phone. "Why don't we exchange numbers so I can keep you in the loop, just in case?"

"Good idea." Des rattled off his and Isa's numbers.

Once Grayson had sent them texts so they would have his number, he turned to Locke. "Ready to head out? I need to grab my stuff and then gas up."

Locke pushed off the bar and straightened. "Ready." He shot Isa a look. "I'll talk to you later."

Her disdainful sniff followed them out.

chapter 3

Cass

TODAY IS GOING TO SUCK.

Cass leaned against Grayson's sedan, sipping a surprisingly good coffee, considering it came from a convenience store. She soaked in the early-morning sun as it crept along the low-lying mountains that trailed from Boulder City into Vegas. Out on Highway 93—which was no longer hampered by congestion, thanks to the newly installed Boulder City Bypass—traffic clipped along. She'd been grateful when Grayson had offered to stop. Not only was it a chance to stretch her legs, but it also meant she could put off facing her parents and the emotional blowout that would follow. A noxious mix of grief and something older and uglier twisted painfully in her gut, but she forced down another sip.

Maybe she would ask Grayson to take her to the funeral home first. Afterward, she could catch a rideshare to her parents' place. That way, he wouldn't be obligated to stick around. Thanks to their road-trip-sharing sessions, she figured he was the type who would make that kind of offer, and that wasn't something she wanted to take advantage of, no matter how tempting.

A *ding* and *whoosh* floated through the air. She turned to see Grayson walk out of the store, a doughnut clenched in his teeth as he snapped a lid on a coffee cup. He caught her watching as he grabbed his doughnut and shot her a charming grin.

Being on the receiving end of it ignited a warm combination of attraction and appreciation that inched back the cold, deep press of sorrow that had settled since she'd answered the phone at work. During the hours-long car ride, that strangely hopeful feeling had gained strength, and despite the timing, she found she really liked him. When they first hit the road, they'd asked the typical getting-to-know-you questions, which morphed into lists of favorites before moving on to the more entertaining versions of two truths and a lie.

Then somewhere along the line, they meandered off into more personal conversational gambits that bumped between stories of the past, observations of the present, and wishes for the future. She learned that he worked with the Western Arcane Guild as a Key, and although he didn't say much, she got the impression his skills with curse breaking were in high demand—so much so that Locke was nudging him to work with the Cordova Family. As one of the premier Arcane Families in Phoenix, the Cordovas had access to the best, so if they were offering to bring Grayson aboard, he had to be a top-tier mage.

When she asked if he was considering the offer, he gently brushed her off with a noncommittal "It's something to think about."

Though her curiosity was a pesky bitch, she allowed him to shift their conversation to swapping amusing anecdotes of slinging drinks. His tales predated his mage career when he worked the Vegas nightclub scene. She matched him story for story, with her vast collection earned from a variety of southwest venues from a time before she'd put *bar owner* on her résumé. Despite the initial reason for their car trip, it was one of the best first dates she'd ever had.

"I left the doors unlocked," he said as he approached the car.

"It's cool. I wasn't in a rush to get back in."

He stopped next to her, leaving a couple of inches between them as they enjoyed their coffee and watched the passing traffic. The next minute or so passed in relaxed quiet. As loath as she was to break it, there was no rest for the wicked.

"I was thinking..."

"Sounds dangerous," he murmured.

She shot him a look and caught the amused curl of his lips. "It could be," she teased. "You mind dropping me off at the funeral home?" Her voice cracked on that last bit.

He angled closer, his shoulder brushing hers. "I can do that," he said gently.

Whether he intended it or not, she took comfort from the brief touch, leaning in a little when he didn't move away. She scrounged up a small smile. "You don't have to stick around. Especially if you've got things to do."

She made the mistake of looking at him, and since he was maybe five or six inches taller than her five foot six, he was close enough that she could see the striations of gold that flared into a thin dark ring that bled into a tiger brown. Flustered, she looked back at the road, feeling heat wash under her skin.

"Got nothing going on. So I'm happy to play your driver." When he paused, she looked back to find him watching her. "Besides, I made Des and Isa a promise."

There was no mistaking his concern, and it threatened to weaken her white-knuckle grip on her grief. She tried to clear her throat, where a lump had taken up residence, and looked away. "I'll be fine."

"Mm-hm." There was a hefty amount of disbelief in his response, but he only said, "You've got good friends."

"The best," she agreed before taking another sip from her cup.

"Makes me think if they're worried enough that they asked someone they don't know to have your back, maybe I should stick around."

"They're worrywarts." *And they have reasons for that worry.*

His silence was loud with unvoiced opinions.

She sighed. "My family... they're complicated."

"Most are."

That was true, but hers took the cake and threw it out the window. "Isa and Des don't like my parents, which isn't a surprise considering my parents are difficult to like." *Or love.*

He cautiously stepped through the door she'd opened. "You mentioned you left home at sixteen."

"Yeah."

"Your choice or theirs?" There was no judgment in his voice, just curiosity.

"Depends on who you ask." She didn't try to mask her bitterness because it was an old wound and had left a scar. From the corner of her eye, she caught him turning to her. When he didn't push for more, she added, "I'd say both of our choices. But if you ask them, they'll tell you it was all me."

"And your grandmother?"

Memories assaulted her, wrapping phantom arms around her heart in a painful embrace. "She's the reason I was able to get out when I did." The urge to hold that connection close spurred her to share more than she normally would. "My parents have very strong opinions on how their daughters' lives should go, and they ensured that we didn't think of deviating from the set path. My yaya, on the other hand, believed her granddaughters should walk their own roads, even if it meant collecting skinned knees and bruised hearts or taking an unintended path. The difference of opinions created a crack in our family that widened, especially after—" She stopped short, realizing what she was about to reveal.

"After...?" Grayson asked.

Cass shook her head and changed tracks. "After I got older. Mainly because I inherited my yaya's stubborn independent streak, except stronger. This did not go over well with my parents, so when things came to a head and that crack turned into uncrossable divide, me and my yaya ended up on one side, my parents on the other."

"Isa mentioned a sister. Where did she land?"

His question twisted the knife of well-worn guilt and sorrow. Cass had to swallow hard before answering. "Sofia got caught straddling the middle. She'd barely turned twelve when everything went down, so she didn't really understand what was happening." Honestly, neither had Cass. Not until later, when she finally confronted her mother. "What sucked worse was that I had my own damage to deal with, and by the time I had my shit together, it was too late to try and make amends. Whatever chance there was to salvage our relationship was long gone." Which had left her with the second biggest regret of her life—failing her baby sister. The first regret... well, that was a hell she wasn't revisiting. "Yaya tried to help. She'd take us both out to lunch, to shop, whatever, and did her best to mediate, but..." Her shoulders rose and fell in an uncomfortable shrug. "Sofia and I, we're not close, but at least we're cordial now."

A car playing music with a heavy bass line drove past. Grayson waited until the thudding beats had faded then said, "I'm sorry."

She managed a strained smile and did her best to nudge the familiar sorrow back into its box. "So am I, but that's life, right?"

"Maybe, but doesn't make it hurt any less." Something in his tone told her he got it.

"What about your family? Do you have siblings?"

She caught a fleeting shadow that dimmed his normally sharp gaze before he looked down to his coffee cup. "Yeah, younger brother, older sister." He brought the cup up, blew across the top, then took a sip.

She tucked away the fact that he didn't mention parents. "Middle child, huh?" That earned her a chuckle. "Are you close?"

There was a wry twist to his lips. "Some days, yes. Others, I wish we weren't."

His dry tone made her laugh and dispelled the lingering traces of their earlier conversation. "I get that. When Isa and Des clash, I've learned to duck and cover."

"I just get the hell out of the way."

Cass huffed out a chuckle. "Smart." She straightened, taking a moment to roll up to her toes and lift her arms—and cup—high as she arched her back. The knots that had set up shop in her lower back unwound, and she sighed in relief before releasing her stretch. "We should probably get going."

She sucked back the rest of her coffee and then went to step around him. She didn't get far because he caught her wrist gently, holding her in place. "Cass, I know things are..." He grimaced, shook his head, and tried again. "You've got a lot going on, but I just wanted to make sure you were okay with me sticking around."

"Why?"

"Why?" he echoed.

She nodded, an unexpected anxiety skating along her nerves as she waited for his answer.

"Because I like you, or at least what I've gotten to know so far, and I wouldn't mind a chance to get to know you more."

His thumb brushed the inside of her wrist, igniting an internal swarm of butterflies.

Ignoring the delicate shiver that ran down her spine, she twisted her wrist until she could take his hand and thread their fingers together. "I like you, too, Grayson." When his eyes darkened at her admission, a thrill shot through her, making her voice rough. "So yes, I'm okay with you sticking around."

"Good." Without letting go of her hand, he tugged her closer until mere inches separated them. "So, your grandmother first, then your parents?"

She managed a nod despite being caught in a disconcerting state of anticipation. Part of her wanted to get lost in his magnetic pull, but the unrelenting grip of her looming reality refused to loosen. "Can you promise me something?"

"What?"

"Let me know if it gets to be too much." When it came to her family, that was an inevitable outcome.

He didn't answer right away. Instead he searched her face. She had no idea what he was looking for, but after a few tense moments, he must have found it, because he said, "I can do that."

"Good." Sweet relief rushed through her, and she leaned in to press a quick kiss against his jaw. She pulled back quickly, her face heating. "Sorry."

His grin was downright wicked as he let her go. "Don't be. I'm not." He stepped back until he could open the passenger door and, with his cup in hand, motioned toward the car. "After you."

She couldn't help but grin as she settled into the seat. "Thank you."

"You want me to take that?" He indicated her almost empty coffee cup.

"Sure." She handed it over.

He took it, shot her another grin, then closed the door.

Cass watched him round the hood and head to the trash bin, only to be blinded when the glass door to the store opened, reflecting the early-morning sunlight directly into her eyes. She turned away and blinked, clearing the white star-bursts, until the parking lot reassembled itself. A dark smudge on the roof of a nearby car caught her attention. She blinked twice until it took the shape of an overly large raven, its inky eyes focused on her. Those dark orbs held her captive as it opened its beak to give a harsh trill that mimicked chuckling. Its call joined a rush of whispered warnings that deafened her with a wave of confused noise and trepidation.

Wincing, she closed her eyes and rubbed her forehead. "Not now." It was stupid to ignore the signs, but she never claimed to be smart when her magic was involved.

The driver's-side door opened then closed as Grayson's weight settled in the car. "You okay?"

She opened her eyes, dropped her hand, and managed to fake a reassuring smile. "Yep, just tired."

He paused. She had no idea if he was buying her excuse until he said, "Why don't you input the address for the funeral home then try to rest?" He started up the car.

She did as he suggested, but once she sat back and closed her eyes, it wasn't rest that found her but a murky knot of worries.

chapter 4

Grayson

GRAYSON FOLLOWED a quiet Cass into the funeral home, where the air of somber elegance surrounded them. He couldn't help but note the runes subtly placed throughout. The bulk of them were Divine sigils that ranged from offering solace for mourners to providing eternal rest for those who were gone. But he picked out a couple of necromancer runes in the warding patterns. That was to be expected, considering the clientele.

Cass left him to follow the funeral home director into a privacy room where she could say goodbye to her grandmother. When she reemerged, whatever respite the brief nap in the car from Boulder City had granted her was long gone, replaced by drawn paleness. Grayson went to her side, noting the careful way she held herself and the reddened eyes behind her glasses. He didn't think she'd welcome his touch, though it was hard not to offer comfort. She remained stiff during the conversation with the director until he reassured her that the logistics were being taken care of as instructed by her grandmother's will, not her parents. Only then did her shoulders ease, and she inched a little closer to his side. He didn't hesitate to curl an arm around her waist and take her weight. Somber goodbyes were exchanged, and he led her back out into the bright morning light.

Without removing his arm, he walked with her across the parking lot. He dug the car remote out of his pocket and clicked it, releasing the locks with a soft beep. They stopped at the passenger side, and he gently tugged her out of the way as he opened the door. Before he could usher her in, she turned fully into him and dropped her forehead to his chest. He tugged off her glasses then tightened his arms and bent his head over hers, holding her close as she buried her face against him. Her grief was a quiet storm of tears dampening his shirt as her frame was wracked by the occasional shudder. It left him battered at the edges, but he gave what he could—a safe harbor for her pain. The feeling was old and familiar, but he turned away from the memories and concentrated on the here and now.

Eventually, the tears and tremors stopped, but she didn't pull away, so he didn't let go. Instead, he waited, letting her dictate the next step. He wasn't surprised when it didn't take long for her to regather her composure and lift her head, her attention aimed at the car, not him.

"Sorry," she mumbled as she swiped fingers under her eyes.

"Nothing to be sorry for." Grayson handed over her glasses, and she took them with a sigh and pulled away. He let her go so he could open the door. "Did you get a chance to let Isa and Des know you made it to Vegas?"

"I sent them a text earlier." Cass, glasses back in place, pulled her phone out as she settled into the passenger seat and snapped the seat belt in place. "I also sent one to my parents, letting them know we were coming."

Not that it was his place, but... "You sure you want to head over now?"

"Better to get it over with."

"All right." It was her choice.

He made a motion to close the door, but she put her hand out and stopped him. Then she waited until their gazes met. "You sure you want to stick around?" The tone of her question was teasing, but it couldn't hide the worried shadows in her eyes.

He scrounged up a reassuring smile. "I'm good, Cass."

She studied him for a long moment before she dropped her hand. "Okay. Just remember, you promised to let me know if that changes."

Since he figured that wasn't going to happen, he simply said, "Put in your parents' address."

⸺ ✦ ⸺

Grayson wasn't expecting the GPS to lead them away from the tourist trap of the Las Vegas strip and west toward Spanish Elms, one of the ritzier neighborhoods and home to a variety of high-profile people, including one of Vegas's leading Arcane Families. The million-dollar custom homes populating the eleven neighborhoods ranged from ostentatious to intimidating, and the manicured golf course and multiple green spaces that spread across six hundred forty acres were a far cry from the xeriscape neighborhoods surrounding it.

His surprise must have shown on his face, because Cass asked, "What?"

He dared a glance at her before going back to driving. "You don't strike me as the Spanish Elms type."

"I'm not," she said with a hint of defensiveness. "My parents moved in right before I left home."

A quick mental calculation told him they'd lived there for at least twelve years. "Where were you all before that?"

"With my yaya in Summerlin. My parents wanted something bigger and closer to their business clients, so we moved." Her even tone held a sliver of resentment.

"You were in high school, right?"

She fiddled with her seat belt. "Incoming freshman when we switched over."

Which meant she'd most likely lost her circle of friends and had to start all over with a new crowd. "Sounds rough."

Cass looked out the passenger window. "It was."

Her two-word agreement held an unspoken warning, so he backed off. "I'm curious—what is your family's business?"

There was a long pause. "Ever heard of Pythia Strategies?"

The name tickled but didn't find purchase. "No. What do they do?"

"Strategic business forecasting."

"Sounds..." Grayson wasn't sure how to finish that sentence.

"Boring? Uptight? Pretentious?" she supplied wryly.

Although he agreed, he still raised his eyebrows at her word choice. "How about I go with expensive?"

She gave a cute huff. "They can definitely be that." She was quiet a moment. "My grandparents started the company. They kept it small, picking and choosing which businesses to partner with, but after my grandfather passed, Yaya turned it over to my parents. Since demand was high, it didn't take much for them to expand the company."

"I'm guessing they wanted you to be part of it."

"I can't remember a time when I didn't know that was the expectation. As the oldest, and as someone naturally inclined to the work, I was supposed to eventually take the helm. Problem was, that wasn't what I wanted. My mom and I would get into these arguments, and no matter how much I tried to explain, she'd shut me down. It didn't help that I had no clue about what I actually wanted, just that I wanted nothing to do with Pythia."

He could picture a younger Cass facing down a demanding mother. "It couldn't have been easy standing up to her like that."

"No, it was far from easy, but it was necessary," she said. "And if I hadn't left, I wouldn't have Isa, Des, or Wonderland."

He tagged along with her shift in conversation. "And that would be a real shame, because your bar is the shit."

That earned him a surprised laugh. "Thank you?"

"Just sharing the truth."

He kept the conversation light until they turned off Tropicana and drove along the curved turnout to the gate guarding the neighborhood. As Grayson slowed to a stop next to the brick facade of the guardhouse, a man stepped out.

Grayson powered down his window and heard Cass undo her seat belt. Placing a hand on his thigh for balance, she leaned over. "Hi, Luca."

The guard bent down to see inside, and his expression went from blank to warm. "Good morning, Ms. Alcmene."

"Cass," she corrected with a familiar ease. "How's the family?"

"Good." He put his hand on the roof of the car. "Amelia's starting kindergarten this year."

"I bet Caro's happy to get some alone time."

He shook his head, and wry amusement filled his face. "She switches between happy and sad, depending on the day."

"It's hard to watch little ones grow up. Tell them both hi from me and give Amelia a big hug."

"Will do. I'm so sorry to hear about your grandmother," he said, his tone softening.

Cass's smile dimmed, and the hand on Grayson's thigh

tightened, but her warm tone didn't waver. "Thank you, Luca. I appreciate it."

"Share my condolences with your parents, please." When she nodded, Luca swept his gaze over Grayson, gave the roof a pat, then stepped back. "You take care of yourself, Cass."

"You too," she said.

As Luca disappeared inside the guardhouse, she sat back. Grayson powered up the window as the warmth of her touch faded. Once the gate opened, he pulled through and followed the GPS directions along the tree-lined streets. He'd been here once before for a job, one that involved a wealthy client who had pissed off the wrong woman and, by extension, had earned the guy a very nasty curse. It wasn't officially recorded anywhere, since his services could be obtained discreetly for the right price. And that price was pretty steep for a man who didn't want the reasons behind his inability to sexually perform made public, especially to his wife.

With each passing moment, he could feel the tension emanating from the woman sitting next to him. Her hands were knotted together in her lap, her gaze focused straight ahead, and her breathing modulated. If he hadn't been clued in that things were rough with her family, this mental and emotional donning of armor would have been a clear indication that whatever lay in wait would not be good.

He hit the southern edge of the private neighborhood and followed the quiet street lined with massive homes set back from the road. A row of old-growth trees partially obscured the cement block fence that kept the busy road on the other side. As Grayson came to the final T, Cass directed him to the third house on the left, a white two-story Spanish-inspired home with pale-beige roof tiles, sitting among towering palm trees. The house wasn't as grand as some of the others, but it was impressive. The architecture hinted at its age, but the modern color scheme of startling white accented with the black glass garage doors and the dark privacy tint on the arched windows made it clear that recent renovations had been undertaken. Unlike its neighbors, there were no gates keeping the curious back from the home's meticulously land-scaped front yard. Instead, a half-moon driveway bypassed the multicar garage, where a silver-gray sedan was parked. Grayson turned in, pulled the car through the porte-cochere—leaving it clear for other visitors—and parked near the end of the drive.

He shut the car down, and they sat in the heavy quiet for a few moments. As he wasn't in a rush, he was more than willing to give Cass whatever time she needed. He checked the rearview mirror, but there was no movement from the house.

Cass blew out a long breath and undid her seat belt. "All right, let's get this over with."

He met her out on the drive, and together, they walked across the polished concrete to the heavy glass front door set in an iron frame. He stayed at her back when she rang the bell. The tint on the glass was dark enough to obscure details, but it wasn't long before a shift of shadows preceded the door opening to reveal a slender young woman in tailored linen slacks and a fitted dress shirt.

"Cass." She stood in the doorway, one hand on the door, the other on the frame, as her gaze swept over them. "You're here."

He wasn't sure if her words held accusation or relief. When Cass replied with a quiet "Hi, Sofia," and the young woman stepped out of the door and pulled Cass into her arms, Grayson settled on relief. He waited as the two women held each other and wasn't surprised when Cass was the first to draw back.

"You doing okay?" She tucked a strand of Sofia's gold-streaked light-brown hair back from a wan face that carried hints of shared traits. The mutual loss was there in the bruised circles under her eyes and fine lines bracketing her pale lips.

Sofia's shrug was jerky, her brown eyes bright with unshed tears. "Do I have a choice?"

Before Cass could answer, a woman's voice sounded from inside. "Sofia, who's at the door?"

Cass's body went wired, her hand falling to her side and curling into a fist.

Sofia took a step back from Cass then twisted to look back through the door. "It's Cassandra, Mother, and—" When she turned back to them, her earlier softness was gone, hidden behind a composed mask as her gaze landed on him, her perfectly arched eyebrows rising in question.

"Grayson," he supplied.

"Grayson," Sofia finished then moved to the door, pushed it wide, and motioned for them to enter.

When Cass simply stood in place, Grayson came up to her side and caught her fisted hand. Her hand uncurled, and he wove their fingers together, giving her something to hold on to. She took a bracing breath and stepped inside.

He immediately saw he was right about the renovations. The herringbone pattern floor spread through an open space leading from the front to the back with very little interruption. To the right was a white baby grand and a formal sitting area that spilled into a heavily influenced euro-style kitchen with clean lines. Above them, soaring ceilings and glass partitions on the second-floor railing added to the illusion of space. A floating chandelier of glass birds caught in mid-flight hovered over the sunken living room, where two crescent-shaped cream-colored couches surrounded a natural-stone boulder that served as a table. Along the far wall was a low shelf filled with various bits and pieces, including potted greenery. All of that sat in front of floor-to-ceiling glass doors that opened onto a luxurious patio with a resort-style pool. As tasteful as the house was, it was clearly a showpiece, not a home.

Behind them, the whoosh of the front door closing made the hair at the back of his neck rise, but before he could process that unsettling moment, the steady clip of heels against the light wood floor preceded the appearance of a woman who had to be Cass's mother. The three females were close in height. Like her daughters, Cass's mother wore her hair long. Unlike theirs, hers was a striking combination of silvers, whites, and grays set off by a black V-neck tunic, her natural curls carefully tamed into a polished wave. The older woman's eyes, though, were the same startling gold, browns, and greens that Cass hid behind her glasses. And at the moment, those eyes were aimed at Cass, with pain flashing through them before they turned assessing.

Cass's mother stopped a few feet away and didn't open her arms for a hug. "Why do you insist on wearing those hideous glasses, Cassandra? You don't need them."

He felt Cass's fingers twitch in his hold, but her voice was pleasantly polite. "Hello, Mother." Her attention shifted to the equally urbane dark-haired man who came up behind her mother and stopped at her side, his hand coming to rest at her back as they faced their oldest daughter. "Father."

"Cassandra," he returned, his gaze going to Grayson.

Cass caught the silent prompt and introduced him. "This is Grayson. He's a friend."

"Grayson." Her father held out his hand. "Elias Ambrose."

Not Alcmene? He made a note to ask Cass about the last name later as he shook the man's hand. "Grayson Beck."

"And since our daughter seems to have forgotten her manners, I'm Rhea."

"Rhea," he acknowledged even as her deliberate jab set his teeth on edge. He inclined his head. "My condolences on your family's loss."

There was a minuscule thaw in her brittle composure that

disappeared as fast as it had come on. "Yes, well..." Rhea murmured with a curious detachment, her attention shifting to the hall behind them.

He pivoted with Cass, the two of them moving in tandem, as two men walked toward them, one close to their age, the other older. The younger man gave them a curious look but clasped the older man on the shoulder before moving to Sofia's side. He curled an arm around her waist, pulled her close, and bent his head to say something too low to hear. At Grayson's side, Cass gave a jerk that Grayson more felt than saw.

The older man continued forward, joining the small group. He wore his dark slacks and light button-down shirt like a well-worn pair of jeans and a T-shirt. His hair was cut short, minimizing his receding hairline, and his eyes were sharp behind the understated frames on the prominent bridge of his nose. His gaze landed on Cass, and that sharpness softened while a welcoming curve eased the stark line of his lips.

He set his leather folder on a nearby entry table then moved to Cass, his hands extended. "Ms. Amb... Alcmene, I hadn't expected you so soon."

Cass stepped forward and took his hand briefly before letting him go. "Mr. Swanson, I presume?"

"Yes, so sorry." Flustered, he nudged the bridge of his glasses. "I should've introduced myself formally, but you look remarkably like your grandmother."

"Thank you."

When she moved stiffly back to Grayson, he did the only thing he could to offer comfort—he set a supporting hand at her hip. Cass's smile was strained at the edges as she leaned into his touch.

"And no harm done," she said graciously. "I recognized your voice." When Swanson's attention went to Grayson, she put a hand on Grayson's stomach. "This is my friend Grayson."

Swanson's gaze flicked to the others behind them before coming back to her and Grayson. "It's good to have friends at your side, especially during such difficult times."

Something in his voice held a warning, and it tripped Grayson's protective streak. Not that he had any right to one when it came to Cass, but standing in the middle of what felt like shark-infested waters, he didn't think twice about issuing his own warning. "Cass is family, and we tend to take care of our own."

A flare of approval was there and gone. "Well, then." Swanson cleared his throat and redonned his professional demeanor. "Did you get a chance to see her?"

"Yes, thank you."

Swanson dipped his head.

"Will you be staying here, Cassandra?" her father asked politely.

The hand at his stomach fisted his T-shirt as she held on to him. Since he was feeling a bit surrounded, he gave Cass's hip a gentle squeeze before, as subtly as possible, he rotated their position, herding Swanson into the center so he and Cass were facing the rest of the family.

"If so, I'll need to prepare the guest room," her mother added, her tone indicating such an accommodation would be a massive chore.

"I—"

"Cass is staying with me." He felt her stiffen but ignored it as he took his own jab. "She didn't want to impose." He didn't know what was up with this family, but whatever it was, Cass didn't need the added weight of their shit on top of everything else. "Thank you, though," he tacked on, not bothering to hide the lack of sincerity in his words.

A hint of color swept over Rhea's cheeks as her eyes

narrowed. "Impose? She should be here, doing her duty to her family."

He held her glare, refusing to look away. He wasn't the one being a bitch. That was all her.

"And what exactly is my duty, Mother?" Cass had clearly had enough. Her question hit the air like a bullet, slamming into her parents, who jerked as if they'd been electrocuted.

chapter 5

Cass

As Rhea sputtered, Cass met her mother's glare with equal fire. After not even ten minutes in her parents' presence, it was clear she wasn't welcome. An old rage seeded with hurt came roaring back with nauseating familiarity. *Family duty? What a crock. They have no idea what family really means, but damn, can they ride the duty train into hell.*

"Your grandmother is dead," her mother all but hissed.

And whose fault is that? Cass fought not to let the vicious, illogical accusation tear free and instead ground out, "I'm very aware of that, which is why I am here."

"Truly, Cassandra? You've never been one to care about presenting a united family front."

She jerked under her mother's ugly insinuation and vaguely felt Grayson's body go rock solid. She tightened her grip on his shirt as unexpected pain sliced through her. She should have known this would happen. Her mother was nothing if not predictable. *But why does it have to still hurt?*

And just like always, she proved she was her mother's daughter by striking back. "I'm not here for you or Pythia." It was her mother's turn to flinch, but Cass was too pissed to care. "I've come because it's about Yaya, who's the only one around here who knew what it meant to be family."

Her mother gasped. It was echoed by Sofia, a result Cass had not intended. Her father did what he always did—he stayed out of it—but he did lay a hand on Rhea's arm. Cass caught the silent sign of support, and resentment flared. Without fail, the two always stood as one, regardless of who they faced down. Which meant nothing had changed. She wondered why she kept expecting it to.

"Okay, I think maybe we all need to take a breath here." The man at Sofia's side stepped between Cass and her mother, his hands up, palms out as he tried to take things down a notch. "This is a difficult time for everybody."

A thin layer of condescension rode under his words and slithered over Cass's skin. With some serious effort, she bit back the two-word response that would have sent her mother into an apoplectic fit. It didn't help when Sofia stepped up behind him, her hands twisting together, her face a shade beyond pale, her shoulders hunched. Seeing her sister like that was another cut, just as painful as the first. Sofia's response was the same every time Cass and her mother got into it—a visual reminder of the collateral damage their clashes inflicted on her.

Coming here was a mistake.

"Russ is right," Swanson said. "Perhaps we should take just a minute. Maybe sit down with some coffee."

"No." Cass held her mother's icy glare and her father's equally disapproving one for a long moment before turning to face Swanson. Her lips felt rigid as she forced them into a polite curve as she reached for, and found, a calmer tone. "No, thank you. We're going to go." There was nothing to be gained by sticking around.

Swanson inclined his head. "Of course."

Following her lead, Grayson turned her toward the door so they could leave, but Swanson's brief touch on her arm brought them to a stop. His face held sympathy and concern. "You have the information on the service?"

Doing her best to ignore her silently seething parents, Cass managed a nod.

"Good," he continued. "Perhaps you'll have more time after the reading."

Gods, she didn't want to come back. Hell, she didn't want to be here at all. She managed another, stiffer nod and headed toward the door.

"Cassandra, the reading of the will will be for family only," her mother bit out.

With freedom just a few feet away, Cass stopped, forcing Grayson to do the same. She caught Swanson's mouth tightening into disapproving lines at her mother's all-too-obvious power play. Turning just her head and matching her mother's frigid tone, she informed her, "As Grayson stated earlier, he is family. My family."

Russ shot her mother a frown, but then Sofia reached out and touched his hand, gaining his attention. When he turned to Sofia, she shook her head. Russ's expression darkened, but he simply pulled her into his side. Sofia was tense for a second and then relaxed as if startled by his touch, but he wasn't watching her. He was watching Cass and her parents with an unsettling intensity. Whoever Russ was, he meant something to her sister. What he wasn't was an Ambrose.

Cass looked at Swanson and asked quietly, "Will he be there?"

The arrogant amusement that flashed over Russ's face set her teeth on edge.

"Yes," Sofia answered before the lawyer could. She glanced at their parents as her tongue touched her top lip, a nervous tell, before she turned back to Cass. "Russ is my fiancé."

The unexpected pronouncement left Cass stunned. Fortunately, Grayson stepped in with his congratulations. Only when she caught Sofia watching her did Cass get her shit together and gave her sister a hug. "Congratulations, baby girl."

Sofia's arms tightened. "Thanks."

When they separated, Cass said, "I'd love to hear about how you two met. Can we do lunch or something?"

Sofia looked at Russ, who inclined his head, then she turned back to Cass. "Perhaps brunch tomorrow. I can text you an address."

"I'd love that."

Sofia's small smile didn't quite reach her eyes. "Me too."

Caught in the emotional storm raging in her mind, Cass barely paid attention to where Grayson was going. Not that she didn't care, but grappling with the toxic brew left in her family's damaged wake took more effort than she remembered. Only when a screaming fire truck sped through an intersection and yanked her out of a spiral of emotional dysfunction did she realize they were stopped at a light.

"Where are we going?" she asked.

"I'm taking you to my place."

"You don't have—"

"Stop, Cass. You haven't slept, and you're running on fumes. You've got enough to deal with without adding the headache of finding a place to stay." Grayson's tone left no room for argument.

Not that she had it in her to fight. Hell, exhaustion was a relentless bitch, and at the moment, she was grateful to have one less thing to deal with. "Thanks?"

He shot her an amused look before the light turned green. "Are you asking me something?"

His levity snuck through the emotional fog. "No. Seriously, thank you. I just don't want to put you out or anything."

"You aren't," he promised. "We've got about fifteen minutes before we get to my place, so why don't you call Isa or Des and let them know where you're going to be?"

She pulled Isa's number up and called her, doing her best to keep the details about what had gone down with her mother as vague as possible, but Isa was familiar with Cass's family dynamics and accurately filled in the blanks. After that, she didn't hesitate to share a few pithy comments.

"Well, I'm glad Grayson is there, then," Isa said.

"Yeah, me too," Cass said softly. It was a little disconcerting how much she liked having him at her side. "Oh, by the way, Sofia's engaged."

Isa's derisive snort filled her ear. "Let me guess—he works with your parents."

Cass hesitated. "Probably."

"What?"

Cass frowned, confused. "What, what?"

"That tone," Isa said. "It's the one you get when you're trying not to judge. Need I remind you who you're talking to? I want you to judge, so judge away."

She sighed. "It's not like I have much to go on, Iz. We exchanged maybe five sentences."

"Well, obviously it was enough, so spill."

Highly aware Grayson was listening, Cass debated stopping the conversation, but because it was Isa, she shared the nebulous impressions swirling in her head. "All right. Well, he acts as if he's the prodigal son my parents never had. In fact, he met with Swanson without the 'rents or Sofia. Fiancé or not, why would he be meeting with the family lawyer?"

"Good question," Isa said. "Unfortunately, I don't have an answer that would fit."

"Neither do I." *But I need to find out because it is beyond odd.* "And you know how my mother is—she'd never let her venom spew in front of outsiders, especially if they're part of the business."

Because a division in the family was bad for business. That fact that her mother hadn't hesitated to let Cass have it with Grayson, Swanson, and Russ standing witness boggled Cass's mind.

"Yeah, she's rabid about maintaining the professional image that hides the bitch underneath," Isa agreed. "If she let fly with the fiancé around, she not only likes him—she trusts him too."

"Maybe, but something tells me that's going to come back and bite her in the ass."

"Let it," Isa said with vicious satisfaction.

"If it was just Mother, I would, but there's Sofia to consider," Cass said. Those little flinches when Russ had touched her baby sister had worked their way under Cass's skin, setting off alarm bells all over the place. "I swear she's scared of him."

There was a tense pause from Isa. "Do you think he's hurting her?" she asked cautiously.

Doing her best to set aside her emotions, Cass replayed the events from earlier. "Physically, no, but something's not right there." She closed her eyes and pinched the bridge of her nose, skewing her glasses. "I asked her to brunch tomorrow."

"And...?" Isa asked.

"And..." Cass opened her gritty eyes and adjusted her glasses. "She said she'd send me an address. I'm sure he'll be with her."

"No doubt. Will Grayson be with you?"

The last was asked with concern, not the teasing Cass would normally expect. Still, she resolutely kept her eyes off the man in question. "I haven't asked."

"Ask," Isa commanded. "Have him keep the fiancé busy while you drag Sofia to the bathroom and get some answers."

"You and I both know that would be a minor miracle." Cass's younger sister made it her life's mission to be the perfect daughter, no matter how much it cost her.

"You have to try," Isa said.

"I know," Cass said. If she didn't try, she'd add another painful regret to the pile she already carried.

"And if things are bad, you know Des and I are here. We'll get her safe."

This time Cass's "I know" was quieter but no less firm.

If Sofia was at risk, Cass would use every resource at her disposal to not only get her safe but also ensure that she stayed that way. Unfortunately, she couldn't shake the feeling that those actions would leave the Ambrose family in ruin.

chapter 6

Grayson

"YOU CAN SLEEP IN HERE." Since the blinds in his bedroom were drawn, Grayson hit the switch to illuminate the space.

Cass stood in the short entry hall as she looked into the room then back at him. "I'm not taking your bed."

Since he was pretty sure offering to share it with her would get him slapped, or worse, he throttled his hormones into maturity. It didn't take much, especially since the recessed lighting made it hard to miss the physical signs of her exhaustion.

"My couch is a sleeper, Cass. The bedroom gives you privacy, plus it has an en suite." He left her at the door and set her bag on his bed. "The second switch will open the blinds. The windows have a privacy tint, so no worries about giving the neighbors a show."

That earned him an amused snort. He turned and found that she had followed him and now stood next to his bed. Her expression stated that she was going to push back on the sleeping arrangements.

Since he wasn't inclined to argue, he kept speaking,

motioning to the opening near the dresser and opposite the bed. "Bathroom's through there. Since I did laundry before I headed down to Phoenix, the towels and sheets are clean, so we're good there."

She sighed then sat on the edge of the bed, her shoulders slumping as she fiddled with the strap to her bag. "Thank you, Grayson."

Despite her quiet tone, her sincerity came through loud and clear. Still, it was obvious that events were catching up to her in a big way. He wasn't surprised to find he wanted to go to her and hold her, but that wasn't who they were. Give it a few more days, and maybe he could get away with it, but for all intents and purposes, they'd only known each other for less than a day, even though it felt longer.

"Hey." He waited until she looked at him. "What can I do to help?"

Color chased away the wan shadows in her face, and her smile held a hint of the woman who caught his attention back at Wonderland. "Okay, I know how this sounds, but are you for real?"

He leaned a hip against his dresser and folded his arms. "In what way?"

"All of this," she said, canting her head to the side as she held his gaze. "Driving a complete stranger six hours in the dead of night? Standing at my side through some serious family drama? Opening up your home? You're being remarkably friendly to a stranger."

He put a hand to his chest. "And here I thought we were becoming friends."

The color in her face deepened. "I think we are…"

He took pity on her. "But…?" When her gaze slid away, he laid it out. "You're wondering if there's something more here, right?" He was surprised by the burst of anxiety he felt as he waited for her nod, but when she did, he went to the bed and sat on the edge. They were close enough that when he cocked his knee, it brushed hers. "Look, Cass, I'm thirty-four years old and no stranger to relationships. I know what I like when I see it. I saw you, and I liked what I saw. The fact that I could be of help when you're dealing with heavy shit—that was an unexpected opportunity, and I'm not one to waste a chance like that."

As he spoke, her lips took on a gentle curve, and she tucked her hair behind an ear. "Well, yay for me, then."

He couldn't help but smile back. "Yeah?"

"Yeah." Then she leaned in, and a warm mix of vanilla and jasmine teased his nose as she brushed her lips over his jaw. "Thanks for not wasting your shot."

The butterfly touch unraveled his intentions. When she started to pull back, he cupped her jaw. She froze in place as he brushed his thumb over her lower lip, mesmerized by the softness. His heart beat harder as an undeniable craving woke with a vengeance. He wanted to learn her taste. He met her gaze, finding an answering need in her eyes and a heightened flush in her cheeks. Slowly, without breaking eye contact, he lowered his head. Grayson stilled when she grabbed his wrist. Instead of pulling away, she held on and closed the remaining inches between them. He didn't mind when it was she who initiated the kiss instead of him. Not this first time. He was grateful when she dared a soft swipe followed by a gentle nibble. Taking her cue, he opened for her then took his time, learning her taste and enjoying the way she returned the favor. Minutes stretched and got lost in the rising tide of hunger and heat. When they drew back, both were breathing hard. He cradled her jaw and shifted a bit because his breathing wasn't the only thing that was hard, but he couldn't stop touching her.

Cass leaned into his hold, her lips brushing his wrist, her eyes a little hazy. "Okay, wow," she murmured.

Her reaction made him smile. "Yeah, *wow* works."

She pulled away reluctantly. They stared at each other for a long moment that was broken when she yawned then looked surprised. She managed to cover her mouth with a hand as he chuckled.

She shook her head. "Okay, as much as it sucks, because I really would like to keep going..."

"You need sleep." He let her go.

She nodded.

He stood, grateful that his shirt was long enough to hide his body's reaction. "Rest. When we wake up, we'll figure out what to do for food. I'm going to grab an extra set of sheets and a pillow for the couch from my closet."

"Sounds like a plan," she said.

He left her and collected what he needed. When he returned to the room, Cass had her bag open and was setting toiletries on the bed.

Unable to stay away from her, he put a hand to her hip then dropped a kiss to the top of her bent head. "Sleep well."

Her "You too" followed him out of the room.

———— ✦ ————

Grayson managed a solid four hours on his couch before a cramped calf muscle snapped him awake. The hours behind the wheel had done him no favors. He stumbled to the half bath, where he kept a couple of pain-relieving amulets that a grateful med mage had crafted for him, and he activated one. With hands braced on the sink, he waited the handful of moments until it kicked in and forced the stiff muscles to relax their painful grip. Only then was he able to straighten and do a careful stretch. Definitely awake, he used the bathroom, washed his hands, splashed his face with water, and then ran his hands through his hair to bring some kind of order to it.

Order groceries, check email, figure out dinner.

With a plan in place, he padded out of the bathroom and into the kitchen to grab a cold drink. Then he did a quick inventory of what he had on hand and placed a grocery order before heading to the desk tucked in the corner of his living room. Not once did he hear any sign of movement from his bedroom.

Good. She needs the break.

Grayson powered up his laptop and filtered his email. After eliminating the junk, he was left with three job offers—a construction company that wanted to verify that their malfunctioning equipment wasn't retaliation from a disgruntled ex-employee, a private account with a vague description of a cursed inheritance, and an Arcane Guild job involving a corporate litigation case. Since the Guild provided the bulk of his contracted jobs, he responded to them first. The construction company was next as they'd been recommended by another client. For the last offer, he asked for more details. When it came to curses, clients tended not to share all the necessary details of how and why they might be a target. Whether it was ignorance, embarrassment, shame, arrogance, or a combination thereof that kept their mouths shut, by the time he got into untangling their mess, the truth would come out. After a couple of early close calls, he stopped being polite with potential clients and got blunt real damn quick, especially since he liked being able to afford his health insurance coverage.

His phone vibrated on the side table next to the couch. He got up and checked his screen to see a short text from his brother, Shep, asking if he was going to be in town and wanted to do dinner in a few weeks as he was heading to Vegas for a work thing. Since Grayson would be in town then, he responded, and they set it up. He was about to sign off when the three dots appeared, indicating that Shep was still typing. Grayson waited, and when the text came through, he felt his shoulders tighten and his jaw clench.

You heard from Dad lately?

Fingers stiff, he punched out, *No,* and hit Enter. He thought about not adding the next question but knew if he didn't, he'd regret it, so he typed, *Why?* Then he stared at the annoying revolving dots while Shep typed.

Rae mentioned he reached out last week. Wondered if he was making the annual rounds.

Grayson did the mental math and realized Shep's assumption might be right. Some of his tension eased because if that was the case, he'd do what he'd done the previous year and let his father's calls go to voicemail. He exhaled and typed, *Probably.*

Shep responded with a thumbs-up emoji, basically ending their conversation. Grayson set his phone aside, knowing there would be further discussion during their upcoming dinner. Grateful for the reprieve, he deliberately turned his mind to the question of what to make for tonight's dinner and headed to the kitchen. He didn't get far when a cry came from his bedroom.

Pulse pounding, he was at the bedroom door in moments, pushing it open. He rushed in and found Cass tangled in his sheets, whimpering. Clearly, she was having a nightmare. He sank to the edge of the bed and cautiously reached out. He stopped short of touching her, not wanting to make things worse.

"Cass," he called softly. "You're okay. Come on, wake up, Cass."

She continued to whimper, her hands clawing at the mattress, her head shifting side to side.

He tried again, a little louder. "Cass, wake up for me. You're good."

Her hands stilled, then her head, but she still didn't open her eyes.

Worried, he decided to risk touching her. He covered her fist with his hand and squeezed. "Come on, Cass, open your eyes."

Her lashes fluttered, and when they finally rose, she stared blearily up at him. For a second, he swore they were milky white, but with the only light being a thin ray from the hall, the shadows were heavy in the room, so it was probably his imagination.

She blinked once, then twice, and when she spoke her voice was scratchy. "Grayson?"

"Yep," he said, unable to hide his relief. "I'm right here. You okay if I turn on a light?"

The hand under his twitched. "Sure."

He traced the illumination rune on his nightstand, and a low glow lined the edge of his headboard, nudging the shadows back. He turned back to her. "You okay?"

Cass tugged her hand out from under his and awkwardly pushed herself up until she was sitting tailor style. She pushed her tangled hair back from her face, and her gaze darted around before coming back to him. "Sorry. Bad dreams."

He couldn't help but notice the fine tremor in her hands. "Probably should have expected that, considering recent events."

She licked her lips then caught the lower one in her teeth before nodding.

Recognizing her discomfort, he gave her knee a squeeze and stood up. "How about you take a few minutes then meet me in the kitchen? We can discuss our dinner options."

She looked at the blackout blinds holding back the early-evening sun and frowned. "What time is it?"

"Closing in on six. I've got some groceries coming, but it's up to you whether we eat in or out."

"In," she quickly responded.

"Sounds good to me." He turned to leave. "I'll see you in the kitchen."

"Okay," she said quietly, the word following him out.

chapter 7

Cass

IT TOOK Cass twenty minutes to pull her shit together. Unlike what she'd told Grayson, it wasn't a nightmare that had stalked her but a kaleidoscope of potential futures. Most of them were centered on her family. Maybe she should have expected it, considering the amount of stress she'd been under, but foolishly, she hadn't. She'd gone to sleep with the heavy shadow of grief over losing her yaya, worried about Sofia, angry at her parents, bemused by the man waiting in the other room, and haunted by ghosts of a past she didn't want to deal with. That had been enough to tempt fate into messing with her head.

She stood in the neat bathroom, hand under the running faucet, and stared at her reflection. The warm water ran over her palm, but she barely felt it as she tried to recapture the images that chased her from sleep. She edged around a jumble, trying to bring them into focus, but they remained indistinct. The emotional resonance was easier to untangle—shock, hurt, then a strange sense of rightness—but it still wasn't enough for an actual seeing, which left her beyond frustrated. This was not an uncommon occurrence when it came to her Mystic-based abilities as an Oracle, especially after the stunt she'd pulled as a teenager, when her use of a second-rate hex to bind her clairvoyant abilities had broken something intrinsic with her magic and almost killed her.

But desperate times and all that. A desperation born of a soul-shattering loss, along with the unrelenting demands of her parents, especially those of her mother, had backed her into a corner where she'd finally considered death as an actual escape option. If not for her yaya's quick thinking, there was no way she'd be alive now. She wouldn't have met Isa and Des or chosen to make amends as best she could. With age and hard-won wisdom, she knew if she could go back to her younger self and slap some sense into her, she would, but what was done was done, and all she could do was deal with the results, no matter how murky they were.

Granted, the magic that memory mages like Oracles played with was wildly unpredictable, which was why they needed mad skills and a titanium will, especially if they wanted to remain sane. There were three classifications of magic: Elemental, Mystic, and Divine. Memory mages were in the psychic-based Mystic class. They further branched into four categories—Sage, Muse, Oracle, and the rare Divine version, Sibyl. Each one required years of rigorous training for memory mages—even the gods-maddened Sibyls—to wield their abilities effectively. Oracles could see all the various futures based on current decisions, a step up from Sages, like her mother and sister, who saw past events and accurately foretold future possibilities. One of her friends, Shelby, was a highly respected Muse who'd spent years refining her work with magically manipulated or trauma-induced memories, earning a top spot in her field. It was Shelby's mentor who, at Yaya's request, had shared the critical tools that allowed Cass to function in the maddening world she'd found herself in after the self-imposed hex had been broken.

"Cass?"

She jumped at Grayson's voice and blinked, the sound of running water filtering back in along with a steady beep.

He stood behind her, frowning, her phone in one hand, the other on her shoulder. "You okay?"

Flustered, she dropped her gaze, yanked her hand out from under the now cold water, and shook it off. She turned off the faucet and grabbed the nearby hand towel. "Sorry. Kind of zoned out for a minute."

"I heard this go off a few minutes ago." He held out her phone. "I knocked when it kept going, but when you didn't answer..."

She took it from him and hit the button to silence it as she did her best to ignore the urge to lean into him. He was radiating heat that slipped through the flimsy barrier of her sleep shorts and oversized T-shirt, leaving goose bumps in its wake. "Thanks."

He let her go and shifted to her side, setting his hip against the counter's edge. He folded his arms as he eyed her. "Our options for dinner include spaghetti, hamburgers, and tacos."

She set her phone on the counter and adjusted her angle so she could face him. He was wearing a T-shirt and lounging pants, and she did her best to keep her eyes on his instead of roaming over his chest and lower, where his well-worn pants hung on his hips. "Tacos."

"Tacos it is." Instead of leaving, he stayed put, his attention focused. "I like it."

Not quite following, she asked, "Like what?"

"You without the glasses."

"Umm, thanks?"

He chuckled. "You've got beautiful eyes, Cass. It's sad to have them kept behind glass."

The corny observation made her laugh. "Dude, seriously?"

It was his turn to blush. He dropped his arms, straightened, and then ran a hand through his hair. "Sorry, yeah, that was cheesy." He turned to leave. "I'll just let you..."

Instantly, she realized he'd been genuine, so she caught his hand, stopping him. "Cheesy or not, thank you, Grayson, for the compliment." He turned to look at her, his eyes holding an amber tint as the gold striations appeared to glow. "Yours are gorgeous too," she said. It slipped out.

He grinned. "Good to know."

Flustered, she let him go and gave him a slight nudge. "Go, make me tacos. I'm hungry."

He pulled off a half bow. "Your wish, my command." He was at the door when he asked, "Do you need your glasses? I can grab them from the nightstand."

She shook her head. "No, I'm good."

He stopped outside the bathroom door and cocked his head, his expression quizzical. "You don't need them, do you?"

She met his gaze in the mirror. "What?"

"Your glasses," he said as she continued to watch him. "It was something your mother said."

There was a lot her mother had spewed. She gave him an honest answer. "No."

He didn't push for an explanation. "Leave them off while you're here?"

His question, strung between them, was anchored in something deeper. She wondered if he understood what he was asking. When he continued to hold her gaze with an alluring steadiness, she took a chance and gave a hesitant nod.

His grin widened, and he tapped the doorframe with his hand twice before guiding their conversation back into safe waters. "Okay, you've got fifteen minutes, then I'm going to need you on lettuce and tomatoes."

"I'll be there."

He disappeared, and she waited until she heard faint noises of pans being pulled out before she blew out a long breath. Meeting her eyes in the mirror, she admonished herself, "Get it together, Cass."

She sped through brushing her teeth, taming her hair into a loose bun, and putting on more substantial clothing. Then she finally checked her phone to find a text from Sofia.

11 at Broken Hen on Charleston?

She wandered into Grayson's kitchen, where he was browning meat at the stove. He turned to her and motioned to the counter behind them with the spatula. "Got stuff out for you."

Cass found a cutting board, knife, a half head of lettuce, and a couple of Roma tomatoes waiting for her. "On it." She took one of the bar stools. "Sofia texted."

"Yeah?"

"Mm-hmm. Wants to meet at Broken Hen on Charleston at eleven."

"Not a problem."

"You sure? I mean I can go rent a car while I'm here so you're not having to play driver."

He half turned so he could see her. "Cass, it's five minutes away. It's fine. I've got nothing going this weekend since I was just going to chill until Monday, so I don't mind taking you where you need to go. Now, if you want to rent a car, I can take you there as well. You tell me what you want to do."

Since she'd probably either have to rent a car to get back to Phoenix or get a last-minute flight, she preferred to take it easy on her checking account. Not to mention that she liked spending time with Grayson. "I'd rather have you drive for now."

"Works for me." He went back to the ground beef.

She added a thumbs-up emoji to Sofia's text then got to work on the vegetables. Conversation stayed light as they finished making dinner, and it wasn't until they were sitting side by side at the counter, tacos and napkins at the ready, that it veered back into personal matters.

"How do you expect this to go down tomorrow?" he asked.

She grimaced. "Awkwardly."

"You mentioned you and your sister weren't close, but she seemed relieved to see you when she answered the door."

"I caught that too." While on the one hand, she couldn't stop the flash of hope that Sofia might be ready to meet her halfway, on the other, there was too much history for it to gain strength.

"But...?"

Cass used a broken piece of taco shell to move some diced tomatoes and shredded cheese into a little pile. "I think the relief was just that there would be another target for Mother to aim at." And nope, that wasn't a crap ton of guilt still plaguing her about leaving her baby sister alone to deal with their parents' shit.

"Yeah, your mom's a piece of work." Grayson sounded far from impressed.

"I did warn you." She scooped up the bite-sized veggie pile with the tortilla shell and popped it into her mouth.

"You did. What's the deal with the fiancé?"

She nudged her plate away, braced her elbow on the counter, and rested her chin against her hand as she looked at him. "So it wasn't just me?"

He gave her a side-eye glance and shook his head.

She exhaled, grateful that she wasn't the only one not feeling Russ.

"I know you're worried," Grayson added, and she raised an eyebrow. "You mentioned it when you were talking to Isa."

Right. "I don't know what it is, but something's not right there. Sofia's not normally so..."

"Jumpy," he supplied helpfully.

She nodded. "She's uptight, thanks to my parents and their need to be the picture-perfect family, but she's never jumped at her own damn shadow." And that discrepancy in her sister's behavior left her with some dark suspicions.

Grayson cautiously asked, "Do you think he's hurting her?"

Since he was the second one to ask that, she gave it serious thought. There were no visible signs, but Cass knew that some of the deepest hurts were invisible. "Physically, I want to say no."

He studied her carefully. "But...?"

"But emotionally, I can't." Frustrated, she sat back, pulled her leg up, and wrapped an arm around it. "I've got a gut feeling that I'm missing something, and not just because I don't like his attitude."

"To be fair, he does give off heavy vibes of douchery."

She appreciated his attempt to lighten things, but it didn't ease the heavy knot of dread. "While gross, it's not illegal to be a douche."

"True." Grayson pushed his empty plate away then turned until they were facing each other. He propped his bare foot on the rung of her barstool, his leg brushing against hers. "Do you think," he said carefully, "you could get Sofia to talk to you if you two were alone?"

"You and Isa must be twins," she muttered.

"No, I think we both know you'll do what you need to save your sister."

His comment curled around her like a hug. "I'd say my odds are fifty-fifty."

He held her gaze for a long moment, something working behind his eyes. She had no idea what he was thinking, but even though her mind was spinning with worries about Sofia, Cass couldn't help but appreciate the fact he was willing to not only listen to her but let her talk it out as well. There had been no judgment about her broken relationship with her family, just quiet support and unabashed honesty.

He brushed a strand of hair back behind her ear and then dropped his hand to her knee. "So, it's worth a try?"

That two-step gentle touch went deeper than skin. Her voice was husky when she said, "Definitely."

It would be easy to fall for him.

That realization didn't scare her per se, but it left her a little off-kilter because Grayson Beck was the last thing she'd expected to walk into her life. But now that he was there, she really wanted him stay.

Oblivious to her ah-ha moment, Grayson's hand tightened on her knee as he smiled. "Good." He let her go and sat back. "If that doesn't work, we'll get his last name and whatever other information we can get out of him. Then we'll run with that and see what we can dig up."

A little bit of the knot loosened. "Your internet-stalking skills are that good?"

He chuckled. "Not as good as some, but I can get around. What about yours?"

She thought of the searches she, Isa, and Des ran on the regular. "I'm sure I can keep up."

"That sounds—" A knock at the door diverted his attention, and he frowned. "Hang on a second." He got up to answer.

Curious, but not wanting to appear nosy, Cass stood, collected their dirty plates, and rounded the counter to the kitchen, keeping her ears trained on the short entry hall.

chapter 8

Grayson

GRAYSON HAD no clue who was knocking on his door, but with the echoes of his brother's text warning, he knew a visit from his dad was a real possibility, and he couldn't chance ignoring it. He braced, checked the peephole, and then opened the door to a familiar face. "Miles, hey. What's up?"

His college-aged neighbor rocked from foot to foot as he dragged his hand through his longish hair. Considering it was standing up at all angles, this had not been the first time he'd done that. "Hey, Gray, man. I'm so glad you're home. I kind of need your help."

Grayson heard his sink go on and figured Cass was cleaning up their dinner. "Is it urgent? I've got company."

The younger man looked embarrassed. "Kind of."

Sighing, Grayson stepped back and held the door open. "Come on in."

Miles mumbled his thanks and shuffled through.

Grayson closed the door then led the way into his condo. When he hit the kitchen, he found Cass at the sink, setting the last plate in the drainboard. "Cass, this my neighbor Miles. Miles, this is Cass."

Miles's anxious air dimmed long enough for him to say

hello and once again offer an apology, which Grayson waved off. "Just tell me what's going on," Grayson said.

Miles drew in a big breath. "Okay, well, you know how Jenna and I are moving to Denver?"

Clearly, this was going to be a story, so Grayson braced a hand on the back of one of his bar stools and settled in. "At the end of month, right?"

"Yeah. Since that's, like, right around the corner..."

Amused, Grayson silently corrected to *More like two weeks*.

"We decided to have one last get-together with our friends the night before last, but it got a little out of hand."

Familiar with Miles's tendency to understate, Grayson had to ask, "How out of hand?"

Miles winced. "They kind of trashed our place." When Grayson didn't say anything, Miles rushed on. "One of Jenna's girls, an air mage, she, like, got into a fight with her guy, a water mage, and the next thing we knew things were flying around, and he was using the kitchen sprayer to ward it off, and by the time we got them separated, the place was a freaking mess."

"Was anyone hurt?" Grayson asked, considering how bad things could turn when it came to hurt feelings and upset magic users.

Miles shook his head, his hand wrapping around the back of his neck. "No, everyone's good. Now."

"Okay, so what's the problem?"

Red rode under Miles's face, and he avoided Grayson's gaze as he dropped his hand. "Jenna and I kind of need the security deposit for the new place 'cause money's tight, you know. We did our best to get the condo back into shape, but when it wasn't looking good, Jenna suggested we use this spell she got from one of her friends. They told her it would put everything back the way it was, but I think it expired or something, because right now, my bed is on my ceiling, I've got chairs pinned to my walls, some of our baking pans are, like, melded to our cabinets, and I don't know what to do."

Maybe don't cheap out on a rune? Grayson looked at the floor and swore he heard Cass choke back a giggle. Not that he blamed her.

"Can you help?" Miles was begging at this point.

It would take a better man than Grayson to refuse such a request, but that didn't mean he had to like it. He blew out a breath and looked at Cass, who stood at the sink, fighting a smile. He didn't even have to say a word.

"Go," she told him. "I'm good."

"You sure?"

She glanced at Miles, sympathy and amusement on her face, then back at Grayson. "Yep, go see what you can do."

He straightened. "Give me five, and I'll meet you at your condo," he told Miles.

Miles rushed forward and hugged him. "Thank you so much, Gray. I so owe you." He let him go and turned to Cass. "I'm really sorry to interrupt things, but thank you too."

"Good luck," she said as Miles headed toward the door, his relief obvious.

When it clicked shut, Grayson muttered, "I shouldn't have answered the door."

Cass laughed and came out of the kitchen to stand in front of him. Her hands went to his chest as she looked up at him. "You're a good man, Grayson Beck."

He shook his head. "I'm a sucker, more like." He pressed his lips to her forehead then went to put on some shoes and grab his work bag before heading over to redecorate Miles's condo.

Over an hour later, Grayson let himself back into his condo, set his bag on one of the barstools, and walked into his living room.

Tucked into the corner of his couch, Cass looked up from her phone, those fascinating eyes of hers warming. "How did it go?"

He dropped down next to her in a sprawl. "I swear to all that's holy, they need to create warning labels for second-rate spells."

She set her phone down on the arm of the couch then changed position so she could face him. "I'm not sure that would help, considering why people go for them in the first place."

Grayson laced his hands behind his head and crossed his feet at the ankles, feeling the stretch through his spine. "Maybe, but cheaping out on spell work generally leads to spending way more in cleanup." He listened to her soft chuckle. "I don't know what the hell the original caster was thinking, but I'm pretty sure they were high as a kite when they created it."

"That bad?"

He gave her a pained grimace. "Undoing it was like walking backward and blindfolded through an acid-trip mine-field. I'm surprised it held together as much as it did without opening a portal to another dimension." He was only half joking. There had been a couple of bowel-loosening moments during the unraveling process.

"But you got it done."

"Yeah, I got it done." He dropped his hands to his stomach and shifted a little deeper into the couch. "Just not quite how Miles hoped, though."

"How so?" Cass scooted closer until she was pressed against his side and rested her head on his shoulder.

He tucked away a thought about how he liked her doing that. "How much do you know about how Keys work?"

"Just the basic premise. You guys are magical code breakers, right?"

"That's one way to think about it."

She tilted her head back, revealing a small frown. "Is there another way to think about it?"

"Yeah, considering a Key is defined by their specialty." Or specialties, in his case. When she continued to study him, he realized she was waiting for more. "Right, so you know how Keys can run the gamut from unraveling a simple cyber-code hex all the way up to undoing a complex hex threat, like a plague dealer?"

She nodded.

"Okay, so that's where the specialties come in. Basically, Keys reverse engineer spell work, so depending on their area of expertise and what kind of magic they're dealing with, they're further divided into either Static or Agile Keys."

Her frown deepened. "What's the difference?"

Too many to count. But for this conversation, he didn't want to get into a dissertation, so he did his best to keep it simple. "Do you know how hexes work?"

Her frown disappeared under exasperation. "That's like a Magic 101 question, Grayson." When he raised his brow in a silent taunt, she heaved a sigh then said, as if reciting a text, "Hexes, also known as curses, are created from active and dormant casts."

Following her subtle teasing cue, he feigned a professorial tone. "And casts are...?"

She gave him a bratty look but continued to play along. "Elemental energies powered by the caster's intent."

Enjoying himself, he grinned and pressed a quick kiss against her pouty lips. "A-plus work, Ms. Alcmene." He pulled back, ignoring her rolling eyes and flushed cheeks. "When a mage casts a spell, that hex, or curse, will take on markers unique to the individual mage."

"Like a fingerprint?"

"Not quite to that detail level. More along the lines of a power signature," he said as she resettled her head back on his shoulder. "Say a water mage decides to cast a curse but doesn't want it tracked back to them. The base thread of the rune powering the hex is influenced by their intent, which will in some way touch on the particular elemental magic of the water mage and hold a pattern unique to the way the magic is crafted. Then they'll continue to shape that cast, or rune, by weaving in other magic—like Elemental or Mystic-tied powers—to bury the fact that the initial thread is linked to water. Keys not only have to identify if a hex exists—they also have to determine if it's active or latent, and even further, they have to figure out how to unravel it without setting it off or destroying it, which means singling out the pattern and base element. And Keys don't just defuse curses—they also do cleanup once a curse has been set off."

"So Keys are the magical equivalent of the bomb squad."

He'd never thought of it quite like that. "Yeah, I guess."

"Which brings us back to the question: What's the difference between Agile and Static Keys?"

He shifted to wrap an arm around her shoulders and bring her in close until the loose top knot of her hair brushed against his jaw. The scent of her shampoo, chased by a subtle hint of jasmine, filled his nostrils. "Agile Keys work with curses built from an active cast base. If we keep with the bomb squad metaphor, that means Agile Keys work with complex, ready-to-blow bombs set for specific targets."

"Like cursing an ex with a case of horrific acne."

"Exactly like that. Static Keys work with latent curses, which are a secondary level of spell work that not only uses dormant casts as their base structure but also require specific conditions to work successfully."

She rested her hand on his abdomen, the heat of her touch no match for his T-shirt. "So instead of acne, that kind of hex would be like every time your ex opens his mouth to lie, the truth comes out, but only when hitting on other women?"

"Yep."

She was quiet for a moment. "Those sound way more dangerous than active curses."

"Either type can be dangerous, just in different ways."

She pushed up until she was facing him. "And which type of Key are you?"

He searched her expression—for what, he wasn't sure. "I'm both."

She blinked. "You're a Dual Key?" When he nodded, she let out a quiet "Wow" then resettled against him. "No wonder you're in such high demand."

"There's no shortage of work—that's for sure."

"I'm guessing Miles's situation was more the cleanup type than the disable type."

"Yeah. Unfortunately, the rune's initial intention was poorly constructed, so when the intended magic tried to 'set things back to normal,' it matched the base materials in their furniture and belongings to core materials like the wood framing of the condo or the metal pipes in the walls. I got their stuff back to its normal state, but they've got a good three or four hours of cleaning to do, and then quite a few holes to patch and paint, if they want to salvage their security deposit."

"Even with you undoing the hex?"

He made a noncommittal noise as he continued to play with her hair.

She tilted her head back, a little smirk playing around her mouth. "Wait, is this your way of teaching Miles a lesson?"

"Maybe." When she shook her head and went back to her

previous position, he added, "Hey, I didn't charge him my normal rate." *Or any rate, actually, since there was no way the kid would be able to afford it.* "And hopefully, next time, they won't use a knockoff hex."

Cass's laugh was soft. When she didn't say anything else, he enjoyed the moment of quiet intimacy—him playing with her hair, her idling tracing circles on his stomach. He thought about what was on deck for tomorrow and knew there were a couple of questions he needed to ask.

Grayson looked down at her bent head. "I've been wanting to ask you something."

Her fingers stilled, and she tensed a little but didn't look up. "What?"

Something told him to tread lightly. "When you mentioned your family's business, you said something about being naturally inclined to do the work."

He stopped, not sure how to ask what he needed to know because it might lead to him revealing more than he was currently comfortable sharing. She let go of his shirt and flattened her hand against his chest as she tilted her head back to study his face. Whatever she saw eased the stiffness from her body.

"Is that your polite way of asking what I am?" she asked with a hint of teasing.

He cleared his throat and did his best not to squirm. "Yes."

"The Ambrose name is my father's, but the Alcmenes are my mother's family. They also happen to be one of the Arcane twenty-seven."

Now it was his turn to tense. After the carnage of the witch trials and the eventual creation of the Mystic Accords, twenty-seven Arcane Families had fled Europe. Some landed in America, where they forged agreements with the existing people of the First Nations, which led to the creation of the First Nation lands and the Mystic States. That had lasted until the late 1800s. Tensions exploded into a brutal civil war, and when the dust settled, three ruling powers emerged—the First Nations, the five-seat Arcane Council, and the US government. The First Nations and the Arcane Council held much more sway than the government, which represented the nonmagic-user faction known as Traditionalists. The majority of the five-member Arcane Council could trace their lineage back to one of the twenty-seven families, the true movers and shakers of the modern Arcane world.

"Unlike the other big-name Families," she continued as if reading his mind, "my maternal line prefers to stay out of the limelight, which is why no member ever sat on the council."

"That's unusual."

"It is," she agreed. "But it's also necessary."

"How so?"

"Well..." Cass said reluctantly. She looked away and finished in a rush. "The Alcmene line is one of Seers."

Grayson's body locked with shock. "You're a Memory mage?"

At his sharp tone she started to pull away, but he tightened his arm, keeping her close. Stilling, she said cautiously, "You know that's a misnomer, right?"

"What?" he asked, too agitated to focus.

"Memory mage? The only ones who really work with memories are Muses, and because the classification of Seer was originally Memori, everyone got smacked with the label of Memory mage." She sounded disgruntled.

Grayson was still trying to wrap his head around her revelation. "Okay, then, what kind of Memori are you?"

"I'm an Oracle." She winced. "Well, a broken one."

He wanted to dig into that, but he was drowning in a sea of relief, grateful that he might not be forced to walk away from her. *An Oracle, I could handle...* If Cass had said she was a Muse, he wasn't sure how he'd have handled it. His experience with Muses had nearly destroyed his family.

Cass watched him. "Are you okay, Grayson?"

He shook his head. "I'm good." Before she could press, he asked, "You said your maternal line is of Seers?"

Cass gave a slow nod.

"So your mother is..."

"A Sage, like Sofia and my yaya."

The tension riding him took another step back.

Cass didn't miss it. "Grayson, what's going on?"

"I've got issues with Muses," he said, determined to be as honest as possible.

"What kind of issues?"

"Big ones. It's something we can get into later," he said. Cass didn't need the added weight of his baggage at the moment.

Fortunately, she went along with his suggestion. "I'm going to hold you to that."

He gave her a reassuring squeeze before circling back to her earlier comment. "What do you mean by broken?"

It was her turn to deflect. "How about I share that story when we've been together a little longer than a week, or when you share yours?"

Which implied she was hoping this would last longer than the weekend—something he could get behind. Grayson covered the hand on his chest and curled his fingers around hers. He was relieved when she returned the gesture.

"Deal." He brought her hand to his lips and pressed a light kiss to the back of it. "What about your dad? What's his contribution?"

"He's a pattern mage from a family that made serious money in the tech industry. That cash was helpful when he and Mother decided to expand the family business." She made air quotes around the last word.

The man bought his way into an elite family. Interesting. "Gotcha. I wasn't aware strategical planning was such a profitable business, but considering your family's magical bent, I guess that makes sense."

She gave an amused huff. "It does and it doesn't."

"Not following."

Her lips tightened as her shoulder rose and fell in a jerky shrug. "When it comes to accurate predictions, Pythia is the best of the best—hence their ability to charge top dollar. It's also why their main clientele come from the Arcane Families and their businesses."

He heard her thinly veiled distaste. "And that's a bad thing?"

Cass's gaze roamed over his face, and the shadows that drifted through her eyes hinted at deep hurts and a deeper anger. "It is when the right price ensures that the predictions are in your favor."

Why that surprised him, he didn't know. The Families were nothing if not ruthlessly capitalistic, but to shift actual events to meet their ends... "They can do that?"

She nodded.

A shiver of disgust crawled over him. "That sounds remarkably..."

"Illegal? Unethical?" she offered.

Evil would be his choice, but instead, he said, "Either. Both."

Her soft "Yeah" was followed by a harsh exhalation. "I shared that opinion with my parents."

"I'm sure that went over like a lead balloon."

"Let's just say body armor became de rigueur for family dinners. It got worse when they realized I had no intention of ever working for Pythia. Then Yaya got involved and sided with me. The arguments got so bad she eventually chose to step down rather than continue to play a part in the business."

He had a feeling there were a lot of details she was leaving out, but her story did, in part, explain the rift with her family. "Can't say I blame either one of you." He squeezed her hand. "Does Sofia know what's happening at Pythia?"

"I don't know. It's not like it's an easy thing to prove. The company's never been sanctioned, never faced any legal repercussions or things like that. It's more whispered comments than anything else, and whispers are easily squashed when you've got heavy hitters that can back you up."

"The Families."

She nodded. "They don't want to risk losing their crystal ball, so..."

"Your parents continue to call the shots."

"Exactly. No one at Pythia will stop them. Last I checked, eleven Sages of various strength were employed there, and each one had some sort of tie to my parents. They're not going to screw their paychecks by speaking out."

"So the natural-inclination thing means Oracles aren't a common occurrence?" he asked.

"There's maybe one per generation."

"That explains why your parents wanted you on board."

"Yes. There is an Oracle on staff. A first cousin to my mother. He's about twenty years older than me. When he joined Pythia under my grandmother, he negotiated an iron-clad contract that allows him to pick and choose which clients he works with and when. Under that contract, my parents have to be very selective of when and how to use him because Oracles don't have a long career life."

That doesn't sound good. There was that pesky protective streak again. "Okay, you need to elaborate."

She gave him a long, considering look before she answered. "Unlike with most mage-wielded abilities, Oracles don't become better at mastering their abilities the more they use them—they can actually get worse."

He frowned. "How does that work?"

She plucked at his T-shirt. "When an Oracle is asked to forecast, they don't just 'see' one path but all the possible paths. Most of the time, an Oracle will stick to the clearest and most obvious path for their forecast, but sometimes an Oracle will go too deep into a seeing, losing track of the reason they're forecasting in the first place. That's when, if they're not careful, it's easy to take a wrong turn and get lost. Think of it like a tree of never-ending what-ifs. The trunk is the clearest path forward, but each choice a person makes forms a branch, and each branch leads to another choice, creating another branch, and so on."

Picturing it, his brain ached. He couldn't imagine having to live that reality.

Cass kept talking. "For an Oracle to get back to the trunk of reality, they have to be rooted in reality, but the more times they climb the tree and the farther out they go, the weaker the root becomes. In the cousin's case, he's got another five, maybe ten, years left so long as he doesn't cascade out."

The grimness of that last description set Grayson on edge. "Cascade out?"

"Being an Oracle requires a mental strength that can be difficult to maintain, which is why we train almost from the moment we can think and all through our lives," she said somberly. "It's our way of trying to strengthen that root holding us in the present. But if it splinters, so do we. It's what we call a cascade, and the chances of recovering from it are slim."

"This cascade thing—can you stop it once it starts?"

"You can if the Oracle has a strong enough anchor to pull them back."

A chill raced down his spine and settled icy links around his chest. "And your parents wanted you to risk that possibility on a regular basis?"

"They did," she confirmed. "I did not, and neither did my grandmother."

"What the hell, Cass?" He didn't bother hiding his revulsion at her parents' attitude. "That's some serious bullshit."

She stayed quiet, and he realized this wasn't the worst of it. "You said you were broken." Something flared in her eyes, striking a chord in him. Before he could put a name to it, she pushed away from him. "And as I said before, that's a story for later."

Recognizing her self-recrimination and sorrow, he tightened his hold, keeping her at his side. He softened his tone. "Okay, we can circle back to how that came about, but for right now, I need to know—was it them that broke you?" If so, he'd make damn sure to severely limit how much air they got to share with her.

"Not them." Her voice was rough. Then she swallowed hard and touched her tongue to her lips in a nervous tell. "That was all me."

chapter 9

Cass

As Grayson cruised through the parking lot of the Broken Hen the next morning, Cass scanned for her sister's car. The sporty two-seater should have been easy to find in the sea of SUVs and sedans, but so far, no such luck.

"I think we beat them here," she told Grayson while he pulled into a parking space.

"We're about five minutes early." He shut the car down, got out, and came around to meet her.

As they crossed the parking lot and headed toward the restaurant, Cass said, "She considers that late."

"Could be that Russ drove."

She gave a soft snort and adjusted her glasses. "Doubt it. She likes to be the one behind the wheel."

They got to the door, and Grayson pulled it open, letting her go first. They hit the host station and the young man behind it. After exchanging greetings, Cass gave her sister's name.

"This way, please," the man said.

They followed him across the busy floor to the back door that led to a small outdoor patio surrounded by lush potted greenery and a couple of strategically positioned trees. Sunlight drifted through the foliage and chased dancing shadows over the handful of customers enjoying their meals as the low murmur of conversation filled the patio. She spotted Sofia and Russ drinking coffee at a table to the left. Sofia caught sight of her and lifted a hand in greeting while Russ pushed his sunglasses to the top of his head.

Cass returned Sofia's wave as a breeze drifted through, ruffling the leaves of a nearby tree. For a disconcerting moment, Sofia's welcoming smile turned into a distorted, almost skull-like grimace. Horror slid over Cass, bringing her to an abrupt stop, but then Grayson brushed a hand down her spine, and the shadows disappeared, leaving behind a frowning Sofia.

Grayson leaned in and asked quietly, "What's wrong?"

Everything. She swallowed her apprehension and did her best to keep her tone casual. "Nothing." When he continued to study her, she reached out and took his hand. "Come on." She tugged him forward, and they continued to the table.

When they got close, the other couple stood. Sofia gave her a brief hug and an air kiss, and Russ held out his hand to Grayson. "Since we haven't been formally introduced, I'm Russell Seagraves, but you can call me Russ."

Cass did her best not to roll her eyes.

Grayson took his hand and shook it. "Grayson Beck."

"Gray," Russ repeated, trying to sound chummy.

"It's Grayson."

Irritation flashed in Russ's eyes, and his chummy smile lost a bit of its charm. "Right. Sorry, Grayson." He retook his seat next to Sofia.

Grayson pulled out the chair across from Sofia for Cass and helped her settle in before taking his across from Russ. The weight in Cass's gut deepened because up close, there was no missing the signs of strain on Sofia's face under the artfully applied makeup. As the server handed out menus and did a round of coffee and water pours, Cass leaned into her.

"You okay?" she murmured.

"I'm fine," Sofia said, brushing off her concerns with a brittle smile.

Far from reassured but with no way to push it, Cass sat back and perused the menu even as she plotted to get her sister alone. For a few minutes, they compared orders and made minor changes then shared their final decisions with the server when he returned.

Cass was stirring cream into her coffee when Russ said, "So, Cassandra, I've heard a lot about you."

Funny, I haven't heard a thing about you. Without moving her head, she looked over the rim of her glasses as she tapped the spoon and then set it aside on the saucer. "Is that so?"

"Yes, Sofia says you own a bar down in Phoenix." His car-salesman smile held a hint of a sneer. "That must be quite the experience."

"I'm part owner," she corrected as she picked up her coffee and cradled it in both hands. "And yes, it can be." She met his gaze. "And what is it that you do?"

He sat back and stretched a proprietary arm over the back of Sofia's chair, the image of the young business professional. "I'm an acquisition manager at Pythia."

She looked at her sister, who had been fiddling with her napkin. "Is that how you two met?" When Sofia didn't look up or respond, she nudged, "Sofia?"

Her sister lifted her head and blinked. "Sorry?"

Cass's earlier worry returned with a vengeance, but she did her best to keep up the getting-to-know-you gambit. "I asked if that's how you two met. At Pythia?"

The distracted haze drifted away, replaced by a bright light. "No, we actually met in the wild." She leaned into Russ's side, her expression softening. "I was out with some girlfriends for Double-M and crashed into Russ. Literally."

"Sounds like that's a story," Grayson chimed in.

Russ chuckled. "I was grabbing a drink at the bar, turned to go back to my table, when I got knocked back by a beautiful blonde. The rest, as they say, is history."

"He's being romantic." Color rode under Sofia's cheeks. "I was a klutz, which happens when you mix new heels and a couple of martinis on an empty stomach." She looked at Cass, and for a moment, it was as if all their years of painful interactions had never happened. "You know how it goes."

"You always were a lightweight," Cass teased. "Okay, so, got to ask. What is Double-M?"

Sofia gave a cute giggle. "Martini Monday. It happens every few weeks when a group of us from the office get together after a particularly rough Monday and vent." Sofia gave Russ a small smile. "Lucky for me, that Monday ended on a high note."

He leaned in and touched his lips to hers then pulled back. "Definitely a high note." He looked at Cass then Grayson. "So, what about you two? How'd you meet?"

The question caught Grayson mid sip. Over the rim of his coffee cup, his gaze met Cass's, and a whisper of warning drifted through her mind. "Through a mutual friend when Grayson was in town for a job," she said, purposely vague.

Russ's gaze sharpened. "Job? What is it you do?"

Grayson set his cup down and followed her lead. "I'm a Key for the Western Guild office."

Because she was watching him so closely, Cass noticed Russ's momentary stillness. When he opened his mouth, the charming-fiancé role was a thing of the past. "A Key and a bartender, huh? Must be some sort of joke in there."

While Cass gritted her teeth so as not to rip into the

jackass, Grayson appeared unruffled. He cocked his head. "How so?" he asked in a decidedly cooler tone.

Russ's friendly guise gained a flustered edge that was tucked away before it could fully form. Before he could respond, Sofia stepped into the awkward pause. "So this is a long-distance thing, then?" she asked sharply, motioning between the two of them. "I mean, knowing how dedicated Cass is to her bar and friends, I can't imagine you two get too much time together—not if you're here with the Guild and she's there."

Cass tamped down her irritation at her sister's unspoken criticism, a practiced move that had been repeated often during their past interactions.

"Oh, we make it work," Grayson said as he aimed a wicked grin Cass's way. "Don't we, sweetheart?"

Her body did not care that he was playing to the other couple. It simply curled into the flirty implication and wallowed. Before she could respond, their order arrived, and talk faded as they settled into their food. When the conversation picked back up, it didn't stray into anything heavy, and Cass was relieved to see Sofia lose some of her early signs of distress. Even her typical barbs disappeared, for which Cass was grateful. Unfortunately, there was Russ's overt charm to contend with, especially as he seemed to be making inroads with Grayson, whose slight coolness from earlier seemed to be thawing.

Either that, or Grayson deserves a freakin' Emmy.

It took a lot of restraint to ignore the little digs Russ threw in every now and again, but the fact that they only seemed to get to her, not Grayson, kept her in check. A couple of times, she had to remind herself that she loved Sofia and going scorched earth on the overbearing jackass would not end well. Throughout the back-and-forth, she learned that Russ's position, which involved reeling in new clients for Pythia, had come about due to an unexpected opening. His role at the family firm and his obvious attitude of self-importance went a long way in explaining why he got along so well with her parents.

Guess if I want my parents' acceptance, I just needed to add to Pythia's bottom line. The caustic thought stung, but Cass couldn't help it. The guy rubbed her the wrong way.

A flare of irritation ignited when Grayson chuckled at another one of Russ's lame-ass quips. She drained the last bit of her coffee, hoping the cup would hide her lip-curling disgust. When she set it down, her gaze went to Sofia, who was cutting into her breakfast. Cass's spine locked and her stomach rolled in queasy horror as Sofia scooped up a rotten mess of blueberries and strawberries from the curdled whip cream topping. Thin filaments that looked like spiderwebs stretched from the nauseating forkful to the pancakes before snapping free. More of the webbing crawled across the table and crept over the edge of Grayson's plate. She jerked to her feet, her chair scraping across the cement patio. The table conversation stopped abruptly, and everyone stared at her.

"Cass, you okay?"

Grayson's question sounded like it came from far away, but she was too busy keeping her stomach from revolting to answer. Something warm and firm curled around her wrist, and suddenly someone was between her and the nightmarish meal on the table.

"Cass?"

Her lungs found air, and she blinked up at a frowning Grayson. "I'm good." She forced the lie from her mouth and tried not to look at the table. Her mind scrambled for an exit. "Sorry, I just..." She waved her free hand, absently noting its slight tremor. "I just need to use the restroom."

Grayson's gaze shifted from her face to her hand and back, concern darkening his eyes. She kept her attention on him, needing the visual anchor to hold back the grim portent. He must have known something was up, but other than a reassuring brush of his thumb over the back of her wrist before he let her go, he didn't push.

Gathering her tattered composure, she forced her lips to curve up and turned to Sofia, deliberately keeping her eyes away from the food. "Want to come with me?"

Sofia studied her then set her fork down. "Sure." She put aside her napkin and leaned into Russ to press a quick kiss to his cheek. "I'll be right back."

Cass couldn't help glancing at the table as she turned away. Fortunately, the spoiled, contaminated food was gone. As unobtrusively as possible, she blew out a shaky breath of relief. Sofia pushed her chair in, and then the two women followed the signs to the restrooms. The short trip was not long enough for Cass to figure out how to approach Sofia without tripping over the multitude of triggers that existed between the sisters, and she couldn't erase the disturbing vision that was messing with her head. She was still struggling with what to say as they stood at the basin, rinsing their hands, when Sofia took the lead.

"What did you see?" There was a brittle edge to her question.

Cass met Sofia's gaze in the mirror, seeing the resentful light that her sister couldn't hide. "A warning."

"About...?"

She studied the stubborn set to Sofia's jaw. "I don't know."

"Bullshit," Sofia snapped, turning away to the hand dryer on the wall. She hit the rune next to it, and the dryer roared to life, making further conversation impossible.

Cass shook her hands over the sink then used one of the

paper towels tucked in the corner so Sofia couldn't storm out while the second dryer was going. She turned, taking in Sofia's stiff shoulders.

As soon as the wall dryer fell quiet, she said, "Sofia—"

Her sister spun around, anger suffusing her face. "If you don't want to tell me, fine. Just don't lie."

The betrayed hurt underlying Sofia's fury tore at Cass's heart. She was struggling to find a way to salvage the conversation when Sofia landed an even deeper cut.

"You know, I don't get it."

"Get what?" Cass asked cautiously.

"Why you did what you did."

Cass tensed under the venomous lash of Sofia's accusation. She didn't need to be an Oracle to know where this was going. Sofia didn't give her a chance to respond as years of resentment finally boiled over in a heart-shredding mess.

"Even when Yaya tried to explain to me, it made no sense. So make it make sense, Cass," she demanded. "Tell me why you tried to kill yourself." *Tell me why you left me.*

Cass heard the unspoken demand loud and clear. Hell, it had echoed in her ears for years even though Sofia had never actually said the words. "That wasn't what I was doing," Cass managed to choke out through the devastation of years of remorse. "I just wanted it to stop."

"Wanted what to stop?" There was the merest bit of snideness in Sofia's question that tore open old wounds.

Cass didn't resort to her normal habit of being careful with her words. Instead, she gave Sofia what she wanted. The truth.

"All of it, Sofia. The visions, the pressure, the guilt." *The demand to see only the paths that lined Pythia's accounts, regardless of the human costs. The pressure to become Mother's pet monster—a pressure I broke under.*

Sofia threw up her hands in agitation. "Oh, boo-fucking-hoo. You know you weren't the only one to lose Thena. She was my sister too."

The beloved name landed like a bomb between them, exposing the fracture that never closed. "I'm aware."

"Are you?" Sofia's eyes glittered with unshed tears and fury. "Because it sure as hell doesn't seem like it. Not when you made damn sure everything was about you after she died."

Anger, hot and bright, seared through Cass, and resentment charged in behind it. "Fuck you, Sofia. That's so far from the truth it's laughable."

Sofia's features were twisted and red, a testament to the depth of her rage. "Do you see me laughing, Cass?"

"No, but you sure sound like Mother." The accusation was out before Cass could stop it.

Sofia flinched but quickly recovered and sneered. "Let me guess—this is all Mother's fault, right?"

Refusing to acknowledge the flare of remorse that flickered under her rising frustration, Cass folded her arms. Maybe it would keep her from grabbing and shaking the shit out of her youngest sister. "Yeah, actually, it is." Icy fury dripped from each syllable.

"Funny," Sofia all but hissed. "I don't remember Mother buying the messed-up hex that about killed you or walking out the damn door. That was all you."

Cass felt that hit deep, but Sofia was far from done.

"And you leaving meant she needed a new heir apparent. It didn't matter if I had other plans. All that mattered was that an Ambrose would run Pythia. Even if there was only one Ambrose left, and it wasn't her precious Oracle or her beloved Harbinger. Just a barely average Sage who could never meet her ridiculous standards no matter how hard she tried. Mother decided, so it was a done deal."

The pain in her sister's voice made it hard for Cass to talk.

"And you think, what—that if I'd stayed, things would be different?"

That cut through Sofia's fury and pulled her up short. "Well, yeah."

"You're wrong." Cass's soft response fell between them.

Sofia's temper flickered then faded into cautious confusion as she held Cass's gaze. "I'd say you don't know, but..."

"But yeah." Then Cass shared a dark truth that had been buried for over a decade. "I tried to save Thena, you know. I warned Mother about what I saw, but she brushed me off." She tried not to react when Sofia's eyes widened with shock. "She told me I wasn't reading it right. It didn't matter how much I argued—she was right, until she wasn't. And afterward..." Cass fought back the lump in her throat. "Afterward, I looked, Sofia. I tried to find another way to survive her intentions. Every decision but one led to the same result within a year."

Horrified realization was creeping in, erasing the angry flush and leaving Sofia pale. "What result, Cass?"

Cass held her gaze, refusing to voice it because there were some things even an Oracle didn't want to tempt, and death was one of them. But her sister was an Alcmene. She *knew*.

Sofia swallowed hard and spun away to brace her hands on the edge of the sink. Her head dropped, and her shoulders slumped. Cass watched her, giving her space even though everything in her screamed to wrap her baby sister in her arms.

Finally, Sofia muttered in a choked voice, "Dammit, Cass."

As the leading edge of the emotional storm eased, Cass carefully closed the distance between them so she could run a comforting hand down Sofia's spine. "I'm sorry I hurt you."

Sofia lifted her head, her eyes watery as she met Cass's gaze in the mirror. "But not that you left."

Unwilling to lie, Cass shook her head.

A storm of emotion flickered then faded as resignation filled Sofia's face, and she looked away. "Yeah."

She pushed away from the sink and straightened, forcing Cass to drop her hand. She turned until she could lean back against the sink and hugged herself as if cold. She studied Cass for a long moment. "Yaya knew, didn't she?"

"She's the one that encouraged me to leave."

Sofia's small smile had a bitter twist. "She loved you."

"She loved you too."

The bitterness disappeared. "Oh, I know." Sofia was quiet. Then in a soft voice, she said, "It was easier, you know, when Yaya was here."

"What was easier?" Cass asked cautiously.

Sofia waved a hand in the air. "Dealing with everything— Mother, the wedding, all of it. Now, though, without Yaya to referee, I don't know…" She shook her head. When she looked up, the poorly hidden signs of strain were back tenfold. "Everything's a fight, Cass, and I'm tired. Russ is no help. Something's going on at work, and Dad keeps looping him into these late-night meetings, which means it's just me dealing with Mother's edicts for the wedding. Without Yaya stepping in, things are only going to get worse."

Guilt seared through Cass. As much as she wanted to offer to help with the wedding plans, there was no way Sofia would take her up on it. Not when putting Rhea and her oldest daughter in the same room was akin to lighting the fuse on unstable dynamite.

"What about Russ's parents? Are they helping?" Cass asked.

"He lost them years ago, and he says he just wants to know when to show up. He's leaving it all up to me and Mother."

In an effort not to share her opinion that maybe Russ needed to think about Sofia instead of kissing up to his soon-to-be in-laws, Cass bit her tongue.

Sofia rubbed her forehead as tears welled in her eyes. "I miss her, damn it," she muttered.

Cass didn't know if she meant Yaya or Thena or both.

A tear rolled down Sofia's cheek. She wiped at it viciously. "I hate this."

Unable to stand by while her sister was in so much pain, Cass gathered the younger woman into her arms and held her tight. "It sucks."

Sofia dropped her head to Cass's shoulder as a shudder worked through her body. "It sucks hard, Cassie."

Hearing her childhood nickname in a choked sob just about broke Cass's heart, but she powered through. "I know, Sofie, but we'll get through this. We always do."

It was the wrong thing to say. Sofia stiffened and pulled back. "Yeah, I guess." Her words were stilted, and she avoided Cass's gaze as she turned back to the sink to erase the evidence of her tears and focused on her reflection. "The warning. What was it?"

Cass looked at the mirror to find Sofia watching her, her face composed. Her eyes held a grimness that hadn't been there before, and Cass knew Sofia's question was a test. One she couldn't afford to fail.

"Rotten fruit and spiderwebs."

Sofia's eyes narrowed. "Death and ties."

"Or lies and influence," Cass countered.

Sofia's "Hmm" didn't convey much. She straightened as she balled up the damp paper towel. "How long are you staying in Vegas?"

Cass fought a wince. "A few days, at least. Longer if I need to."

Sofia nodded as if that confirmed something. "We should probably head back." She turned, tossed her used paper towels in the trash, and headed for the door. "Russ has to get back to the office."

Cass caught Sofia's arm, stopping her. "Are we okay?"

Her spine straight, her body rigid, Sofia was quiet for a moment. "I don't know," she said in a barely there voice before pulling out of Cass's grip to open the door and walk away.

chapter 10

Grayson

THE HEADACHE that had flirted with Grayson at the Broken Hen had gone into full-on stalker mode by the time he released the security wards and led an unusually subdued Cass into his condo. He tossed his keys onto the counter and headed to the couch, where he collapsed with a relieved groan. He laid his head back, closed his eyes, and pinched the bridge of his nose.

"You okay?" Cass asked, the first words she had uttered since saying goodbye to Sofia and Russ.

What's it look like? The snappish thought came out of nowhere as he concentrated on breathing through the throbbing ache. "No, my head's killing me." He dropped his hands, and as the cushions next to him moved, he braved opening his eyes just enough to see her settling into the couch.

She was watching him with a worried frown. "You need me to grab some aspirin?"

Over-the-counter medicine was not going to be strong enough to keep his head from exploding. "There's a pain amulet in the hall bath. Can you grab that for me?"

Grayson closed his eyes again as she got up. He focused on

a slow and steady inhalation- exhalation pattern instead of the strange simmering irritation bubbling under the dull pain.

When she came back, she took a seat next to him, curled her fingers around his wrist, turned his hand palm up, and set the amulet in it. "Here."

He muttered his thanks, activated the charm, then pressed it against his forehead. A soothing wash of magic encircled his head, easing the worst of the pain, and the resulting relief took the edge off his temper. He dropped his hand to his lap, felt her take the amulet, and listened as she tossed it onto one of the end tables. The muscles in his neck and shoulders eased, and his breathing deepened.

He wasn't sure how long they sat there in silence, but he could hear her typing on her phone. From the stops and starts, he figured she was texting someone. Likely Isa or Des. At one point, Cass got up, but he was happy to drift in that semi-aware, hazy state. He felt her come back but not to sit next to him. Instead, she settled on the floor in front of the couch, her shoulder brushing his calf. When the familiar snick of playing cards crept into the quiet, a distant curiosity stirred then floated away. Eventually, even that small noise dissipated, and he drifted in a sea of quiet.

"Grayson," she called softly. When he responded with an equally low questioning hum, she asked, "Do you normally get migraines like this?"

Not wanting to jar anything, he kept his eyes closed. "Not a migraine, just a headache."

"Okay, so do you normally get headaches like this?"

The exaggerated patience in her voice made him want to smile. And he would have chanced doing just that except he worried the movement would worsen the ache in his head. "Sometimes. Generally, it's because of allergies and stuff like that." Or if he worked for an extended time on extremely diffi-cult curses.

There was another long pause. "What if it's not allergies?"

Her question dragged him out of the comfortable haze and invited the lurking curiosity to settle in for a chat. He opened his eyes and dared to lift his head and look at her. The afternoon sun was stuck behind half-open blinds, which allowed just enough light to bathe the room in a soft glow. Fortunately, she hadn't turned on any lights, and his careful movements weren't aggravating the stubborn ache in his temples.

"What?" he asked.

Still sitting on the floor, Cass twisted so she could see him, her arm resting on the couch next to him. She wasn't wearing her glasses, and her gaze was steady and grave. "What if it's not allergies? What if it's something else? Something magic related, not pollen related?"

He tried not to take offense but wasn't sure he managed. "I think I'd know if I was hexed, Cass."

She bit her lower lip and looked back at the coffee table, where colorful cards were laid out in a familiar cross pattern. "I don't think you're hexed, Grayson." She tapped a card lying crosswise over a center card.

He carefully leaned forward so he could make out the image. "Erinyes?"

"Seven of swords. Symbolizes deceptions, and it's covering you."

He nudged aside the haunting picture of three older warrior women who were clearly related, each armed with lethal-looking swords and wearing various crowns of skulls, snakes, and bone. The card underneath it held three profiles of a younger black-haired woman. Illuminated on each forehead were a waxing, a new, and a waning moon. The center image had tears of fire and held a key and an adder. All three profiles struck a chord deep within him. He traced the card with his finger and raised a brow at Cass.

"Hecate. In other decks, this is the Magician card." She dropped her attention to the card. "It represents you." She nudged the Erinyes card back into position.

"You're doing a tarot reading? Of me?" He winced when he caught the edge of skepticism in his voice.

Cass's back went tight, and she shifted away from him, picking up the pile of unlaid cards.

He caught her wrist, stopping her. "I'm sorry. That came out wrong."

"It's fine." She didn't look at him, but she didn't pull away either. "Not everyone is comfortable with readings."

She was giving him an out, but he refused to take it. "It's not that. It's just..." Since he had no idea where he was going with this, he lamely ended with "Why?"

She sighed. "It wasn't supposed to be about you. There's something going on, something I can't see, and sometimes the cards help clear the lens, so to speak."

Considering she was an Oracle, he'd be an idiot to brush off her concerns. "Okay, so you played with the cards and—what? They just landed on me?"

She twisted her wrist, breaking his grip, and shot him a narrow-eyed look. "I don't play with cards, Grayson. This isn't a game."

Knowing he'd blundered yet again, he held up both hands, palms out in a conciliatory manner. "No, it's not."

He dropped his head and rubbed his temples, hoping to ease the lingering ache. *Why am I being such a dick about this?* Cass hadn't struck him as a drama queen, so if there was something that worried her, he needed to listen.

Resolved, he lifted his head and took in the ten-card spread. "All right, tell me what we're looking at."

Cass searched his face, probably trying to see if he was serious. He waited her out. The tension in her body slowly faded, and she turned back to the cards. "Do you know anything about tarot?"

"Outside the fact that it's a divination tool, no."

"Right, so this deck has been in my family for generations." She fanned out a few cards from the pile she held, showing him the vibrant imagery. "The Alcmene women descend from a line of Greek Seers, hence the gods and goddesses instead of the typical Major and Minor Arcana titles." She set the stack of unused cards aside and then went back to the ones lying on the table. "This layout is a Celtic Cross, and it can either provide in-depth answers to specific questions or help guide you on general ones. Since I couldn't nail down what's bothering me, I needed something to help me cut through the noise. I wasn't intending to ask anything specific and was surprised when you became the focus."

He studied the striking artwork on each card. It was vivid and mesmerizing and, despite its age, didn't look like it had survived generations of hands and shuffling. His attention drifted back to the Magician card. "Why Hecate's card?"

Cass's shoulders went solid, and she tucked her hair behind an ear, a nervous tell he'd spotted earlier, right before they kissed. What she didn't do was look at him as she spoke. "Depending on its position, it can represent someone who doesn't let emotions rule but uses them to enhance their skills. This person tends to be detail oriented, extremely good at what they do, and an inspiration to others."

He could recognize some of those traits in himself, but no one was that good. "Sounds a little too perfect to be me."

That brought her head up, and a flash of humor was there and gone. "Oh, it's not all rainbows and glitter, because it can also represent someone unsure of themselves and their abilities, leaving them constantly off-balance. They may be more inclined to talk a big game than actually pull it off, which makes others wonder what they're up to."

"Not sure I like any of those either."

She gave a soft chuckle. "This card fits you in that you're steady, you know what you want, and you're sure of your skills."

A warm feeling wrapped around his heart. "Okay, I can work with that." He decided to move them along. "And that one?"

"That one would be our current problem. The Erinyes card tends to signify some kind of illusion or deception."

"I'm not hexed." He didn't know why her continued insinuation irritated him so much.

"That's not what I said, Grayson," she shot back with strained patience. "I said you're being negatively influenced somehow. Look." She got up on her knees and started pointing out the various cards, beginning with the one to the left of Hecate. "This represents your past—things that are impacting the now."

The card showed a woman lying in a flower-strewn pool, her eyes half open as if asleep or dreaming, but it was upside down. "Naiads? What's it mean?"

Cass looked uncomfortable. "It's the ten of cups, reversed. It signifies a broken family, disharmony, conflict, and emotional turmoil."

He tensed, not liking how close her interpretation skirted to the truth, but before he could comment, she moved on.

"This one"—she touched the card sitting to the right of his card—"indicates the possible future if we don't change things."

It was heavily shadowed, with a bare sliver of moon illuminating a male profile with an angled chin. The name at the bottom said *Erebus*. His stomach knotted as he noted that it, too, was upside-down.

"The Page of Swords, reversed, indicates that if things

remain the same, you'll start to question what's real." She reached for the card sitting above his. It reminded him of Cass —dark hair, golden eyes, and witchy face set against a star-studded sky and surrounded by shadows that could be either grasping hands or feathered wings. "This is the best outcome if we continue forward without making any changes."

He read the name at the bottom of the card. "Chaos? That doesn't sound good."

That earned him a small smile. "Actually, the Ace of Swords in this position shows you'll eventually see through the lies."

"How about not having to deal with them in the first place?"

"Yeah, that would be ideal." She skipped over the grim visage of the card sitting directly below his, instead picking up the last card of four placed in a column to the right. "This is the Knight of Pentacles, Zephyros, which warns us to move carefully as we deal with all of this."

This card was done in shades of white, gold, and silver. A man with gold wings faced to the left, his profile lovingly detailed but his body a vague impression of smoke.

"And this one?" He took the card she had skipped over. It showed a black-armored, horned, helmeted warrior holding a three-headed puppy. "Let me guess—Hades is the Devil?"

She nodded as she took the card from him and put it back. What she didn't do was talk.

"Cass, what does it mean?"

Instead of answering, she said, "I made a call to Des and asked him to do a search on Russ." She took a deep breath and faced him. Her gaze was worried but steady. "He found out that Russ is an Auctori mage."

Shock shoved his dull headache aside for a moment. "He's sure?"

She nodded. "The card that sits below yours—"

"The Devil card," he said grimly.

"Indicates that there are unknown factors driving the current situation," she finished.

That would make a sick sort of sense if Russ was an Auctori mage. This particular mage class was notorious for fucking with people's heads, and their influence could span from minor influence to almost complete mind control, depending on where they sat on the power spectrum. That made Russ dangerous.

Cass turned back to the spread. "Hades can also symbolize other things, like entrapment, addictions, temptations, and transformations."

"Transformations?"

"Think of breaking free of bad habits or influences."

"So, which is it here?"

"I think in this case, it's saying you're being manipulated by others, and once you recognize what's happening, it's going to flip some emotional triggers."

Every muscle locked as his mind raced, putting the pieces together. He really didn't like the picture it was forming. "You think Russ's managed to get into my head and fuck with it."

Old rage seethed and burned through the locks holding it deep in his psyche. Unable to contain the fallout, he shoved himself to his feet and started to pace the living room, needing an outlet that wouldn't raze everything in its path.

Cass kept her seat on the floor but watched him. "I think he tried."

Grayson dragged a hand through his hair and gripped the back of his neck. "Let's find out."

Grayson spun on his heel and stormed to his bedroom, hearing Cass call his name. He went to his closet and shoved aside a rack of jackets to reveal an in-wall safe. He undid the wards and then coded in the combination that would release the lock. Inside was his personal stash of charms, spells that he'd created to counter the shit he dealt with on the regular. He quickly found the one he wanted, grabbed it and returned to the living room.

Cass was now standing and had moved around the coffee table. She watched him stalk back in. "Grayson—"

He cut her off with a sharp shake of his head. "I can't—not until I know for sure, Cass."

She studied him for a long moment, her head tilted as if listening to—or for—something. Then she gave in. "Okay, what can I do to help?"

He headed to the squat coffee table. "We need to put this off to the side."

Together they moved it to the edge of the room, making sure not to disturb the cards on top. Then he had her help him shove his sofa back so that the area rug was clear. They rolled it back, revealing an intricately etched design.

"Here, hold this for me." He handed Cass the charm bag.

She took it as she studied the markings. "You have a circle carved in your floor?"

"Unlike Miles, I'm not planning on getting my security deposit back." He went to his kitchen and began putting together the items he needed. "Worth it, though, because sometimes I have to work on stuff at home. I didn't want to have to redraw it every time I need the added protection or power." Hands full, he came back to where she stood and set the chosen items on the coffee table next to the cards they hadn't finished reading, before taking the charm from her. "Do me a favor—set up the four points for me?"

She nodded and picked up the salt, athame, unlit candle, and roughhewn crystal. He moved to the circle's center and sat, crossing his legs lotus style. He waited as Cass finished positioning the items and stepped back.

Grayson loosened the leather cord holding the deep-indigo

bag closed and spilled out the combination of bones, stones, and dried herbs into his palm. He closed his eyes and breathed, forcing his thoughts to slow and finally still. Only then did he reach for the magic that lived in his veins, pulling it up and wrapping it around him like a blanket. He let it grow until it lay thick and heavy around him.

When it was bucking at the reins, he opened his eyes and whispered, "*Ignis eum.*"

Power ran through him and spilled into the circle. With an ease born of years of practice, he wove his magic through the lines of the complex spell that would warn if someone was fucking with him. Reddish-gold threads of fire ripped through the runes on the floor then swept back to curl around him as if directed by an invisible hand, until he was wrapped inside a glowing cocoon. Power washed through him and lapped at the edges of the circle before sweeping back toward him. With each pass, the magic grew until the force of it tangled his hair and scoured his skin.

He was busy taking stock and only vaguely noted that Cass stood still and wide-eyed as he worked. It didn't take him long to identify the markers Russ had left behind. Auctori mages were known for being sly and tricky, part and parcel of wielding a magic that relied on manipulating a person's perception until it matched what the mage wanted their victim to believe. Their initial cast could easily go undetected, but once it found an anchor and went to work, a skilled Key could spot the differences.

Grayson pinpointed the small dark knots currently fucking with his head. Either Russ had been rushed, or he was a half-assed mage. Either way, the magical lines of influence scraped across Grayson's nerve endings, and outrage at the blatant violation surged, turning the flickering red of his protection spell into a pulsating deep ruby. As a Key, this kind of thing shouldn't happen to him, but there had been other things on his mind, so he hadn't noticed the insidious tendrils setting up shop.

He shoved down his anger to deal with later and concentrated on unraveling the lures Russ had set. They weren't deep and were barely holding on, which explained his headache and prickly attitude with Cass. He made quick work of unraveling the distorted knots before incinerating them to nothing. Only then did he go in and reinforce his personal protections, determined not to give the asshole another shot.

When he was done, he opened his eyes and found Cass sitting outside the circle across from him, her expression serene as the glow of magic danced between them. "Everything okay?"

"It is now." The dull ache in his head was gone, and so was his earlier irritation. In its place was a grim determination fueled by an underlying fury that wasn't going away anytime soon. "You were right."

He expected a flash of satisfaction at his admission. Instead, her expression didn't change. He touched a rune by his hip and pulled his magic back. The lines of power faded and then winked out, but he didn't move from his position. "What does he gain by turning me against you?"

A frown marred her brow, and she tapped her fingers on her knee. "Distraction. If I'm busy arguing with you, I won't keep pushing Sofia."

"So if he's arrogant enough to try to manipulate a Key, why wouldn't he just cut out the middleman and go straight to fucking with you?"

Her lips curved, and her eyes hardened, giving her face a merciless cast. "Because Oracles have a natural resistance to magical manipulation. Fate's a bitch, and She's not inclined to bend for anyone, nor does She like people interfering with Her mouthpieces."

Uh, learn something new. "And you're sure he didn't mess with you?"

Warmth chased away Cass's cold edges, leaving a genuine grin in its wake. "I'm sure."

Not fully convinced, Grayson held out his hand in silent invitation. She shook her head but got to her feet and took his hand. He kept hold as she stepped carefully across the lines until he had her where he wanted her. He pulled her down so she was sitting in front of him, their knees touching as they mirrored each other.

He claimed her other hand and then held both as he unfurled his magic, reigniting the lines. "Ready?"

She nodded.

The red tendrils curled around her with a slow grace, and he sank into his power, studying the woman before him. Searching another person for possible curses meant studying their magical fabric for any unnatural imperfections. In the simplest terms, it was like examining a unique coat for tiny rips and tears, but first, you had to learn what the coat was supposed to look like. He let go of her hands and lifted his to hover just above the crown of her head. He watched her intriguing eyes widen.

"Your eyes..." she said.

They were probably glowing in that freaky way they did when he opened the throttle on his magic. "It's all good," he reassured her. "Ready?"

Her throat worked as she swallowed, but she gave him a decisive nod.

He moved his hands apart and swept them down either side of her at a slow, steady pace. Cass's coat came together in his mind with a wash of silver, gold, and stormy white gray. The colors were ever shifting, like a churning sea. The constant movement made it difficult to find things that didn't belong. Absently, he noted a few spots where her magical material appeared to have been mended. He gently brushed a metaphoric hand over those imperfections, testing them even as Cass's breath hitched. When they resisted his touch, he moved on, searching intently, but nothing appeared out of place. When he was sure she was clear, he pulled back, his power once again draining away. He sat there, holding her hands in his, as they stared at each other in the quiet.

She was the first to speak. "You feel better now?" The question carried a gentle tease.

"I do."

She squeezed his hands. "Good." She let him go, got to her feet, and held her hand out. "Come on. Let's clean this up."

He let her pull him up, and they cleaned up the circle and put the living room back together. Cass was preparing to gather up her cards when he stopped her. "You didn't finish telling me the rest of the reading."

"There's not much left to share." From the top of the four-card column, she picked up a gold-washed card of a man in chains, hanging upside down. "The outcome. Prometheus, the Hanged Man. Basically just confirms that the future is uncertain and we need to watch for a new path to present itself."

Not exactly helpful, but then again, divination never offered clear answers. He touched the card now topping the column. "This one?" When she shot him a worried frown, he asked, "What?"

"Out of all the cards, this tends to be the most challenging to read."

"Why?"

"It's supposed to address the hopes or fears surrounding the question, but sometimes it can represent both."

He studied the gold-laced full moon that rose behind a white-haired woman, her face half shadowed, her gaze contemplative. "Selene."

"The Moon card." She picked it up and studied it. "Considering all the other factors at play, my guess is she represents the fear of losing the ability to choose."

He didn't like how his stomach tightened at the implication. "That makes sense, especially if Russ has no issues about exploiting others."

"No wonder Mother and Father like him," she muttered as she tucked the card into the deck. She reached for the last card sitting above the Hanging Man, but he got there first.

"What about this one?" He picked up the card showing a blond woman crowned by black roses, her arms filled with pomegranates and roses.

Cass cleared her throat. "Persephone, the High Priestess." She went to take the card from him.

He held onto it and took in Cass's flushed face as she avoided his eyes. "And in this position?"

"She represents the external influences." She tugged on the card, but when he continued to hold it, she finally met his gaze.

"She's you," he guessed.

Cass gave him a small, hesitant nod.

The flash of vulnerability tugged at him. "Tell me about her." It was a gentle demand, but a demand nevertheless.

She dropped her eyes to the card he held, her thumb brushing over the image. "She's the epitome of duality, representing a highly intuitive person, someone who offers whispers of wisdom to guide others. She's more than she appears." Cass met his gaze and held it, a war brewing in the depths of her gold-shot eyes. "She can also be someone who is emotionally cold, unable to maintain deep connections for fear of being hurt, and she can easily disconnect from the world around her."

He understood her warning, but no one got to their age without picking up a few dents and dings. "No one is all one thing, Cass. That's the beauty of personal choice. We get to choose who we are and how we move through this world. Not everything is set in stone." He let the card go.

"Oh, trust me, I'm well aware of that." Her admission was weighty with experience. Cass tucked the card into the deck. "But sometimes those choices only lead to one end, no matter which road we take."

chapter 11

Cass

Cass walked next to Grayson as a line of sweat beaded along her spine under her simple black dress. Although it was late morning, the Vegas heat was stifling. Even the breeze drifting off the man-made lake that the path curved along couldn't relax its hold. Not that it mattered to Cass. Sometime between stepping out of Grayson's car and walking up to the chapel doors, a numbing cloak had fallen around her, holding the world at bay. She clutched it close, grateful for its emotional protection as she navigated the endless parade of strangers gathered to pay their respects. Within its folds she could pretend she was watching someone else's life play out. Even her mother's chilly disdain, her father's typical disinterest, and Sofia's obvious grief barely penetrated. She sat through the memorial service in the packed chapel as the sentiments washed over her in a deluge of white noise.

The only thing that felt real was the steady hold of Grayson's hand in hers. She took her cues from him—standing when he tugged, sitting when he gently pressed. Fortunately, her yaya had made it clear that there would be no viewing and had insisted the closed casket would be set in place before the memorial service started. Iris had requested that the service in the chapel center on sharing stories of a life well spent, not on the empty shell left behind. Those gathered honored that wish, the stories continuing even as the service's allotted time came and went. Finally, the priest gave a gentle reminder that the majority were invited to stay and continue to share as the family said their goodbyes at Iris's final resting place.

Grayson led her out behind her parents, Sofia and Russ, and a handful of others as they made their way to the family plot. It was nestled in a walled garden facing the serene lake. The group separated into clusters under the shade of the two trees guarding the headstones nestled amid the neatly cut grass. When the dark mound of dirt piled to the side of one of the larger headstones caught her eye, something finally penetrated. A searing pain clawed at her heart, making her chest ache. Her soft, pained gasp had Grayson letting go of her hand so he could curl his arm around her waist and pull her tight to his side. The world steadied, and she leaned into his strength, forcing her attention away from the haunting hole where the curved edge of a casket could just be seen.

Her parents moved to stand with a somber priest and spoke in low tones. Her father's ever-present blank mask was firmly in place, but her mother's face was drawn, and there were dark shadows under reddened eyes. Cass had no interest in their conversation; instead she stayed still and silent at Grayson's side as she waited for the others to say their good-byes. Her parents didn't linger but stood over the grave for long moments before her mother took one of the roses from a nearby arrangement and dropped it on top of the casket before turning away. They headed out of the small garden. Cass deliberately avoided meeting their eyes by keeping hers on Yaya's grave. She wasn't sure she could handle what would be staring back.

Sofia was next, an overly solicitous Russ at her side. Her

shoulders shook as she took two roses and held them close. She bowed her head and pressed her lips to one of them before crouching to set it on top. She kept her hand there for long minutes before letting Russ help her back up. Sofia stepped back, turned, and moved off to the right. Russ went to follow her, but she waved him off. He continued to watch her as she went to a headstone lying under the protective branches of an old-growth tree. She crouched, brushed her hand over the surface, then carefully set the second rose on the marker. The pain in Cass's chest dug deeper, shredding a hole in the protective numbness, and a lump lodged itself in her throat. Although her eyes burned, they remained painfully dry.

Sofia rejoined Russ, who then guided her past them, lifting his chin to Grayson. His gaze slid to Cass before his attention was reclaimed by Sofia, who stumbled. He steadied her, and as they walked by, Cass couldn't stop herself from reaching out to catch her baby sister's hand and give it a gentle squeeze. Sofia's head lifted, revealing a face wet with tears and eyes bruised by grief. She returned the gesture before letting Cass's hand slip from hers as Russ led her away.

Standing at Grayson's side, Cass—too lost in her head to pay attention to her surroundings—barely registered the others saying their goodbyes. Only when Grayson called her name did she shove her way through the hazy fog and realize they were alone.

"I'm sorry, what?"

"We'll need to leave soon to make it to the reading," Grayson repeated, brushing his thumb over her cheek.

"Right." Her gaze went to the casket. "Can you give me a minute?"

He dipped his chin and let her go.

She walked slowly toward the open grave with an etched marble at its head. With each step, the numbness thinned, and a storm of emotions crowded in. She stopped, noting that there was a new date carved into the marker Iris now shared with her beloved husband. The finality of that date shredded the insulating emotional cloak even more. Cass spotted a beautiful arrangement of gold daffodils tucked among the roses and carefully pulled one free from the bouquet. She returned to the grave's edge, dropped into a closed-knee crouch, and set it on top of the scattered collection of roses. The gold blooms were a slash of brightness among the deep reds.

She flattened her hand against the sun-warmed wood. "I miss you."

The three little words released the lock holding everything back. Sorrow ripped the last numbing threads free and bled down her cheeks as she whispered her goodbyes. Somewhere in the midst of the storm, strong arms wrapped around her and held her close. When it finally ebbed, she rested her head against Grayson's chest. Despite the pall of the day, the sun continued to shine down with an unrelenting brightness while a nearby bird sang and was answered—a reminder that death wasn't an end, just a transition, something she firmly believed. In fact, she would place good money on the idea that her grandparents were somewhere else, making the most of their reunion. At that thought, a sweet peace tinged with an irreverent humor seeped in, easing the ache around her heart.

"You two had better behave, Yaya," she whispered with a shaky smile. "I'll see you around, okay?"

Grayson straightened first, holding out his hand to help her up. "Ready to head over to your parents' place?"

Not even in the slightest. But she didn't have much of a choice. "I will be."

She waited for the pins and needles to fade from her legs then turned toward the shaded spot Sofia had visited. Images from the previous day's nuanced reading rose, accompanied by whispers of warning. There had been a few things in the reading she hadn't shared with Grayson, namely the importance of their individual cards and the possibilities they presented. Even though her inquiry was focused on something completely different, the fact she and Grayson were shown as two of the most influential cards revealed the potential for an unexpected, yet powerful, emotional connection.

Relationship, she silently corrected, refusing to lie to herself.

But she was here, at a crossroads, and she had a decision to make because the cards had warned that the nebulous relationship was tempered by an overriding theme surrounding communication and how it could make—or break, if absent—whatever potential they were building. Grayson wasn't the only one with a past full of broken family ties.

She drew in a bracing breath and made her choice. "Can I introduce you to someone?"

"Sure."

He kept her hand in his as she led him over to the corner and under the canopy of leaves, where she stopped in front of an empty patch marred by two rectangular marble headstones set into the ground. The empty spaces between them made it clear that this plot was where the rest of the family would eventually find themselves. The one on the right belonged to her mother's sister Cora, who had died when Cass was a toddler. But it was the marker to the left that she stopped near. It bore the name Athena Alcmene Ambrose and the inscription *beloved daughter and sister* above dates that reflected a life cut tragically short.

"Remember that story I promised to tell you?" She felt his fingers tighten on hers in a silent confirmation. "It starts here." She inhaled deeply and stepped onto the path the Fates had shown her, sharing a story very few knew. "Once upon a time, there were three of us—Sofia, Thena, and me—and we were close. Not just because there were only a couple years between each of us, but also because we spent the majority of our lives knowing that our parents put Pythia before all else. As the oldest, I was determined to buffer Thena and Sofia from that reality as long as I could. Which was why, when I was sixteen, despite my grandmother's objections, I interned at Pythia, hoping my involvement would keep them safe."

Grayson frowned. "Isn't that a little young to be doing that kind of work?"

She shrugged. "You'd think so, especially considering magic and hormones aren't exactly a stable mix." Add in her guilt for being the reason her parents had always been arguing with Yaya. "But my accuracy rate was enough to override whatever concerns, if any, they had. Yaya didn't know, because I refused to tell her, that I had already been supplying predictions at my parents' request for a couple years before that. I officially came on board as a deal with my mother to keep her from dragging Thena into Pythia."

He studied the headstone. "And as the oldest, you wanted to protect them."

"I did, but in the end, I failed them." The pressure in her chest tightened. Yesterday's confrontation with Sofia had left fissures in the walls she'd shoved the dark memories behind. Old wounds had reopened, as raw as the day they were created, but she held tight to her determination to see this through. "There was an especially problematic client at Pythia who required a guaranteed plan to ensure a hostile takeover. Due to the complex nature of the businesses and familial ties involved, creating a predetermined outcome would require every resource Pythia had, including their personal Oracle."

"So why not tap the cousin on staff?"

"Because Yaya had told my parents to not take on this particular client. He'd hired Pythia before, and either she didn't like him or she knew something was up, but in the end, it didn't matter because my parents ignored her misgivings.

She did the only thing she could to slow them down—she cut off their access to the cousin, since his contract was with her, thinking it would bring them to heel."

"But it didn't."

"No. Instead, they came to me, which eventually led to a rip-roaring argument and Yaya walking away from the company." Even now she could remember how she and Thena had hidden in the shadowed landing of the stairs, listening to her parents' cold, cutting comments as her grandmother tried to appeal to whatever was left of their better natures, and when that hadn't work, had made outright threats. "But at that point, between the exorbitantly high price the client was willing to pay and the fact that they were backed by the majority of the board, who couldn't see past the profit margin, my parents were determined to see it through. That left my grandmother with few options other than throwing up as many obstacles as she could."

"She didn't know they were using you?"

"Not then, no. But that wasn't the worst of it. I didn't know they had already started in on Thena." If she had, she never would have allowed Thena to eavesdrop with her that night.

"Why would they do that?"

Instead of answering, she circled around. "Have you heard of the derivative-lineage principle?"

His frown, which hadn't really faded while she talked, came back with a vengeance. "It's a theory that describes how the recessive abilities of two magical genetic lines could come together to create an altered version of the dominant ability."

She had to admit to being impressed. Most people had no clue about the genetic theory because it wasn't widely taught. "Thena wasn't an Oracle—she was a Harbinger."

He canted his head in question. "I don't recognize that term, but something tells me that's not a happy thing."

"No, it's not. It's also not a generally acknowledged ability outside the family because it only turns up every few hundred years, and when that happens, families will lean toward hiding the Harbinger's existence." She finally let go of his hand so she could crouch by her sister's grave. She brushed her fingers along the carved letters. "Harbingers are the darker twin of Oracles, and they rarely end up living happy lives." At one point, she'd naively believed she could change that for Thena, but that was before the Fates had taught her otherwise. "Remember the tree analogy?"

He nodded.

"Right. Whereas Oracles can travel along all the future possibilities, Harbingers zero in on the one branch most likely to achieve the desired outcome, and then they prune all the other branches it to make it happen. And when you wield that kind of power, there are those who have no qualms about exploiting it."

Grayson read between the lines. "Like your parents?"

"Exactly." The familiar bite of bitter betrayal sank its poisonous fangs deep, and despite the press of summer's heat, a phantom chill slid over her, forcing her to her feet. "I spent days following multiple futures for the client, but each ended the same, with the client in financial ruin and legal trouble, which did not go over well with either the client or my parents. However, using my magic for that long left me teetering on the edge of a cascade, which was the only reason my parents allowed me to stop." Mainly because, as they flat out told her, they hadn't wanted to endanger her future earning potential. "The client continued to push. They even went so far as to offer more money, enough to override whatever reservations my parents might have had. That's when they decided to bring Thena in. At fourteen, she was still learning how to handle her wildly erratic magic, but that didn't stop my parents from piling on the guilt until she agreed to do the job. Unfortunately, the client's rival somehow found out about Thena and her ability, and before she could do what my parents wanted, she was kidnapped. Within hours of Thena being taken, the kidnappers made contact. They demanded that my parents pay a five-million-dollar ransom, drop the client, and provide proof of the client's illegal dealings."

She stopped as memories crowded in, replacing her sister's grave with the terrifying days after Thena disappeared. How Sofia had gone mute and silent, like a ghost. How Cass had decided to push her magic to its limits in a desperate search for answers. How her parents had refused to listen to what she saw, which drove her to scream at them until they decided to sedate her.

"I told them," she said.

A warm hand wrapped around the nape of her neck in an offer of comfort. "Told them what?"

"That Thena would die if they didn't give the kidnappers what they wanted." That Thena's blood was on their hands. That Cass would hate them forever. None of it made a difference. "They said Pythia couldn't capitulate to threats. Instead, the board authorized bringing in a hostage-rescue team that specialized in Family disputes. When the team went in to get her, it was a clusterfuck of epic proportions. The kidnappers went balls to the wall, and in the ensuing fight, Thena got caught in a lethal cast. She was dead before the last kidnapper fell."

And when Cass finally clawed her way free of the forced sedation and heard what happened, part of her followed Thena. In the hole her sister's death had created, a bitter brew of resentment, hate, and guilt stewed until it finally boiled over, searing away whatever fragile threads tied her to her parents and damaging the ones connecting her to Sofia and Yaya. "Afterward, I shut everyone out. The only time I spoke to my parents was when we argued, which generally led to me telling them to fuck off. I avoided Yaya and barely looked at Sofia." *Because the guilt was suffocating.*

Using his hold on her nape, Grayson turned her into his arms and held her tight. "Not a surprise, Cass. You were traumatized."

Traumatized. Gods, I hate that word with a passion.

She pressed her hands against his chest as a bitter laugh escaped her. "No, I was a self-centered bitch." She tilted her head back and met his gaze. "As much as I blamed my parents for not protecting her, I blamed myself even more." The cutting remarks of her parents, when they fought, had just added to her suffocating guilt. "What good was my ability if it couldn't save someone I loved? And if it was the only part of me that my parents valued, then I was determined to make sure they never got access to it again. So I got my hands on a subversion spell."

Tension snapped through Grayson, horror brewing in his dark eyes as his hold tightened. "Dear gods, Cass."

A familiar shame slid through her as she looked away and nervously fiddled with his tie. "I know."

"How?"

"There was a guy at school with questionable connections." She left his tie to rest her hands on his waist. "He set me up with a hex dealer." Looking back, she knew she was lucky to have survived, but at the time, she was desperate to get rid of the magic that made her an Oracle. "I was so angry, but even then, I couldn't help but think the risk was worth it. If I died, so be it. At least I wouldn't hurt anymore."

His fingers left her nape and trailed down her back. "You took a hell of a chance, considering high-quality subversion spells have a sixty percent success rate," he said with no hint of judgment. "And even then, some of the long-term impacts can be devastating. For under-the-table spells, those numbers drop significantly." The soothing motion stopped, and the heat of his palm seeped into the base of her spine. "You said you were broken. I'm guessing that's because of the hex…"

She pressed her lips together and nodded.

He gave her a light squeeze. "Tell me."

"It was a few months after Thena died." *After another fight with Mother that left me hollow.* "My parents were out of town, and Sofia was at her friend's house for a sleepover. Yaya had wanted me to stay with her, but I refused and stayed home. It was one of the few times I was alone, so I made the most of it. Yaya saw an omen, knew something was up, so later that night, she rushed over and found me. She called in a family friend who happened to be a Key. By the time she was able to stop it, the damage had already been done. Still, she did her best to repair what she could." Something flickered in Grayson's eyes, so she asked, "What?"

"When I searched you yesterday, I found those repairs." He studied her closely. "Her work is good, Cass. Extremely good. What I think is you're not broken, just a little scuffed up. If it had been a less talented Key, things might not have turned out as well."

She wanted to believe him, but it was hard. "Maybe."

Instead of arguing, he simply said, "Tell me what changed."

She worried her bottom lip. "The best way to describe it is to say my prophetic roots were weakened and warped. If I don't go far into the future, I can still walk the clearest path without distraction, but if I reach too far forward, I tend to get lost, which means I'm more likely to cascade out."

Concern lit his eyes. "So you have to be careful how far into the future you look?"

She nodded. "But that wasn't the only change. Sometimes, the line between the recent past and the near future blurs."

Confusion flickered. "I'm not following."

"Typically, Oracles work only in future possibilities. They

travel along the various paths an individual's decision creates, and if they choose to, Oracles can provide decision points for the person to pick which of the dominant futures they prefer. Whatever trigger the hex flipped gave me the ability to create specific decision points, which in turn allows me to create the future I want to happen, regardless of the petitioner's choice. Even worse, there are times I'm not really aware I'm doing it, because I'm so far along that future path that I don't realize I'm the one creating it."

He studied her for a long moment. "Okay, that's scary."

She grimaced. "Tell me about it."

Even scarier was realizing the only thing that held her back from taking that power and running with it was her personal moral code. The first time it had happened, she'd tried to explain it away, but when it happened again, there had been nowhere to hide from the truth. Already shaken by her close call with the second-rate hex, she'd gone to Yaya, scared and feeling more alone and out of control than ever. Her grandmother hadn't batted an eyelash but instead had carefully curated information that helped Cass learn how to rein in the impulse to play goddess.

"All right, I've got to ask, and not because I'm a dick but because I'm truly curious—how difficult is it not to use it?"

"Very." She wished she could answer differently.

Grayson's expression gentled. "But you've done it."

She gave serious consideration to lying then remembered the cards and gave a slight nod.

"Tell me about it?" It was a request, not a demand.

"Before I do, I need your word that what I tell you, you'll never share." If it got out that an Oracle had forced someone's path, it wouldn't be her parents but the Alcmene Family who would ensure that it never happened again.

The arm at her back disappeared as he brought it between them, his palm facing hers. "Promise."

Reddish-gold power ignited into an oath rune and hovered above his palm. She called up her magic, a stormy mix of pearl white, beaten gold, and flecks of iridescent sparks, which fired into a mirror image of the rune. The two runes merged into one, the colors shifting into rose gold, as the promise was offered and accepted. When the power faded out, he curled his fingers around hers and pressed her hand to his chest.

She lowered her voice, keeping their conversation between them. Not that anyone was around, but this secret involved more than just her. "Sometimes, Des, Isa, and I provide help to those who don't have a lot of options or, for whatever reason, can't trust typical channels."

His eyes narrowed, but he didn't say anything, silently encouraging her to continue.

"The last time, there was a young mother, with two little ones, who needed to get away from their father because he owed some seriously nasty people money, and the debt was secured with a geas that allowed him to use the kids to pay it. When the mother found out, she was desperate to get the children safe. She had no extended family to turn to, and her husband controlled their finances, leaving her trapped. It wasn't like she could appeal to the ones who set the geas, so we offered to intervene. Des and Isa did their part, and I did my thing. Together, we tried to figure out the best and safest way to get her and the kids out of his reach. The problem was, no matter which path we took, it left her, her kids, or both in danger because the one factor that remained constant was the geas." Which wasn't unusual when magical bindings came into play.

"What did you do?" he asked.

She wasn't proud, exactly, but she sure as hell wasn't sorry about her decision, not then and not now. Those children didn't deserve to pay for their father being a selfish prick. Honestly, neither did their mother.

She held his gaze and lifted her chin. "I found the one faint path with a possible loophole and exploited it, changing the terms of the geas so the only acceptable payment came from him. Then I made sure every possible path led to it."

"That couldn't have been easy."

"It wasn't."

Understatement of the year. She'd almost given up on finding a solution when one of the paths shared a glimpse of another crime, one that meant Isa could step in and get the name they needed so Des could pay the individual who set the geas a visit, which eventually created the loophole she used. Only then had she been able to twist the magical vow enough to set things in motion, like a karmic version of dominos.

He smiled, not with humor but with merciless admiration. "You're wrong, you know."

She arched her eyebrows. "About...?"

"About being broken." She opened her mouth to protest, but he got there first. "You're like a kintsugi piece."

Not sure if that was a positive or negative, she asked, "Kintsugi?"

"It's a centuries-old Japanese art form that showcases the beauty of imperfections in repaired pottery by adorning the mending cracks with precious metals." He brought her fingers up and pressed a quick kiss to them. "I think you're exactly who you were meant to be."

A sweet warmth replaced the ache in her chest, and she let her weight sink against him, trusting him to hold them steady. She wanted to believe he was right. For the first time since she'd lost Thena, she wanted to believe she was who she was meant to be.

chapter 12

Grayson

GRAYSON KNEW he was in real trouble, or more correctly, his heart was in trouble. The more time he spent with Cass, the deeper she drew him in and the more she fascinated him. Granted, it had only been a few days, but he had a feeling Cass was someone he could go the distance with, and if he was reading her right, she was feeling the same. While he was honored she trusted him enough to share all that she had, he found he was hesitant to reciprocate her courage. At least not today, when she had enough to handle with saying goodbye to her grandmother and dealing with her family. Later, though, he'd have to share because she wasn't the only one who lived with family-induced guilt and the price it demanded. Hell, his story could hold its own against hers.

They came around the corner and saw that the gathering in the chapel had migrated outside. Clusters of mourners stood under the protective shade of trees near the building, talking in low voices. Others stood in the parking lot, preparing to leave, but it was the group at the foot of the chapel stairs that had his pace slowing to a stop. His gaze stalled on the man standing with Rhea and Elias. He wore his tailored slate-gray suit with an ease that hinted it was his normal attire. His short dark hair was streaked with gray, and his arm was curled around the waist of a stylish brunette a good fifteen years younger than the man's sixty-plus years.

What the hell is he doing here?

"What?"

Grayson realized he'd stopped walking. "Do you know who your parents are talking to?"

She followed the direction of his gaze, and behind her heavily tinted lenses, her eyes narrowed in consideration. "No. Should I?"

"That's Cole Burton," he said without looking away from the small group.

Cass stepped in front of him, brushing a hand down his tie as if smoothing it out. "Sounds familiar, but I'm not placing it."

He looked at her, his hands coming to rest at her hips as if he'd been doing it forever. "Cole Burton is the head of Burton Street Entertainment."

She frowned and tilted her head, clearly still not understanding.

"He's one of Vegas's premier business leaders." He gave her hips a gentle squeeze and lowered his voice. "He's also rumored to be a possible replacement for Councilman Novak's seat."

Her frown disappeared as her eyes widened, her eyebrows rising above the rim of her glasses. "As in the Arcane Council, Councilman?"

"One and the same." His gaze drifted back to the group, and he felt Cass follow suit.

"Interesting," she murmured.

Yes, it is.

Close to a year ago, Jude Novak, one of the five members of the Arcane Council, had been forced to resign, and the details behind that were kept deliberately vague. But Grayson had contacts in unlikely places, who'd mentioned the possibility of treachery and attempted murder. Whatever the truth, filling the seat left empty by one of the biggest powerhouses in the Arcane world took serious time. Grayson was not surprised that Burton, with his immense business influence and money and his old-name Family, was one of three names under consideration. The sight of him talking to Rhea, Elias, and Russ with a familiar ease raised a few red flags, mainly because Grayson was a cynical soul and could think of many unsavory reasons a business mogul who might soon rise in power would consult a highly regarded strategic forecasting company, especially considering the rumors that a decision was imminent.

Or you're letting the past get in the way of logic.

He ignored that rational voice as Cole caught his eye and lifted his chin in silent acknowledgment, a move that wasn't missed by Russ or Rhea. Both turned to look for who had Cole's attention, and when they spotted Grayson standing with Cass, they frowned, Rhea in consideration and Russ in displeasure. Tension spiraled through Grayson, but he returned Cole's gesture.

Cass, who had caught the exchange, turned back to him. "You know each other."

He looked at the woman in front of him. "He knew my parents."

She didn't miss the verb tense, but instead of pressing, she murmured, "Looks like he knows mine now too."

As if hearing her, Rhea lifted an imperious hand to motion them over.

Cass sighed then half turned and took his hand. "Come on. Let's get this over with."

He let her lead the way for a few steps before falling in sync at her side. A slight breeze swept by, rustling the nearby leaves. Dappled sunlight followed them as they headed over.

They hadn't gotten far when Cass stumbled, and a small gasp escaped her.

He managed to keep her steady, but before he could ask if she was okay, she spoke in a low, urgent tone. "Who's the woman with him?"

"No clue." He adjusted his hold from her elbow to her waist as he picked up on her curious tension. "Why?"

She shot him an unreadable look and started to say something but stopped as two older women moved to intercept them. "I'll tell you later."

And that wasn't at all ominous.

The women had been friends of Iris, but they knew Cass enough to give her a hug while quietly sharing their condolences. She handled it with a grace that Grayson had discovered, over the course of the morning, came naturally to her.

When they finally reached her parents, it was Elias who made the introductions. "Cole, this is my daughter Cassandra and her friend—"

"Grayson." Cole's smile was warm and sincere as he let go of the woman at his side and held out his hand to Grayson. "I wasn't expecting to see you here."

Grayson stepped in and shook his hand. "Sir."

"Oh, you two know each other?" Rhea asked as Grayson retook his position at Cass's side.

"We do." Cole reclaimed the brunette. "His father and I worked together off and on through the years."

That earned him a speculative look from Rhea, but Grayson wasn't about to give her an opening to pursue her curiosity. Neither, it seemed, was Cass, who turned to the watchful brunette at Cole's side and said, "Hi, I'm Cass."

The other woman's lips turned up, and amusement flickered in her eyes as if she understood Cass's play and was happy to go along with it. "Hello, I'm Dana Marr." She sobered a bit. "My condolences on your loss."

"Thank you," Cass said before stepping back to Grayson's side. "Were you friends with my grandmother?" Her question was aimed at both Dana and Cole.

Rhea scowled briefly before her features settled into a more neutral expression, while Elias's distant air gained a hint of disapproval.

What is it with these two? Their initial response to every interaction with their daughter was borderline defensive. No wonder Cass no longer tried to play nice. It had to be exhausting to feel like you were walking on eggshells every time you opened your mouth.

Dana shook her head.

"I was, actually. Her and Dorian," Cole said.

For a moment, Grayson couldn't place the name, but then it hit him. *Dorian* was the name etched on the shared headstone where Iris now lay.

"My ex-wife and I spent a great deal of time with your grandparents," Cole said wistfully. "We lost touch with Iris after she lost Dorian. Then Lacey and I divorced, but I always meant to reach out."

A slight grimace flickered on Cole's face. Dana leaned in, her hand coming to rest on his chest, light flashing off the diamond of an unmistakable engagement ring.

"Unfortunately, life has a way of derailing the best of intentions." Cole covered her hand with his and turned his attention to Grayson. "Speaking of, how is your father? I saw him about a year ago, and he seemed to be doing well."

And there it was. The one topic Grayson had no intention of discussing, but manners dictated a response. "As far as I know, he's fine."

An awkward silence followed, interrupted by Russ clearing his throat. "Cole, why don't you come by my office on Monday, and we can finish our discussion on how Pythia can assist?" he said with overdone affability.

Cole fielded the painfully clumsy change in conversation with a nod. "I'll have my assistant call." He turned away from Russ so he could address Rhea and Elias. "Again, so sorry for your loss. Iris was a wonderful woman, and she will be sorely missed." Dana added her condolences while exchanging polite air kisses with Rhea as the two men shook hands. Then Cole turned to Grayson and Cass. "Grayson, it was good to see you despite the circumstances. We should get together sometime."

Grayson gave him a noncommittal "I'll have to check my schedule," as they shook hands.

Farewells were shared all around, and once the couple left, a strained silence swept through those left behind. Cass stepped into the breach, turning to her parents. "We'll meet you at the house."

She didn't wait for their reply before going to Sofia and wrapping the wan young woman in a tight hug. She whispered something to her sister and pulled back to study her. Fresh tears hovered in Sofia's red-rimmed eyes, but she gave Cass a nod, and Cass let her go. She gave Russ a distant chin dip and then returned to Grayson, who took her hand, and without another word, they walked away.

——— +⋅✦⋅+ ———

"You're awfully quiet over there," Grayson said as they headed to her parents' house.

"Just thinking," Cass said to the passenger window.

"About your grandmother?"

"No." Her answer was soft, and when she didn't add anything more, he gave it time. His patience paid off when she turned away from the window and haltingly asked, "Do you... can I just vent for a second?"

Her hesitancy pinched his chest. "Vent away, Cass," he said gently.

"Okay, so I know my sister's grieving, but something's not right with her. Every time she's with Russ, she's this... shell of a person who barely talks and hardly knows what's happening around her. I'm worried he's doing something to her, and not just because he somehow managed to be in the right place at the right time to get a position at Pythia then, within months, hook up with the owner's daughter."

Her concern was legit. The asshole hadn't thought twice about dicking with Grayson, so the idea that he was messing with Sofia wouldn't be much of a stretch. However, it could also be argued that Russ's interference with Grayson was the act of an insecure douche trying to ensure a good impression. Either way, Grayson was all about being Cass's sounding board, and to that end, he decided to play devil's advocate.

"Okay, let's say he is—"

"You don't agree?" Her question was sharp with hurt and outrage.

"I didn't say that. But there are tons of undercurrents in this whole situation, Cass. If we don't want to accidentally sink your sister's relationship, or what's left of your relationship with your family—which, if we confront him, is what will happen—then we need to tread carefully." He glanced over and caught her mutinous frown, a silent indication he was right. "So, if Russ is actively working Sofia, why?"

Cass sighed. "The most obvious would be to get in good with my parents," she said with a hint of defensiveness.

"To what end? He could climb the company ranks by using the same trick on his higher-ups."

"Not necessarily," she said, reflecting. "His magic is all about manipulation, but there are those, like Oracles, whose powers naturally block that kind of control. And with the types of mages at Pythia, a good majority rely on that kind of natural shield because their inherent powers don't like outside interference. Hard to predict what the future holds if someone's messing with your reality."

Good point. "Okay, so this natural shield—I'm assuming your parents and Sofia all have one."

"Some level of one, yes, but Pythia has a Key on retainer who ensures that my parents and most of the C-suite mages can't be influenced. It's a requirement by Pythia's board, to guarantee impartiality." The last was said with heavy sarcasm. "Not that it stops greed, but it looks good to the public."

"What about Sofia? Does the Key's work include her?" he asked.

"I would think so."

"If you had to rate Sofia's natural immunity, where would she fall?"

If a Key was bolstering natural shields, the spell's foundation would only be as strong as the natural immunity of the mage.

"If we put me at the top, Mother and Yaya would fall next, then Sofia, then my father."

"So, if he spent months working on her, he could get through." Like a beetle burrowing through wood. It would take time, but eventually Russ would get in.

"You're not making me feel better here, Grayson."

"It's just speculation, Cass." He held out his hand and waited until she took it, then he gave it a reassuring squeeze. "Maybe it has nothing to do with Pythia. What if she's having second thoughts about her engagement?"

"One could only hope," she muttered. "Unfortunately, I think Sofia's determined to see it through. Either that, or my mother is riding her ass so hard Sofie can't walk away." She was quiet a moment. "If Russ is influencing Sofia, can you break it?"

He thought about what it would take to reverse what was basically a long-term emotional curse. "Maybe," he offered cautiously. "But depending on how deep it's set, there may be lasting scars."

"Shit." The air in the car grew heavy with worry.

There wasn't much he could say or do right now to reassure her, so he decided to switch subjects. "Back at the cemetery, when you saw Cole and Dana, something happened."

Her thumb swept over the back of his hand as she took her time answering. "It wasn't anything specific, just an impression, and not a very clear one at that. It's probably nothing."

He wasn't sure he agreed, because if she was getting visions around Cole, then something was up. Still, she was clearly reluctant to elaborate, and he wanted her to feel safe enough with him to share. "Maybe, but tell me anyway."

She shifted in the passenger seat, lifting his hand so she could cross her legs then resting his hand back on her thigh. "I get the feeling Dana's at the center of something... big. I just can't pin down what the big thing is. It's like this..." She waved an arm around. "Vague possibility."

Dana, not Cole? he wanted to ask, but instead said, "I'm not sure I'm following."

She continued to brush a featherlight touch over his knuckles. "You know how a snail's shell swirls outward from a center point?"

"Yeah."

"Think of Dana as the center point, and the impact of her actions are a line of dominos that follow the spiral pattern."

Okay, that was a visual he could follow. "So your feeling of 'something big' is based on how large the snail shell is?"

"Not exactly. I mean..." Frustration made her voice sharp. "It wasn't a real seeing. More like a snapshot, there and gone."

"Okay, so what's worrying you?" When she didn't say anything more, he risked a glance to find she was biting her lip. "Cass, this is your area of expertise, so no judgment here, okay? I'm just trying to understand."

"Sorry, it's... I'm..." She pinched her nose and blew out a breath. Then she dropped her hand and tried again. "Right, so each ring appeared to connect to people I know. At least, I think they were. The further out it went, the harder it was to make out who and what I was seeing."

His grip on the steering wheel tightened as he picked up on her word choice. *People*, not *person*, which meant more than one. If Dana was the connection point, he could guess at least one, maybe two people.

"I'm going to assume one of those is Cole, and since he was all but bragging about bagging a bigwig for Pythia, another would be Russ?"

"They were the two smallest swirls," she confirmed. "Likely because they're the two with the most direct contact with her."

He felt an uneasy sensation creep in. "Who else?"

Her thumb stilled, and her hold started to tighten. "In ascending order from there, it was Sofia..."

Grayson would put down good money that was because of her connection to Russ.

"Then my mother..."

The person behind Pythia.

"And then Yaya, and then you."

A rogue thought created a crack for doubt to slither through, but he refused to give it voice because he could be completely off base. He could tell Cass was frustrated and struggling to put whatever she was seeing into words.

As if she'd heard an echo of his musings, Cass kept talking. "Which might just be me projecting, considering where we were and why..."

He didn't like the pinch in his chest that her defeatist tone triggered. "Were they the only ones?"

"No, and that's the thing. I could swear that it was Isa, Dev, Locke, and Rory on those far rings. Which makes no sense because where would any of them be connected to Dana?"

Those were not the names he'd expected, especially one of them. "Rory? Like Zev's Rory?"

"Yeah."

"Huh." He wasn't sure what else to say. Cass had a point about the lack of connections. It would be more understandable if it was Cass sitting at the center, but Dana? Yeah, he wasn't quite sure what to think about that particular detail.

Cass sighed. "I don't know what it means or if it means anything at all."

He gave her hand a gentle squeeze. "There's not much we can do right now, so let's get through the rest of today before we worry about what might be coming."

She didn't let go of his hand but remained quiet as they continued to her parents' house. As he drove, the air around her slowly shifted as her grief sifted back in. She turned to stare out the window, and his heart stung at the soft sniffles she tried to hide. He brought her hand to his mouth to brush his lips over her knuckles, a silent offer of support because there was nothing he could say to ease her pain. Her grip tightened.

When he drove through the gate at Spanish Elms, she finally spoke, her voice husky with tears. "Thank you for being with me today, Grayson."

It was all he could do not to pull over and gather her into his arms, or better yet, turn the car around and avoid the impending interaction with her family altogether because he didn't need Cass's magic to know things could go sideways easily.

Instead, he stated with simple honesty, "No place I'd rather be, sweetheart."

chapter 13

Cass

ON ONE OF the two half-moon couches in her parent's living room, Cass sat next to Grayson, a breath away from flying apart. Her emotions bounced along the gamut of apathetic numbness to chafing resentment to a hollow sort of heartache then back, leaving her a mess. If not for Mr. Swanson's insistence that she be present for the reading, she would have asked Grayson to take her back to his condo. Instead, she sat stiff as a board, nails biting into her palms, as she tried not to lose her shit.

Swanson stood between the two couches as he proceeded quickly through the formalities and into the financials. First up was Iris's shares in Pythia. While she had ceded the running of Pythia to Rhea and Elias years before, she still held both her and Dorian's shares, which would now be divided between Sofia and Cass. That little announcement drew frowns from her parents but not the expected angry outburst. Strange, considering that if the two sisters decided to team up, they would be in a position to seize majority control from Rhea and Elias. Insight struck hard, and Cass realized the lack of reaction was because her parents felt confident that Cass would continue her hands-off approach to Pythia instead of seeing Yaya's decision for what it was—an unspoken request that her granddaughters act as the final check on their parents' ambition and greed.

Resentment flickered, quickly followed by guilt. Cass didn't want that responsibility—not after doing everything she could to leave behind Pythia and its twisted ties. A muffled sniffle came from Sofia, who sat next to a stoic Russ on the other couch as Swanson's voice faded into the background. Taking in her sister's grief-ravaged appearance, Cass felt the sticky webs of Pythia tighten, because protecting Sofia took priority. Snippets from her vision at the cemetery teased her mind in a dizzying dance and piled onto her growing suspicions about Russ, weighing them down with the certainty that something much darker was at play.

Her mother's soft shudder of breath caught her attention. Rhea was slumped heavily into Elias, looking far from her normal composed self. Her typical impenetrable mask was gone, fractured by grief and loss.

It's disconcerting to see her being so... human.

A flash of memory slapped aside the childish thought and seared through Cass's brain, the weight of it undeniable.

Cass struggled through the heavy fog of sedation, unable to move, her arms and legs strapped to a bed. The room was dim, but she could make out her mother hunched in a chair next to her. Rhea's shoulders shook as she buried her face in her hands, her muffled sobs seeping through Cass's haze and the heavy press of guilt in the air—hers, her mother's, or both. It was hard to tell them apart.

"And to Cassandra..."

At her name, Cass snapped back to the present.

Swanson shared Iris's personal messages. "I leave my grandmother's mirror as a reminder that what lies behind paves the way forward. To Sofia, I leave my emerald ring from my beloved Dorian as a reminder that love is unconditional and forever. To my Rhea, I leave my locket so that you never forget you have always been one of my most precious gifts."

A sob escaped Rhea as she buried her face into Elias's chest, and Swanson fell quiet. In a rare show of emotion, her father's arms came around her mother, and he pressed his lips to the top of her head. Watching it, Cass's heart broke a little, the ragged edges tearing away old scabs.

Yaya's words from years before, when Cass had struggled to come to terms with the situation surrounding Thena's death, echoed in her mind: "Remember, there is always more to the picture than what you see at first glance, angel." Maybe it was time to grow up—to lower the lenses from her younger self, the ones tinted by resentment, blame, and guilt, and study her family's picture with a nuanced eye.

Swanson cleared his throat and waited until Rhea regained her composure. When she finally lifted her head, he continued. "Iris set up individual trusts for both Sofia and Cassandra that can be accessed on their thirtieth birthdays. Each account totals seven hundred fifty thousand. Her wish was to ensure that her granddaughters had the financial freedom to pursue their own endeavors. The remainder of the estate goes to Rhea." He took off the reading glasses and tucked them into an interior pocket of his suit jacket. He then opened his briefcase and pulled out three small boxes with accompanying envelopes. "She also asked me to give you these personally." He moved to Rhea first, then Sofia, and finally Cass, handing each woman a package and an envelope.

Like the other two, Cass's wasn't overly large and was unwrapped. The wooden box was hinged on one side and just big enough to hold her great-gran's pocket mirror, the one she'd always admired even though Yaya had been careful to keep the antique out of reach. She set it in her lap and then took the envelope Swanson held out to her. Her name was written on the front in her grandmother's familiar looping script, and when she turned it over, she found it sealed with wax. She brushed a finger over the raised lines of the Alcmene crest—an hourglass surrounded by the swirls of an infinity loop—set in the indigo wax.

Grayson's arm around her shoulders tightened, and she turned. He was frowning, his attention on the letter and box. His gaze came to hers, and he gave a barely there head shake. It didn't take a genius to understand he didn't want her to open either item here, and since she'd rather read her yaya's last letter in private, she tucked the envelope under the box for later.

Across from her, Rhea had set Iris's unopened gift in her lap but was slipping the letter free of the envelope. Sofia had done the opposite, setting the envelope aside so she could open her gift. The gleam of the emerald ring their yaya had never been without glinted. Sofia stared down at the ring, her finger gently brushing the faceted jewel as tears spilled down her drawn face.

Swanson returned to his briefcase, collected his files, and tucked them away. Then he addressed the group, his voice gentle. "There are a few forms that need to be signed, but they can wait until Monday."

Elias carefully removed his arm from Rhea and got to his feet. "Thank you, Eric," he said gruffly as he offered the lawyer his hand. "If you can bring those to the offices, I'd appreciate it."

Swanson shook his hand. "Of course. I'll make sure you know when to expect me." He moved to Rhea, who was still seated, her gaze on Iris's letter in her trembling hands. He carefully took a seat on the edge of the stone coffee table in front of her and set his briefcase on the floor. "Rhea." He waited for her attention to switch from the letter to him then reached out and patted her knee. "I'm so sorry for your loss."

Rhea blinked a couple of times as if finding her way back

to the present and set the letter aside. She briefly covered his hands with hers. "Thank you." Her voice was an empty mimicry of politeness.

Swanson let her go, straightened, then went to Sofia and Russ. He shook Russ's hand and murmured something Cass couldn't catch to Sofia as he patted her shoulder. Then he made his way to Cass and Grayson.

"Could you hold this for me?" Cass murmured as she handed Grayson her grandmother's gift.

"Sure." He slipped it into an interior pocket of his jacket.

She rose, feeling Grayson do the same at her side, and together, they faced Swanson.

"Ms. Ambrose."

"Mr. Swanson."

His lips took a slight curve up. "I realize you may want your own legal counsel to review the documents. Would you like me to courier them to someone? Or I'm happy to go over them now."

The lawyer she worked with in Phoenix specialized in business law, not family law. "If you don't mind, I'd rather go over it now," she said.

"Of course." He went back to her parents and picked up his briefcase before asking Elias, "Could we use your office?"

Her father looked from Cass to Grayson then back to Swanson before he nodded. "You know where it is."

"Thank you." Swanson turned back to her and waved her toward the hall. "After you?"

Wanting the support, Cass looked at Grayson. "Come with me?"

His answer was to come to her side and press a warm reassuring hand to the base of her spine. Together, they started down the hall. They reached the set of glass French doors and stepped inside, where book-filled hunter-green walls surrounded an impressive desk with a live edge, which faced two leather barrel club chairs. Various photos of famous people, with an occasional award scattered throughout, sat on the shelves, making it apparent that this was her father's domain. Cass and Grayson took the two chairs as Swanson went behind the desk and pulled out papers from his briefcase.

"Everything's pretty straightforward." He slid documents across the polished surface. "However, there are a few more items we need from you to finalize the trust."

The next twenty minutes went by as he patiently answered Cass's questions. By the time she signed on the dotted lines, Cass was emotionally done. All she wanted was to escape the impending weight of familial duty and the incessant reminders that her grandmother was well and truly gone. Swanson was packing up the papers when raised voices penetrated the quiet office.

Cass shared a startled look with Grayson. "What—"

"You can't be serious!" an irate male shouted.

His tone of outrage spiked Cass's adrenaline and knotted her gut. She rushed to the door, but Swanson was already there, yanking it open and disappearing down the hall. She and Grayson rushed behind him and hit the living room to find her parents on their feet, looking angry and confused, and Sofia facing down a furious Russ. Cass's protective instincts shot to high alert.

"I'm not saying no, Russ." There was the faintest tremor in Sofia's voice, but she was resolute as Russ paced the limited space between the couches. "I just want to postpone the wedding."

He spun around and snapped, "I don't understand where this is coming from."

Sofia's chin lifted, and her eyes flashed, subtle tells that her composure was starting to crack. "Don't you? I've been trying to tell you for weeks that I wanted to slow things down."

"Maybe you should've tried harder."

His remark skated the edge of snide, causing Sofia to flinch and Cass's hackles to stand on end.

Russ flushed and squeezed the back of his neck. "That was..." He shook his head. "I shouldn't have said that."

Cass didn't believe his apparent remorse, but Sofia softened. "Maybe you're right, but now I'm telling you that it's too much."

Rhea decided to wade in. "What's too much?"

Sofia's composure frayed. "All of this. The wedding, Yaya's death." The last came out on a hitched breath that made Cass's chest ache.

"You're just overwhelmed." Rhea's tone was conciliatory, but it was the wrong thing to say.

Color rushed to Sofia's face as her spine snapped straight. "You're right—I am, because no one is listening to what I want." Her voice rose as she gesticulated wildly, light glinting off Yaya's emerald ring, now snug on her right hand. "I wasn't sure about such a rushed engagement, much less a short one, but you both"—she motioned between Russ and Rhea—"insisted it was necessary, something about impressing the importance of family ties to the board, which I still don't get." Her hands went to her head as if it would pop right off if she didn't hold it in place. "I swear, if it wasn't for Yaya taking my side, you would have had me married off weeks ago."

A hint of guilt flashed over her mother's face as she opened her mouth to respond, but Russ got there first. "Which would've worked for me, since I love you, but then again, I thought we wanted the same things."

Sofia dropped her hands and turned to Russ, her expression an uncomfortable mix of remorse and determination. "I thought we did, too, but more and more, it's become clear you're more focused on partnering at Pythia, not with me."

"That's not true."

"Isn't it? How many late nights have you spent at the

office because you're chasing potential clients? How many times have you ghosted me at the appointments with the caterer? The bakery? The florist?" He winced, but Sofia didn't relent. "Yaya stepped in because you wouldn't, and truthfully, I get that you love your job, but it would be nice if you could direct some of that dedication to us."

"I'm not just working this hard for me—I'm doing it for both of us." His response was both defensive and pleading.

Sofia gave him a small sad smile. "I know you believe that, but, Russ, I'm not sure my future is Pythia." Her shoulders rose as she took a deep breath and quietly added, "Or you."

Russ looked as if Sofia had gut punched him.

Where the hell is this coming from? As much as she wanted to cheer whatever it was that flipped the switch for Sofia, Cass was shocked.

Her parents, on the other hand, were quickly leaving shock behind and storming full force into piling on the familial expectations. Rhea caught Sofia's wrist. "Sofia, you don't mean that."

At the same time, Elias said, "Pythia is your legacy."

Their shared panic made Cass wonder what she was missing. Before she could dig for details, Sofia gently pulled herself free of Rhea's grip then took both of her mother's hands in hers. "And if it's not a legacy I want...?"

With a sharp inhalation, Rhea pulled free from her youngest daughter's hold and stepped back into a stiff Elias. Sofia slowly dropped her hands, which fisted by her sides. Anger, hurt, betrayal, and guilt gathered in the long moment of silence, leaving invisible wounds on both sides. The thin hold Cass had on her emotions began to slip.

Swanson ventured into the chasm of uncomfortable tension. "Maybe this discussion is better had when emotions aren't so high. This has been a very difficult day."

When Rhea and Elias remained mute, Sofia turned away

to pick up Yaya's letter from the couch, but not before Cass caught the raw pain that twisted her sister's face. An emotional echo ripped through Cass, tearing away the last of her patience. It was clear nothing had changed with her parents—their demands were just aimed at a different daughter. But as far as Cass was concerned, enough was enough. If they wouldn't protect Sofia, she would. She started for Sofia but only made it a few steps before Russ stepped in her way.

She pulled up short and met his glare even as she felt the air move behind her. "Get out of my way."

He did the opposite, closing in until only inches separated them. "This is your fault," he all but snarled.

"Back off." That came from behind her, where Grayson had her back, and there was no mistaking the threat in his voice.

Russ ignored him and continued to stare her down. "I don't know what you said or did, but this is on you."

Icy disdain rushed through her and dripped from her mouth, each syllable cutting. "No, this is all you." Cass then shouldered past him and made her way to Sofia. "Come on, let's get you out of here." She wrapped her arm around her sister's waist.

Sofia swallowed, her attention centered on Cass as she refused to acknowledge the others and gave a tiny nod. Cass walked with her body between Sofia and Russ, trusting Grayson to keep everyone off her. She guided Sofia out of the space where she was trapped between their parents, Russ, and the couch.

They cleared the couches, moving within arm's reach of Russ, and there was a flurry of movement as he went to cut them off. "You're not going anywhere."

Grayson was faster, sliding between Russ and Cass. "Don't." The one word was a clear warning.

Russ tried to get past him and failed. "Sofia!"

Sofia's steps faltered, but Cass nudged her toward the door. In just a few more feet, they'd be in the clear.

"Your parents were right, Cassandra!" Russ yelled after them. "You're toxic."

Cass heard Sofia gasp. She came to an abrupt halt and slowly turned. Fury seared through her, turning the edges of her vision red. *Not good.* Maybe later, she'd admit to the hurt fueling it, but in this moment, she was just done with everything. Her parents. This asshole. She crossed the scant space, her heels hitting the tile in an ominous stalk. She got to Grayson and touched his back in a silent signal to give her room. It took a moment or two for him to step back, allowing her access to Russ.

"I'm the toxic one?" She held his gaze, refusing to hide the fury and disgust curling her gut as she faced him down. "Really? Because from where I'm standing, it's not me trying to gaslight the heir to Pythia. That's all you."

"I'm not gaslighting anyone, but you're a jealous bitch," he shot back as his mask slipped, exposing a peek into the rage-filled man who was quickly losing control. "It's clear you don't like me, but now, it's even clearer that you're intent on ruining my relationship with Sofia."

"You're right about one thing," she shot back. "I don't like you, but Sofia does, and since I love her and want her happy, I kept my opinion to myself."

His lip curled in a sneer. "Yeah, well, I don't like you, either, but I'm not about to let you take Sofia away from me."

"Sofia or Pythia?" If she hadn't been so close and watching so carefully, she might have missed his flicker of guilt, but she didn't. *Gods, poor Sofia.* "Yeah, that's what I thought," she said quietly. Unable to stomach dealing with him anymore, she turned away and started back to Sofia, who was looking at Russ, betrayed understanding darkening her teary eyes.

"You can't help yourself, can you?" Russ called after Cass.

"You can't stand your family or what they've built, so you're all about destroying them—first Athena and now Sofia. Where does it stop, Cassandra? When everyone's dead?"

Sofia's faint but horrified "Russ, stop!" was chased by Rhea's sharp rebuke of "Enough, both of you!"

Cass turned to see her parents closing in, her mother's glare aimed solely at her. *Because of course Mother would blame me for Russ being a dick.*

Rhea brushed past Cass and wrapped her arm around Sofia's shoulders in a picture of maternal concern, drawing her away from the door. "Sofia, sweetheart, why don't you stay here tonight?"

Sofia was shaking her head and pulling away from Rhea, her gaze going to Cass. "No, I need some space." Her gaze flickered to Russ and back to Rhea, who finally let her go. "From everyone."

Rhea and Russ exchanged glances, and Cass didn't miss the way Russ's jaw tightened.

"How about I stay here and give you the condo for tonight?" he asked.

How about putting Sofia on a plane with a one-way ticket? Not that she'd get away with it, but the thought was tempting.

Sofia gave a jerky nod and wrapped her arms around her middle. "Thank you."

And the fact that she felt the need to thank the jerk for being able to stay in her own place just pissed Cass off even more. For a moment, Cass's vision wavered, and she swore cracks were snaking along the far wall of the living room, but she blinked, and the wall returned to normal. Her gut churned.

But her mother wasn't giving up. She tried for a cajoling tone. "I know things have been stressful for you both, but perhaps tomorrow, everything will look different. Then you two can sit down and talk, figure things out."

Or maybe, if luck is on my side, I can talk Sofia into changing the locks so my sister can get more than a night away from Russ.

"Maybe," Sofia said softly as she moved closer to Cass.

That small concession had her parents exchanging a relieved look. The late-afternoon sun stretched through the wall of glass behind them, throwing a glint of silver over them. A whisper of knowing flashed through Cass, a warning of betrayal.

She guided Sofia behind her as she confronted her parents. "What are you two up to?"

Rhea and Elias both stared at her, her father with a frown, her mother with an arched brow, but true to form, neither one answered. Disgusted, Cass shook her head.

"You know what? Forget I asked. I don't want to know." Which was a lie, but getting Sofia out of there was more important than figuring out her parents' scheme.

"What does that mean?" Elias demanded as Cass started to turn away.

She met her father's disapproving gaze. "It means whatever you all are up to, keep Sofia out of it." She turned to her mother. "She deserves to choose her own life, not be guilted into whatever role you choose for her."

Frustration tightened Rhea's face. "Why do you persist in thinking the worst of us?"

Before she could think twice, Cass revealed the heart-breaking truth, "Because that's the lesson you taught me."

Her father flinched, and her mother's back shot straight.

"Always so willing to blame others, aren't you, Cassandra? Even when it's your choices that ruin everything," Rhea said, doubling down on the snide. Her mother's temper had sunk its claws deep.

Memories of endless arguments after Thena's death rolled back in, threatening to drown Cass in old habits. Instead of letting them suck her down, she anchored herself in the life she'd created over the years, the hard-earned knowledge of her past mistakes, and the acceptance of her chosen family and stood strong.

"You do realize I'm no longer a guilt-ridden teenager, right? I know exactly whose choices led to what, and why. Today, my choice is to keep my baby sister safe."

"Like you did for Thena?" Rhea's bitter question ripped through the room like a bomb. As she blew across the unspoken, shaky line that barely held the mother and daughter together, her face paled, and her eyes widened. "Cassandra, I... I didn't..."

Bleeding internally from a thousand emotional cuts and feeling as if a puff of air would send her flying into a million pieces, Cass struggled not to follow the hazy path spiraling out before her. The siren song of magic was difficult to resist, but staring into her mother's face, she managed.

"What more do you need to lose before you actually listen to something other than your pride and greed?" Cass's voice echoed ominously in the tense quiet. She caught Russ's dark look and returned it with one of her own. "Or maybe it's not just your pride and greed."

Rhea swayed, and Elias moved in, holding her close. His face was drawn, and for the first time, Cass thought the two looked their age, but it was a distant observation that didn't pierce the thickening layer of ice wrapping around her.

She motioned to her parents and Russ. "I don't know what's up between you three, but I don't need to be an Oracle to know you're about to repeat history. The thing is, I'm not about to let Sofia pay the price."

"This is bullshit," Russ snarled and went to push past Grayson.

With unexpected speed, Grayson caught Russ's arm and spun him around. Russ's reaction was immediate—he roared and threw a punch as Cass nudged Sofia farther out of harm's way. Grayson easily dodged the punch and, in a move too fast to follow, had Russ's arm pinned between his shoulder blades.

"Not smart, man."

Undaunted, a red-faced, hobbled Russ snarled back, "Let me go."

"Cassie."

Cass tore her attention from the men and turned in time to see Sofia's eyes roll back in her ashen face as she started to collapse.

chapter 14

Grayson

G RAYSON TIGHTENED his grip on Russ's arm and hitched it higher, forcing a pained grunt from the idiot as he shifted to his toes to escape the pain. What he didn't do was stop struggling, so Grayson turned him away from Cass and Sofia and then let him go with a shove.

Russ stumbled a few feet before catching his balance against the sofa. "Asshole!"

"Sofia!"

Cass's cry made Grayson spin around. She held a slowly collapsing Sofia and was trying to keep them both upright. He rushed to her side as pandemonium broke out behind them.

He got his arms around Cass, bracing her so she wasn't holding Sofia's weight on her own. "I've got you."

Cass turned her head, her eyes wide with panic, and gave him a jerky nod. They did some awkward maneuvering as he shifted around to take Sofia's weight so Cass could kick off her heels and then sink to the floor, folding her legs to the side. Working together, they got Sofia down so Cass could cradle her head in her lap.

"What happened?" He crouched and set his fingers to Sofia's wrist, checking her pulse. He didn't like how pale she was or the series of tiny, unexpected muscle jerks running through her limbs. Behind them, Grayson heard Swanson tell Rhea and Elias to call 911.

"I don't know." Cass's voice shook, and she focused her attention on his fingers.

"Slow but steady," Grayson reassured her as the others joined them.

Sofia's muscle tremors were gaining strength, and under closed lids, her eyes were darting back and forth. He shifted his hold on her hand, his fingers brushing against the emerald ring. A ripple of magic crept along his awareness, and an ugly suspicion rose.

"I think—"

"We should move her to the couch." Russ crouched on Sofia's other side, worry etched on his face. He went to reach for her. "I can—"

"Don't touch her!" Grayson threw out an arm to keep Russ away from Sofia. "Something's not right."

"What?" Cass's voice broke.

Russ drew back with a scowl. "What are you talking about?"

Grayson ignored him and reached for his magic as he warned Cass, "I think she's hexed."

Her mouth fell open but quickly snapped shut as she pinned Russ with a glare. "What did you do to her?"

He rocked back, offended shock wiping away the lines of worry. "Not a damn thing, you crazy lunatic!"

Grayson pinned Russ with a hard glare. "Don't."

Russ flicked him a worried glance, and his throat bobbed, but he kept his mouth shut.

Dismissing him, Grayson gathered Sofia into his arms and got to his feet, with Cass helping him. "I need a room." A sense of urgency was plucking at his nerves. "Now."

The arguing stopped, and Elias said, "Follow me." He led

Grayson down the hall to the second door to the right. He threw open the door, revealing a guest room in shades of beige and white. Worry and fear lined his face as he watched Grayson carry his youngest daughter through the door, with Cass following. "What else do you need?"

"Space." Grayson set Sofia carefully on the bed. He gently tried to position her, but the muscle spasms were gaining strength and lasting longer. He turned to Cass. "Stay with her. I'll need to grab my bag from the car."

"I can—"

He shook his head, already turning to leave. "It's locked in a compartment."

Grayson ran out, digging his keys out of his pocket. He hit the driveway and popped the trunk. Fortunately he hadn't parked out on the street, so it was just a matter of moments to throw up the trunk, undo the rune that locked the compartment where he kept his backup kit, grab it, slam the trunk closed, and run back in.

In the scant minutes he'd been gone, Cass had managed to clear the room, but Rhea, Elias, Swanson, and Russ were all clustered in the hall by the door. Grayson shouldered his way through and, once inside, closed the door in their astonished faces and locked it. He joined Cass and set his kit near the foot of the bed and out of the way of Sofia's twitching legs. Someone started pounding on the door, but they both ignored it.

Cass's voice shook as she said, "It's getting worse, Gray."

The shortening of his name felt good, but he didn't have time to dwell on that because she was right. Soft whimpers were coming from the unconscious Sofia as the tremors teetered on seizures. Whatever was happening was moving quickly. He tore off his suit coat and tossed it onto a nearby chair.

"We need to start with a nullification spell, just until we

know what we're dealing with." He dug through his bag, grabbed a salt-infused piece of chalk, and held it out to Cass. "I need you to draw a protection circle."

She took it from him. "We need to move the bed out so I can close it."

"I'll pull, you push."

He moved to the foot of the bed while she set the chalk on the nightstand and grabbed the edge of the headboard. Luckily, the bed wasn't heavy, but it still scraped against the tile with a few worrisome creaks and groans that sounded like wood splitting. When they had a couple of feet between the headboard and the wall, Cass got to work on the circle.

The pounding at the door stopped, only to be replaced by muffled voices. Grayson and Cass ignored all of it as they worked together to set up a basic protection circle. Once the candle, crystal, antique athame, and herbs were in place, he pulled out a prepped purification packet that was the basis for the nullification spell and moved into the circle.

He waited until she straightened on the other side, chalk gripped in her hand. "Are you clear of the circle?"

"Yes."

He sent a flare of magic into the activation rune on the packet. With a flash of burnished copper, the spell activated, wrapping around Sofia like a blanket. Tension sang through him as he waited. In moments, her muscle spasms started to ease and her whimpers faded, both good signs. If nothing else, the combination of the nullification spell and the protection circle would buy him time to figure out what was happening.

The pounding at the door started up again, and Cass glared at the door. "Go away!" It went quiet. She placed the chalk on the nightstand. "What now?"

He set the packet aside and picked up a second piece of chalk. "Now you stay there and let me work."

She looked at her sister and whispered, "Just hurry."

He didn't bother with reassurances, not when he didn't know what he was dealing with. Instead, he drew in a centering breath, gathered his magic, and sent it through the chalk lines. Magic rose, sweeping through the circle, curling around Sofia, and rushing back to him. His instincts whispered that something was off. Heeding them, he crouched and added a couple of runes to the floor. There was a shift in the magical flow, a tightening as the circle and spell blended into a unified purpose, protecting Sofia. He grasped the magic that made him a Key, and his perception of the world shifted.

He studied Sofia, who, in his mind's eye, was now a flowing weave of pastels. Her magical fabric showed signs of repairs, not quite to the extent of Cass's but close. Not unexpected, considering that they shared certain family traumas. He took his time, noting troublesome knots here and there plus a few spots where her fabric appeared frayed. There was a handful of shadowed threads with random knots that he needed to examine further, but right at the moment, his attention was solely on the ring. It was clearly bespelled because it was currently doing its best to hold back a swarm of ghostly ribbons that flickered from opaque to transparent even as he watched. Whatever the magic's intention was, the thin threads of power hued in a soft rose that delicately threaded through the pastel weave of Sofia's inherent magic kept them at bay. Its subtle flow dipped into fissures and filled in the gaps left behind by the parasitic cluster that kept trying to wrap around the ring's power.

He studied the ebb and flow, trying to pinpoint why it seemed so familiar. When recognition hit, it was quickly chased by a hot rush of anger. *Russ.* The dick was trying to manipulate the woman he claimed to love, but somehow, the ring was denying his magic an anchor.

What an asshole.

Determined to eliminate at least one threat to Sofia,

Grayson gathered his power to put the manipulation mage in his place, but before he could act, a few strands made it past the rose-hued guardian and connected with the bright heart of the ring. Tendrils quickly wrapped around the pulsating heart of the ring as if trying to squeeze it into another shape. Grayson's breath caught as he braced to move, but the tendrils abruptly stilled and withered into nothing.

Iris's message replayed in his head. *To Sofia, I leave my emerald ring from my beloved Dorian as a reminder that love is unconditional and forever.* Puzzle pieces fell into place. Sofia's sudden second thoughts on her engagement and the ring's magical protective behavior were a manifestation of Iris's love for her granddaughter, bound into a protection amulet.

Grayson eased back. Too often, messing with such primally powered magic could make things worse, so for the moment, he'd leave Iris's gift to deal with Russ. He was starting to pull his power back, when there was a shift in Sofia's magic. It wasn't much, just a flicker on the edge of his perception. Like a brush of dark fingers whispering over the lighter strands, the movement caused the pastels to undulate in a jerky motion as they tried to avoid the touch. The insidious fingers were relentless, continually trying to find a path to absorb the surrounding magic and blend in.

Narrowing his concentration, Grayson let his magic drop into the crouch of a stalking predator as he waited for it happen again. It didn't take long. Those darker threads were having a hell of time matching Sofia's magic, mainly because their darkness kept bleeding through. The weave was subtle, but what was more disturbing was the fact that there were no telltale signs to indicate a recognizable signature.

Unless the darkness is the signature.

Uneasy, he crept closer, trying to unravel the complex elements that made up the threads. No way in hell was this

Russ's work. It was too complex. The longer he studied it, the more it disturbed him. Not only did it appear to be fraying Sofia's magic, but the power fueling this hex shouldn't have even existed. It was like blending a thread of silk and steel into mercury—an impossibility.

Without knowing what exactly he was up against, Grayson didn't dare attempt to unravel the hex, but he couldn't leave Sofia like this. What he needed was time. He held his position as he ran through various options then settled on keeping it simple. He layered a stasis spell and anchored it to the nullification spell. Relief trickled in when the dance of the darker threads slowed considerably. With that threat temporarily held at bay, he focused on unraveling Russ's influence by boosting the ring's protections and further disintegrating the Auctori's hold. After burning away the last gray knot, he reinforced Sofia's worn-down shield so Russ couldn't get to her again. He did one final check to make sure he hadn't missed anything else before he pulled his magic back. The world resettled around him as he blinked his vision clear. There was a mild ache at the back of his head, which was typical after work like this.

Cass rose from a nearby chair. "Is she cursed?"

"Yes." His voice was rough, and he hated the fear that replaced her concern at his answer.

"Can you break it?"

He shook his head.

Cass's gaze went to Sofia and back to him. "Why not?"

"Because whoever set this is highly skilled, and I don't recognize the signature."

Her eyes widened, her panic clear. "So, not Russ."

"Definitely not Russ." He flexed his magic, shifting the circle's protections so he could step over the boundary without breaking the spell. Once clear, he locked it back down. "But I don't want to poke at it until I know what I'm dealing with."

"Which means what?" Cass grabbed the chalk from the nightstand and rounded the bed.

He began collecting the random tools and containers and tucking them into his bag as she closed in. "That I need to reach out to a couple people I know, get them to do some digging. Plus, I need to consult with an old mentor."

Cass held out the chalk. He reached for it, but she didn't let it go. "Can't you just call him or her?"

"Him, and it's not quite that easy." He took the chalk, dropped it into the bag, and zipped it close. "He's going to require a favor owed."

"From you or me?"

"Most likely? You."

She looked to where Sofia lay, and all the grief and worry disappeared under a grim determination. "If it saves Sofia and it's within reason, I'll pay it."

He caught her hand and pulled her close until she was leaning into him, her head resting on his chest, her attention on the sleeping Sofia. "He doesn't like people, so that means I have to hunt him down. While I'm doing that, why don't you stay with Sofia? Make sure not to leave her alone with anyone, especially Russ."

Cass lifted her head and stared at him, her worry hardening into something colder. "You said he wasn't behind it."

"He's not, but he has been manipulating her emotions, though your grandmother's ring seems to be helping to undo the damage."

Anger, fast and furious, flashed over her features before worry settled in. "Is she going to be okay, Grayson?"

"We'll keep her safe," he said and prayed he wasn't lying.

Grayson waited until he'd cleared the residential roads and hit the freeway that would take him to Rattler Springs, the small community situated outside Vegas in the middle of nowhere, before using his handsfree.

The line rang twice before being picked up, and a distracted voice said, "What?"

"I'm calling in my favor, Zane."

"About damn time." The sounds of movement came through the car speakers. "Hit me with it."

Grayson checked his mirrors, flicked on his turn signal, and merged over to the far lane. "Get a pen ready because I've got a list of names I need you to dig into."

The clunk of a drawer opening and closing came across the line, followed by an abrupt "Go."

"Russell Seagraves. He works at Pythia Strategies, mid-thirties. Sofia Alcmene Ambrose, his fiancée." Though that might not be true for much longer. "Her parents and Pythia's owners, Rhea and Elias Ambrose. It might be worth it to look into Eric Swanson, lawyer."

"Type?"

"Family, I think, since he's handling the estate of the Alcmene matriarch."

A considering hum came over the line before Zane asked, "Why does that name sound familiar?"

"They're one of the original twenty-seven but like to play behind the scenes."

"And here I was thinking you were wasting my time," Zane drawled. "Any other players I need to look into?"

It was risky as shit to open this Pandora's box, but between Cass's visions and his gut, he couldn't shake the feeling there was something out there. "Two. But, Zane, tread carefully."

"Oh, now you're just being a tease." Predatory anticipation darkened Zane's voice.

"Dana Marr and Cole Burton."

Stunned silence filled the line. "As in Burton Entertainment?"

"Yes."

A low whistle came back. "And the Marr chick?"

"Cole's current companion."

"Dare I ask what kind of shit you stepped into, Grayson?"

The imagery was spot-on. "The kind that can get deep quick."

"Then I'm not the only one who needs to watch my step," Zane said. Before Grayson could respond, Zane went back to business. "What am I looking for?"

"Connections that tie the players together. Whatever kind you can find outside the obvious."

"The obvious being you?" Zane shot back.

Grayson winced. "Me and Cassandra Alcmene."

That earned a knowing chuckle. "Cassandra? Sounds like a story."

"Maybe later."

"I'll hold you to it. What's my timeline?" Zane asked.

"ASAP. I'm dealing with an unknown hex."

"That means you're heading out to Walter's."

"On my way now," Grayson confirmed.

"Need backup?"

Grayson's lips twitched. "You know him. Me visiting is bad enough. No sense in adding to the old man's torture."

"Right. Do me a favor—text me when you're heading back so I know you're alive."

Zane's dry tone lit a spark of amusement. "Will do."

"Right. Let me see what I can dig up. I'll reach out tomorrow. Later."

"Later, Zane."

Forty minutes later, Grayson drove past a diner that had seen better days, its street-facing windows decorated with hand-painted menu specials. He turned off the sun-beaten asphalt and into a dusty parking lot that held a pair of well-maintained motorcycles and a couple of older trucks. He parked in a spot in the far back corner next to a prehistoric pay phone haphazardly perched next to a weathered metal lamppost. Grayson popped open his glove compartment and shuffled through a collection of paper napkins and receipts until he found a small metal tin. He pulled it out and popped the lid. Inside, where mints had once lived, was an odd collection of polished glass and etched bones and stones. He thumbed through them until he found what he needed then put the rest back.

Grayson stepped out of the car, pocketed his keys and the piece of glass, and closed the door, leaving his phone behind. The street was quiet, not a surprise considering that Rattler Springs's business district covered maybe four blocks. No one was out, because it was too hot to be walking around—not that there was much shopping to be had. At least a third of the storefront windows were dark or boarded up. Road trippers heading to and from the bright lights of Vegas might swing into the diner and nearby gas station, but the only other shop that held signs of life was the feed store at the other end of the street. It was one of those small towns that defied logic, somehow supporting a scattered population that might stretch into three digits on a good day.

Gravel crunched underfoot as he took the handful of steps necessary to get to the pay phone. Faded spray paint crawled along the metal sides, and on the sun-worn directions above the receiver, someone had used a sharpie to invite visitors to call Barb. He took a moment to make sure there were no accidental witnesses to what would happen next since Walter was borderline paranoid and violently committed to his privacy.

Grayson contemplated the handset, which was stained

with dust and other things he didn't want to think about, and reached for his magic. He wrapped his power around the rune stone in his other palm and murmured, "*Sýn mér.*"

The rune stone warmed as the sharpie message began to shimmer with a shadowy light. Slowly, it reshaped itself into a set of runic letters. Shaking his head at the abrupt message, he gingerly lifted the handset and held it just above his ear, not willing to risk it getting too close. There was no dial tone, just static. On the keypad, an inky thread dotted with tiny, shimmery pinpricks of white wound around the keys but didn't settle. Grayson set the activated rune stone above the coin slot, and the shimmery ribbon curled around the third key. He hit it, and the ribbon moved to the next number—eight. About four numbers in, he realized what the letters aligned with the numbers spelled and gave an amused huff at Walter's acerbic wit. Filling in the blanks, he hit the last three—six, three, three—in quick succession. The static in his ear fell silent for a long moment.

Then a deep voice demanded, "What do you want?"

"Hello, Walter," Grayson said. "We need to talk."

A heavy pause. "About...?"

"Old business."

The silence lasted longer this time. "Mine or yours?"

"I'm thinking yours," Grayson said.

That got a snort. "I'll send Jack to get you."

"I'm on a tight timetable, so no games," Grayson warned.

"Yeah, well, you called me, so no promises." Then the static was back.

Grayson hung up the phone and reeled in his magic, noting that Barb's calling card was back. He picked up the rune stone and headed back to his car to wait for his escort. He started the car so he could run the AC. He didn't have to wait long. A large raven landed on the pay phone and looked right at him.

He rolled down his window. "Hey, Jack."

The raven cocked its head, its dark eyes bright, and let out a harsh caw. Then it launched into the air.

Grayson followed Jack out of town and toward the desert mountains. The dark shadow led him along a series of dirt roads that wove through the foothills, and roughly fifteen minutes in, Jack angled to the east. Grayson almost missed a set of barely there tire tracks to his right. He turned and slowed even more as the car rocked over the rough path. Five minutes into the bone-shaking ride, he prayed his car would survive the trip. Ahead and above him, Jack dove down and disappeared, and Grayson rounded a bend. The rutted tracks leveled into a graveled yard at the base of a sizable hill, where an older mobile home stood. Its siding was sun faded to off-white, and the once-green trim was now closer to gray. Jack circled between two large acacia trees that bookended the home, their branches offering dubious shade. Under one were two large brindle-coated dogs, no chains in sight. The other had a rusted bike chained to it.

Grayson pulled in next to a rust-covered pickup truck, and the canine pair got to their feet, shaking dust from their coats. As if that wasn't warning enough, there was the disturbing collection of colored beads, bones, and small animal skulls hanging like macabre wind chimes from the weathered wooden porch ceiling. All of it together made visitors want to turn around before a chainsaw started up somewhere. Which was how Walter liked it.

Grayson shut his car down and got out, closing the door behind him. Jack glided down to perch on the wooden railing then spread his wings wide, opened his beak, and let out a harsh screech. The canine pair split apart and began to stalk forward with low bone-rattling growls. Walter's home protection unit had been activated.

Grayson held his position even as his pulse picked up the

pace. He reached for his magic, holding it at the ready, and hoped he wouldn't have to use it. It wasn't the animals' fault their human was fucking nuts.

"Walter, get out here before I have to stop playing nice with your pets."

"They're not pets, idiot." The screen door opened on a squeak, and a tall, thin man in faded jeans and a short-sleeved olive-green button-down shirt stepped out to the porch. "*Varði.*"

The dogs froze like guardian statues and fell silent. Jack closed his beak midscream, resettled his feathers, and started to fluff them as if he hadn't been trying to make Grayson's ears bleed.

"Jerry, Frank, settle."

In eerie tandem, the two dogs backed to their previous spot without taking their attention from Grayson.

Walter stopped at the porch railing and folded his arms. "Didn't expect to see you again."

"That was the plan."

"What changed?"

"I'm dealing with a non-Elemental cast."

In a disturbing mimicry of Jack, Walter cocked his head as he stared. "You're sure?"

"Yeah."

A wolfish curl of his lips turned his frown predatory, revealing the cunning mage lurking under Walter's crabby-loner persona. "Who?"

Grayson really didn't need the old man digging into Cass's family. "Not important."

The curl turned into a sneer. "Bullshit. If you earn a Cabal curse, you're fucking important, and you know it."

Gods dammit. Walter's confirmation hardened the unease that had been roiling in Grayson's gut since he'd left Cass. He hated being right. Most considered the Cabal's existence a cautionary tale about how a group of disenfranchised mages had risen in opposition to the Arcane Families and used corrupted ritualistic spells that twisted science and magic into a fucking nightmare.

"Forget the name. I need to pick your brain."

"What's in for me?" Walter asked.

"If your help leads to breaking the curse, I'll inform my client that a favor is owed."

"From you as well."

And this was where it would get sticky, because he was about to make a promise he wasn't sure he could keep. Cass's panicked face flashed in his mind, and he hoped she would forgive him for this. "From me as well."

Walter studied him. Grayson could almost follow his thoughts. A Cabal target meant someone powerful, and a favor at that level was worth its weight in gold, no matter what Arcane power it involved. Then there was the fact that to get answers, Grayson would have to share specifics of the casting that, given enough time, Walter could appropriate for his own spells.

Knowledge is a two-edged sword.

"Fine." Walter dropped his arms and turned away. "Come on up, boy. Don't got all day." With that, he disappeared inside.

Ignoring the watching animals, Grayson went up the stairs, slowing when Jack stopped his preening to pin him with a beady-eyed stare. Grayson took the next step, and Jack shifted along the rail, stalking him. Grayson dug into his pocket, brought out a bright-blue piece of polished glass, and held it out. "Is this enough?"

Jack snatched up the shiny piece in his beak and, with a series of pleased caws, hopped back. Free to pass, Grayson reached the screen door, pulled it open, and walked inside.

chapter 15

Cass

CASS RAN, chased by the fear that time was slipping away grain by grain. It piled around her feet as she slogged through the deepening drifts, her chest aching as she tried to suck nonexistent air into her laboring lungs. The grit tore at her bare feet as the path twisted and turned with a feral sentience. Sofia called for her from somewhere up ahead, but no matter how fast Cass ran, the distance remained unchanged. An owl dropped from above with a chilling screech, its vicious talons tearing through the night. She covered her head with her arms and threw herself to the side to escape, but she was too slow, and fire whipped along her forearms. The owl lifted on a deafening whoosh of backdraft that left behind a choking cloud of something foul and circled for another attack.

"*Áfise tin!*" The ominous echo of her yaya's voice came from everywhere and nowhere.

The owl veered off with an angry shriek.

Cass scrambled to her hands and knees. She spun in a panicked circle, trying to see through the distorting haze, only to stop when a shimmery, robed figure appeared at the edge of a monstrous forest. It glided toward her as she stumbled back.

"Yaya? Is that you?" Her voice was younger and scared.

She inched away, and something rolled underfoot. She hit the ground with a pained grunt.

In less than a breath, the figure was kneeling at her side. "*Prosékhste.*"

Pay attention to what? She didn't get a chance to ask, because the cowled head lifted, and the unforgiving faces of the Erinyes from her tarot deck stared back. She pointed a bloodied sword to the left. Cass turned and got her answer. The forest parted to reveal a dark pool where the naiad floated, her sorrowful gaze aimed at the shadowy shore, where silent winds tore through trees, changing the landscape with dizzying speed. The water around her rippled ominously as though something lurked in the depths below.

A chill touch brushed her face as her yaya's voice gently ordered, "Go back to the start, angel."

Cass jerked awake so hard she almost fell out of the chair she'd curled into while sitting at Sofia's bedside. Grayson's jacket, which she'd been using as a blanket, fell to the floor with a muffled thump. Her gaze went to Sofia, who lay quietly on the bed under a faint glow of copper from the protection spell. The reassuring rise and fall of her chest nudged some of the panic away, but Cass's heart beat a mile a minute, and her hands shook.

She scrubbed her face, trying to wipe away the remnants of the disturbing dream as she uncurled her legs from their cramped position in the chair. She set her bare feet on the floor, the feel of the cool, hard surface grounding her. She dropped her hands, kept her eyes closed, and stilled her mind as she drew in a couple of deliberate breaths to chase away the shakiness. Resettled, she opened her eyes and looked around, realizing that evening had set in and the room had drifted into dimness. Cass turned on the light on the nightstand and let the soft illumination chase away the gathering shadows.

She went to Sofia and brushed her fingers through her

hair. *She looks so young.* Worry, frustration, and anger battered her heart even as the fear that she was watching history repeat itself lurked at the edges of her mind.

She bent, pressed her lips to her sister's temple, and whispered, "Hang in there, Sofie."

There was no response.

Cass straightened and pinched the bridge of her nose in an attempt to bank her useless tears. *Come on, Grayson, hurry back.*

Logic told her he was doing the best he could, but she hated the fact that she was stuck waiting for him to get back. She picked up her glasses from the nightstand, set them in place, then turned back to the chair. Cass picked up Grayson's suit coat from the floor and gave it a small shake to straighten it out. Something heavy weighed down one side. Frowning, she folded it over her arm so she could search the pockets. When she got to the inner pocket, she hit pay dirt and pulled out her grandmother's letter and gift. Cass laid the jacket at the foot of Sofia's bed then carried the letter and box with her as she retook her seat.

She set the box on the chair's padded arm and turned her attention to the letter. She brushed a finger over the wax seal, tracing the hourglass symbol, and absently wondered if her mother had inherited the seal set that Yaya kept at her desk. Then she slid a nail under the edge of the flap, broke the seal, and carefully pulled the letter free of the envelope. Cass set the envelope aside and unfolded the letter. Her grandmother's familiar loops filled the page.

Dearest angel,

This was not how I wanted to have this conversation, but Fate has a way of ensuring that Her plans play out as She prefers, no matter how much we wish differently. First, I want you to know how much I love you, and how proud I am of the woman you have chosen to be. I know it has not been an easy road, but then, the easy path has never been your chosen mode of travel, has it?

Cass smiled at the familiar question, one she'd heard often growing up.

You're much like my stubborn heart, Dorian, in that regard. Always about forging your own path. Much like him, you love deep and true, but that kind of heart wields a double-edged sword because when betrayed, it has difficulty finding forgiveness. Especially when that betrayal comes from those closest to you. This is a trait that runs true in our family, especially in my darling Rhea, and whether you believe it or not, your mother loves you. (Don't you roll your eyes at me, young lady.)

A watery huff of amusement escaped Cass, and she brushed away a tear.

She may show it in ways even I have trouble understanding, but there are reasons behind her choices. And as I've taught you, others' choices are not yours to make, or mine, no matter how tempting. I had hoped to help guide you two back onto common ground, but it seems I've run out of time, so now I need to ask you to do something I know you'd rather not do—forgive her.

"That's a hell of an ask, Yaya," Cass said even as her chest ached.

I know it's a lot to ask, but angel, you're strong enough to do this. When your heart is ready, take my gift and watch, listen, and try to give your mother some grace as her roads have had their own challenges. Remember that each of us must walk our own path, no matter where it takes us, and when we reach the end, only we can say if the journey was worth it.

Be brave, Cassandra.

I love you.

Yaya

She refolded the letter, tucked it back into the envelope, and then picked up the small box. She tried and failed to open it. Upon closer inspection, she realized there was no seam between the top and bottom. In fact, the hinge appeared to be decorative instead of functional.

"That's not right," she muttered, absently retracing the crest. She remembered this box sitting open on Yaya's dresser, the antique pocket mirror nestled inside.

She ran her finger along the curling loops etched into the wood, remembering her grandmother doing the same on more than one occasion. Iris would hold the box while tracing the crest, her gaze unfocused, and then, without anything obvious, the lid would release. Which meant there had to be some way to open this thing.

"What am I missing?"

She reread Yaya's letter and did her best to recall what Swanson had said at the reading. She remembered Grayson's frown as he stared at the letter and box and his warning head-shake. Grayson, who was a Key.

Realization clicked. "Magical lock."

An heirloom from a family of seers in a seemingly inoperable box. *Like a miniature Pandora's box maybe?*

Intrigued, Cass turned it over and over in her mind. Pandora's story was typical of the misogynistic mythos that stretched back thousands of years. A beautiful woman created to punish men by narcissistic man-gods got curious and unleashed a plague of evil on the mortal realm. When an angry Zeus slammed the lid closed, Hope, who also happened to be female, was trapped inside, unable to help mortal men, and somehow that was also Pandora's fault.

Never mind how all that shit got into the box in the first damn place. Cass stepped back from that particular rabbit's hole and considered the curiosity angle. *Could that be the key?*

No, not curiosity, but something else, something just as strong.

"'What lies behind paves the way forward,'" she said, repeating Yaya's words as shared by Swanson, then looked at the letter with Yaya's last message as she continued to slowly trace the crest.

Forgive her.

Curiosity.

Each of us must walk our own path.

Pieces shifted, and knowledge sparked, born of magic and instinct. Forgiveness required understanding, and Cass had never understood her mother, never wanted to know. But with everything unraveling and Sofia at risk, it was time to find out. The lines under her fingertip began to glow, following the path of her touch. It deepened into indigo, and as she finished with the last swirl, a soft click sounded and the wooden top shifted. Cass gingerly raised the lid. Delicate silver filigree twisted to appear like thread wrapped around the slightly domed lid in a never-ending spiral. An owl, wings open, sat underneath the three phases of the moon. The two faceted moonstones that were its eyes appeared to glow with an inner fire.

Cass carefully lifted the mirror out, set the box aside, and then undid the clasp. There were tiny nicks here and there on the lid, indicating the passage of years, but the two interior mirrors remained clear. Cass lifted the case and blew a gentle breath over the lower mirror, fogging its surface, before she realized what she was doing. She lowered it and reached for the hem of her skirt, only to stop when the condensation shifted and moved. Mesmerized, Cass stared into the mirror.

The mist rose, closing around her until there was nothing left of Sofia or the bedroom. She moved through the thickening haze as if pulled by an invisible thread. The quiet was deafening as if the world was wrapped in cotton. It wasn't dark, but it wasn't bright either. There was enough light to see a few feet around her, but something moved to her left, its shadow drifting along the wall of mist. She went a few more steps and realized the light was getting brighter. Just then, the familiar sound of wings cut through the muffled silence. Ahead of her, an owl burst from the mist and disappeared into the brightening haze. She switched to a run to follow it.

"Wait!" Her voice cut through the strangely muffled world, and the mist snapped apart as if a switch had been thrown.

The abrupt scenery change made her stumble, and she caught her balance against a doorjamb that appeared out of nowhere. But what kept her in place was the two women standing in a nursery, caught in the midst of an emotional storm. A much younger Rhea, looking pale and frightened, cradled an infant protectively against her chest as she stood in front of the aunt Cass only knew through photos. A younger version of her grandmother stood with them.

"Take it back, Cora!"

Cora was equally pale, her expression both anguished and resolute. "I would if I could, but you know that's not how this works, Rhea."

"Fine. Then we figure out how to change this."

Cora was shaking her head. "Every path I take shows the same thing."

Rhea turned away, which left her facing Cass and Iris. The baby stirred, a small hand reaching out to grasp Rhea's pendant. Her mother made a soft shushing sound.

"I've got you, Sofie." She bent her head and pressed her lips to Sofia's head.

The naked pain on her mother's face froze Cass in place. It was raw and uncensored, leaving no room for doubt that this was a tormented woman. "Mom."

But Rhea couldn't hear her because this was a captured memory, locked into the mirror by Iris. Rhea gazed down at her youngest daughter, her fear swallowed by a ruthless determination that was much more familiar to Cass.

"No." Rhea's denial was quiet but unrelenting. "I won't allow it."

Iris flinched. "You can't outrun the Fates, Rhea."

Rhea looked at her mother, obstinate determination clear in her face. "Fuck the Fates, Mama. These are my babies she's talking about, and I'll do whatever I must to keep them safe."

Cass recognized the sorrow that darkened both Iris and Cora's gazes—not just because one sister was breaking the other's heart but also because both knew there was no manipulating the Fates' plans. Any attempt would only lead to more heartache.

Cora started to reach out. "Rhea, you can't—"

"Don't!" Rhea bit out, a flush sweeping through her face as fear was a living fire in her eyes. She kept Sofia cradled close. "Don't tell me what I can or can't do." The tension between the sisters clogged the air, and Sofia started to fuss. Rhea rocked her, softening her tone even as frustration kept her anger alive. "If there's no escaping this, why tell me in the first place?"

"Because you need to know," Cora replied, resigned.

"That's not an answer, Cora!" Rhea snapped.

"Would you rather I didn't say anything?" Frustration edged out Cora's compassion as she matched her sister's temper.

"It'd be better than this," Rhea snarled. "You can't tell me which daughter, you can't tell me how, you can't tell me when. All you give me is some vague warning that one daughter will cost me another."

Cora endured Rhea's accusations, her hands fisted at her sides, and said nothing.

"You're a damn Oracle, so tell me how to fix this."

There was so much pain in Rhea's voice that it left Cass feeling bloodied and bruised. And considering the tears falling down Cora's face, she shared that feeling. Both Oracles knew the cruel truth, and in an eerie tandem, they said, "You can't."

"Can't what, Cassandra?"

Cass looked up and met her mother's gaze, disconcerted as the past and present collided. The world around her shifted back to her parents' guest room. Rhea stood on the other side of the bed where Sofia lay, a frown joining the tired lines on her face. "Cassandra, are you okay?"

Cass shook her head, trying to come back from the past and sync with the present. "Sorry, Mom. Give me a second." The emotional echoes of what she'd witnessed clung tightly, and she barely registered Rhea's shock at the informal address. "I was just..." She went to wave her hand, forgetting she still held the pocket mirror. Shaking her head, she closed the antique compact, put it in the box, then set it and the letter aside. "Must have fallen asleep." She got to her feet, grabbed her glasses, and set them in place, their familiar weight dislodging the lingering hold of the past. "Everything okay?"

Rhea gently straightened the light cover on Sofia, her gaze lingering on the box. "What did you see?"

Still rattled by the past, Cass adjusted her glasses and fought the urge to squirm. "What?"

"The mirror," Rhea said, angling her head toward it. "What did Mother want you to see?"

A tone of accusation had slipped into Rhea's question, setting Cass's teeth on edge, but she struggled past her fundamental rejection of whatever her mother asked her to do and aimed for a mature response. "Why don't we discuss this later?"

Rhea didn't take the hint. "What did you see, Cassandra?"

The haughty demand set Cass's back up. *Fuck being mature.* "You, Sofia, Yaya, and Cora."

Rhea swayed before slowly sinking to sit on the edge of the bed, her face slipping into a shade past pale. Her shoulders hunched as she closed her eyes and pinched the bridge of her nose. "Dammit, Mama, you just couldn't leave it alone."

The words were not quiet enough to escape Cass's ears. "Leave what alone?"

Rhea dropped her hand, opened her eyes, and pinned them on Cass, frustration and fear swirling in their depths. "What purpose does it serve to show you that?"

Even though there was a chance the question wasn't intended for her, that glimpse of fear pricked Cass's curiosity. "Maybe she wanted me to know."

Red suffused Rhea's face, and she looked away. She tugged at the blanket then smoothed it out, agitated. "Know what exactly?"

The knee-jerk reaction to snap back rode Cass hard, and she opened her mouth to retread old roads, only to close it. She studied her mother, taking in the shoulders braced for a blow, the set jaw, and the fidgeting hands, all of it screaming guilt and grief. Two things she never associated with Rhea. Raging and railing at her mother might make her feel better, but in the end, what would it change?

The answer was simple: Nothing.

Sofia was in danger. Her yaya was gone. Thena was still dead. And Cass? She was still an outsider in her own family. Hell, her mother could barely stand to be in the same room with her. At least now, thanks to Yaya, she knew the reason why—a shitty one to be sure, but it had to count for something, right?

Rhea lifted her head and asked again, "What did she want you to know?"

"That you're human."

Rhea blinked, her face softening as her lips curved into a sad, bitter twist. "Oh, sweetheart, I've never been anything but." The unexpected endearment stunned Cass, but Rhea wasn't done rocking her daughter's world. "I know you don't believe me, but I never blamed you."

There was no way to stop Cass's disbelieving snort. "Could've fooled me."

"You know, as thrilled as I am that you've inherited a great deal from our family, the holding-grudges thing, I could do without."

The subtle parental reprimand deducted years from Cass's age, and she shot back, "Can you blame me?"

"Yes." Her mother didn't even take a breath before nailing her with that agreement.

Cass rocked back. She was still trying to figure out how to respond, when Rhea apparently decided it was time to air out all their nasty laundry.

"You were never one to forgive easily. If someone hurt you, they had to work to get you to listen. Your sisters were the exception, but not me. You girls were so close, so protective of each other, and I adored that." Rhea brushed a hand over Sofia's hair. "Until you all turned it on me." She faced Cass with no mask in sight, just raw, unfiltered emotion—pain, frustration, and through it all, a terrible kind of love. "I understand now. Then?" She shook her head. "I couldn't see it. Didn't understand how that bond would turn you and Thena against me just when I needed you both to trust me. My mistake was doing everything in my power to steer you both off the path Cora warned me about, and by doing so, I all but guaranteed it was the only one left for you both to take. And Sofia, she would follow her sisters anywhere. It made me desperate because without Cora, I had no way to know if my decisions were the right ones. It didn't matter how many outcomes I tried—I couldn't get things to change."

As her mother shared, Cass returned to the chair, sinking down to perch on the edge, her hands fisted in her lap. She tried to put herself in Rhea's shoes. It wasn't easy getting free of the emotional quicksand and finding that pitiless point where she could observe without influencing, but she managed.

"And when you realized Thena was a Harbinger?"

Her mother held her gaze without flinching. "I thought together, you two could change the future so all three of my girls would survive."

So much of this would hurt later, but while they were actually talking, Cass clung to her impartiality with a desperation that wasn't pretty. "Then why didn't you listen when I warned you about what would happen to Thena? Why didn't you ignore the board and go after her?"

"We did." Rhea's admission sent fissures through Cass's heart, but her mother was far from done. "Your father and I, we sent in a friend—a powerful friend—to get her out, to save her. He failed. We failed." Guilt seeped through her voice and pores, staining the air. "I knew better, but I was determined to cut Fate off. I was an Alcmene. We're Her instruments, and if anyone could thwart Her, it would be us." She lifted a hand and softly corrected, "Not us—me. Because these were my daughters, my precious ones, and I'd served the family faithfully." Rhea's arrogance was back, hotter than before. "I made the hard choices, ensured that the essential pieces were in place so my girls wouldn't have to walk Her path. Cultivated the favors I would need, manipulated the alliances that would provide critical resources, all because they deserved a future, even if that future didn't include me." She paused, her temper draining away like water. "It was risky, but if it meant the three of you would be alive, even if you hated me, it would be worth it. You, Sofia, and Thena, you were my everything. I did what I thought best to protect each of you, and in the end, I lost all of you."

There was so much there, so many heavy things to address, that Cass had no idea where to start.

But Rhea wasn't finished. "I was a mess after Cora died. I was so angry, so determined to outrun Fate, that I ignored Mama's warnings. Told her I knew what I was doing. She tried so hard to make me listen but..." Rhea shook her head and looked away. She took a couple of broken breaths as she gazed down at Sofia, her voice softening as if she was talking to herself. "I didn't understand why she wouldn't fight back—why she wouldn't help me fight Cora's vision."

Cass knew why. "Because fighting it makes it worse."

"So I learned."

The resignation in Rhea's voice widened the cracks in Cass's heart as she finally saw the full picture. Why her parents and Yaya had argued so much. Rhea's relentless pressure on Cass and Thena to master their magic. Why Rhea and Elias were so focused on deepening their connections to the Arcane Families. All of Rhea's choices spread out in front of Cass like a crystal spiderweb, each inexorable thread leading from one decision to the next, an impossible construct meant to protect the daughters sitting at the heart of it. Instead, it had become a trap of her own making because Fate had other plans, and She was the queen of grudges.

Cass's heart broke. "Oh, Mom."

Rhea met her gaze, a toxic look of remorse and self-recrimination swimming in her eyes, as she brushed her fingers over Sofia's hair. "And now I have to wonder which decision led to this. What did I set in motion?"

chapter 16

Grayson

IT WAS close to ten thirty when Grayson put Cassandra into the passenger seat of his car. He closed the door and turned, only to run into Elias's glare. "When will you be back in the morning?" The older man's frustration came through loud and clear.

"As soon as I have everything I need to help Sofia." He rounded the hood, not giving a rat's ass if Elias found his answer lacking, and got behind the wheel. After his conversation with Walter, Grayson didn't trust either of the older Ambroses as far as he could spit.

He was pulling out of the drive when Cass asked, "You sure she'll be okay?"

As they drove under the muted streetlights, he glanced over to see Cass staring straight ahead, unnaturally still, her hands fisted in her lap. He turned back to the road but not before taking one hand from the wheel to cover hers and give it a comforting squeeze. "The stasis spell will hold the curse in check."

"But it won't stop it."

"No, but with the addition of your grandmother's protection, it should last until morning." He let her go and took the freeway exit.

She shifted in her seat. "What did you find out that you didn't want to share in front of my parents?"

He wasn't surprised by her perception. "The hex on Sofia is based on a Cabal spell."

Instead of the disbelief he expected, he got a shocked "Cabal? You're sure?"

"Positive." He knew he looked as grim as he sounded. "And Sofia's not the only one."

"What do you mean?"

"According to my source, over the last year, there have been some alarming incidents that involve a handful of the original Families."

"Alarming how?" When he didn't say anything, she demanded sharply, "Grayson, alarming how?"

He kept his attention on the road. "Magical experimentation on unwilling mages, demon pacts, big-money fraud, kidnappings, and hexes for hire. The kind of things the Families don't want made public."

She was quiet for a moment. "The curse victims—they survived?"

It was futile to hope she wouldn't zero in on that particular issue, but he wouldn't lie, not to her. "Not all of them."

She sucked in a breath and, on a choked sob, whispered, "Oh gods, Sofie."

"Hey." He reached out, found her hand, and held it tight.

She held on as words tumbled from her in a panicked rush. "You told my mother you could reverse it, but mixing dark magic and science—that's not the same."

"It is and it isn't, Cass." He forced his voice to stay level. "A Cabal-based spell is complicated because of how it's created, but that doesn't make it impossible to break."

With her free hand, she rubbed her forehead and

muttered, "Okay, okay," as if trying to convince herself. When she tugged on her other hand, he let her go. A tense minute passed before she regained her composure. "All right. According to your source, the ones behind Sofia's curse are part of the Cabal?"

He nodded.

"And they're sure? I mean, like, you believe them?"

"I do."

"Why?"

Old oaths prevented him from sharing details such as Walter's name or how, in a previous life, Walter's work with Cabal casts had been legendary. Instead, Grayson stuck with the simplest answer. "We have a business arrangement based on mutually assured destruction."

"Seriously?"

It was one word, but in it he heard her flickers of doubt. He needed to head them off before they found fertile ground. Frustration and desperation left his voice hard. "There have been times when I've had to work with less-than-legit players, and one of those times includes this source. I can't—not won't, Cass, can't—share beyond swearing to you that he would not risk the repercussions of lying to me."

He waited, tension knotting his gut. The seconds stretched into eternity.

Then came her quiet "Okay."

"Okay," he repeated, relief loosening the knots as he flexed his bloodless fingers on the steering wheel.

"You said Russ wasn't behind the hex."

"He didn't set it, but that doesn't mean someone else isn't using him as a stalking horse." He gave it a beat. "Do you have any idea what the Cabal would gain by targeting your sister?"

She didn't rush to answer. "I don't know." She fidgeted with the hem of her skirt. "There's always a chance she's got a client who's the target, but unless things have drastically changed, her clients wouldn't rate that kind of attention. High-level clients, the kind more likely to earn Cabal attention —those would be handled by my parents."

If that was the case, Zane would sniff it out.

"But..." she said.

When she fell quiet, he prodded, "But...?"

"Okay, I need you to stick with me because this convoluted, but it makes a twisted sort of sense when you consider the services Pythia provides."

He caught a glimmer of where she was headed. "Prediction."

"Right, and the majority of Pythia's mages are Mystics."

"Because predictive magic is intuitive in nature." He caught her nod as he checked his mirrors.

She turned in her seat until she was facing him. "Which is directly opposed to what the Cabal practice."

She wasn't wrong. The Cabal earned their nightmarish reputation by having zero qualms about mixing horrific science with darker magics, and they had less than zero reservations about using the results to get what they wanted.

"If they're behind all these supposed 'incidents'"—she used finger quotes on the last word—"and trying to stay off the Families' radar, they would have two choices to get what they wanted. Hire Pythia or cripple it."

His gut soured, and he hated that he had to even ask. "Would your mother work for the Cabal?"

"Knowingly? No." She sounded resigned. "But if a client waved enough money around, she wouldn't ask questions."

That was far from reassuring. "The second option?"

"To cripple Pythia's operations and keep them from getting in the way, they'd be more likely to target my mother, not Sofia."

Maybe. He flipped the turn signal for the upcoming exit as an ugly suspicion crept in. "Cass, how sure are you that Iris died of natural causes?"

She stared at his profile. "No, that's not..." she said, her voice cracking. She turned away, shaking her head. "No, if anything was hinky with Yaya's death, Mother would be on the warpath."

He didn't say anything because he had his doubts and Cass had had a hell of a day. Still, it might be worth adding a deeper dive into Rhea's client list to Zane's research. He turned onto the surface streets, grateful that the traffic was light.

Accurately interpreting his silence, Cass touched his knee. "It wasn't murder, Grayson."

He didn't want to hurt her, but from the outside looking in, her family was a problematic nightmare. "How can you be so sure?"

"Because my mother would have looked," she said calmly.

Right. Because Sages can see the past. "But would she?"

"Yes."

The depth of her certainty threw him off. "You sound awfully sure." He shot her a look. "What happened while I was gone?"

"She and I had a long-overdue conversation."

As she shared the details involving her aunt's prediction and her mother's resulting decisions, he didn't miss the hints of compassion and flashes of anger as she repeated Rhea's justifications. Cass was struggling to come to terms with what her mother had revealed. But the more she shared, the more his concern grew, and he had to wonder if she was too emotionally tied to the situation to see the same glaring warning signs he saw—Rhea's deliberate decision to climb into bed with the Families, the way she manipulated situations and people to get what she wanted, and how she justified hurting those she loved. That last one tripped his personal trigger in a big way and made him wonder just how far Rhea would go to get what she wanted.

He didn't like the answer.

When Cass stopped talking and fell quiet, he picked his words carefully. "Does it help, knowing all this now?"

"I don't know," she admitted softly, almost sadly. "I've spent years with this image of her in my head, and now..." She sighed. "She was right about the holding-a-grudge thing because even now, after everything she told me, part of me wonders if it's all some sort of ploy."

Trying to ignore the way his chest loosened at her admission, he focused on playing devil's advocate. "To what end?"

"That's the thing. I don't know."

Well, maybe he could help with that—at least he hoped she'd view it that way. He cleared his throat. "Just so you're aware, I have someone looking into Russ and your parents."

Fortunately, her response was more resigned than outraged. "Probably a good idea."

He pulled into the condo's parking lot. "I'm hoping he'll bring me something by early tomorrow."

"That's fast."

"Zane's that good, and he knows I'm working against the clock." He turned into his assigned spot and noted someone had parked in his visitor's lot. Not that he minded. The compact wasn't Zane's truck and probably belonged to someone visiting a neighbor. He shut the car, popped his trunk, and undid his seat belt.

"So, what's the plan?" Cass asked as she undid hers.

"I've got Zane grabbing a couple of items I need, so I can dive into the leads my source gave me."

"What leads?"

"I'll show you."

They got out and met at the trunk. Grayson lifted the lid, and Cass frowned. "What are those?"

He picked up the two heavy leather-bound books, shifted them to one arm, and then closed the trunk. "Research journals," he murmured.

She matched his tone. "Research?"

"The kind that shouldn't exist," he admitted as he curled his free arm around her waist. Together, they started toward the condo.

Her eyes widened, but she followed his example and, despite no one being around, kept their conversation quiet by mouthing the word, "Cabal?"

He nodded as they passed under the streetlight and hopped the curb to the path that led through the complex. The faint sound of a car door opening and closing came from somewhere behind them.

"That means you'll be staying in and studying?" she asked.

"Unless I need to go out and grab something. Why?"

She worried her bottom lip. "I need to do a divining, maybe get a better idea of what we're up against."

They turned into the breezeway, and under the outdoor lights, he studied the weary slump of her shoulders and the shadows darkening her face. The circles under her eyes were obvious even through her tinted lenses.

He tried to be diplomatic. "You're exhausted, Cass. Maybe you should rest first."

"I'm fine," she lied with a tight smile. He raised his eyebrows, and her smile turned genuine as she leaned in and bumped shoulders with him. "Okay, not exactly fine, but fine enough. Besides, you'll be there, so I won't stay under long."

Remembering her warning about spiraling out, he waited until they'd climbed the exterior stairs to the second floor and then asked, "And if you cascade?"

Determination wiped out her faint humor. "I won't go deep."

They got to his door, where he undid the locks and then

the security rune before holding it open for her. "I'm going to hold you to that."

She moved to pass but stopped in front of him, her hands resting on his chest as she pressed a quick kiss to his jaw. When she pulled back, she held his gaze. "I'll be fine."

He brushed the back of his hand over her cheek. "I know." He would make certain of it.

Cass smiled, and she walked inside, leaving him to follow. "You mind if I take a quick shower?"

"No." He closed the door and reset his wards to sentry mode as she headed toward the bedroom. Not that he expected unwanted company, but you never knew who would drop by. He tossed his keys on the counter and set the books on one of the barstools as she disappeared. "You hungry?" Grayson called out as he went to the refrigerator and opened it.

"Not really. If you have tea, I'll take that."

He closed the fridge and turned to his cupboard. After digging behind a box of cereal, he found what he was looking for. "I've got orange spice, Earl Grey, and one called wild raspberry hibiscus."

"The raspberry works."

"Got it." He pulled it out then unearthed an electric teakettle his sister had given him after swearing that microwaving water for tea was uncivilized.

He heard the shower go on as he set the kettle to heat. Grayson leaned against the counter and pulled out his phone. He was about to check his notifications when someone knocked on the door. He straightened, tension coiling through him. It was late, too late for a casual visitor, and Zane would have given him a heads-up if he was on his way over. A check of the wards showed a steady, uninterrupted green, not the angry red indicating a threat. Like many Keys, he understood the value of a security system that was both proactive and reactive.

Wary, he reached for his magic and the invisible weave of spells that protected his home. He got to the door and, with one hand on the handle, pressed his other to the door's surface. His magic hummed back, steady and quiet.

He checked the Judas hole and jerked back with a hiss. "Are you fucking kidding me?" He undid the locks, yanked the door open, and then kept his body solidly in the opening. "What the hell are you doing here?"

The man on the other side was an older version of him, just a bit wirier and more worn down. There was gray in his hair and a hint of hollowness in his dark eyes. "Hello, son."

"Why are you here, Dad?"

Dylan Beck took no offense at the less-than-welcoming question. "Because if I called, you wouldn't pick up."

Grayson refused to deny or apologize. "I'm busy."

"So I've heard," Dylan deadpanned.

Grayson narrowed his eyes. "What's that supposed to mean?"

"Can I come in?" his father asked.

Grayson folded his arms. "It's almost eleven."

"And I've been waiting since nine."

Grayson clenched his teeth, locking down the growl that wanted to escape. His father wasn't going away. "Fine." He dropped his arms, stepped back, and waved the man in. As Dylan crossed the threshold, Grayson said, "I've got company, so make this quick."

He closed the door then stalked down the short hall to find his dad standing at the counter bar, his attention shifting from the books on the stool to Grayson. Grayson fought the urge to snatch up the books. Instead, he went to his bedroom door, through which he could still hear Cass's shower, pulled it closed, and retraced his steps. He stopped a few feet from his dad, who had used a finger to lift the cover on the top book.

Dylan stared down at the pages. "Why are you messing with Cabal spells?"

"I'm a Key. Spells are my business."

The older man let the cover go and studied him, his expression hard and his eyes dark as a muscle jumped in his clean-shaven jaw.

Years before, that look would have made Grayson flinch. Now he didn't give the first damn what his dad saw. He just wanted him gone. He stood with his arms folded and waited for the old man to start talking. It didn't take long.

"I got an unexpected call today."

Oh, for fuck's sake. Like I'm a kid or something. Grayson blew out a frustrated breath. "Burton."

Dylan's gaze went to the closed door and then came back. "What are you doing working with the Ambroses, boy?" he asked grimly.

Grayson narrowed his eyes as his temper started to churn, but he held it in check. "First, I'm not a damn boy. Second, none of your business."

"It is my business when it appears my son is following his mother's footsteps."

"Fuck you, Dad."

The words were out before Grayson could stop them—not that he tried. Oh, hell no. He was too pissed to see straight, and after everything that had happened that day, he was just done. "You and I both know it was your work that killed Mom, not the other way around." He ignored his father's flinch. "I don't need you coming in here and shoving your fucked-up guilt in my face."

For a moment, his father's mask slipped, revealing the scar honed by the pitiless claws of regret and heartache. Then he blinked, and it was gone. "That's not what I'm doing."

"Isn't it?" Grayson didn't give him a chance to respond. He'd heard it all before. Instead, he stuck to the important stuff. "Why the hell is Burton calling you, anyway?"

Dylan rested a hand on the back of the barstool. "He's a friend. He called—asked if I was in town and wanted to get together for dinner at some point. I agreed, and then he mentioned running into you and where. Imagine my surprise when he shared you were with the oldest Ambrose."

"Alcmene," Grayson corrected.

"Excuse me?"

"Cass prefers Alcmene over Ambrose."

"Cass, is it?" He looked at the bedroom then back at Grayson. "Just how serious is this?"

"Again, none of your business."

Dylan threw up his hands in frustration. "That's where you're wrong. Not only is my son walking into a pit of vipers, but based on this"—he motioned to the books—"you're sliding back into shady shit, and you think I'm going to ignore it?"

Grayson ignored the whispered echo of guilt that had been birthed years earlier. "It's what you do best, isn't it?" he drawled.

Hurt flashed over Dylan's face, but his spine snapped straight as he pinned his son with a narrow-eyed glare. "Are you serious with that?"

"Yeah, Dad, I am." Realizing he couldn't hear the shower anymore, Grayson decided it was time to move the old man along. He dropped his arms, stalked to his father, and lowered his voice. "You shared your opinion, for what it's worth. Now, leave."

"No," Dylan shot back. "Not until—" He broke off as the bedroom door opened, and the unmistakable tension swirling between them leveled up.

Grayson turned his head to see Cass in the doorway, her

wet hair in a sloppy bun, wearing one of his shirts and her leggings. She adjusted her glasses and turned her attention to Dylan. Whatever she saw there made her stiffen, drop her hand, and angle her chin warily.

"Is everything okay out here?" she asked.

He shot his father a dark look of warning. Then he went to Cass and set his hands on her hips. "It's fine."

"Liar," she said softly, holding his gaze. "Introduce me?"

He ground his teeth. That was the last damn thing he wanted to do.

Her fingers brushed along his clenched jaw as if willing away the tension. "Please."

Unable to deny her, he relented with a terse nod. He turned, keeping her close to his side. "Cass, this my father, Dylan Beck."

"Hi." Whether it was because Grayson kept his arm around her waist to hold her back or because his dad was glaring at her, Cass didn't offer her hand but gave a small wave.

"Evening." At least the old man was polite enough to offer a tight nod. Unfortunately, he couldn't have been more obvious about the fact that he didn't welcome Cass's presence.

"I'll just grab my tea and leave you two alone," Cass said uncomfortably.

Grayson felt his temper start to boil over. She started to move to the kitchen, but Grayson tightened his hold in silent demand, and she stilled. He glared at his father. "He was just leaving. Right, Dad?" he said coldly.

A flare of frustration washed through Dylan's face as he glared right back. "I guess I am, but this conversation isn't finished."

Grayson curled his lip, not in a smile but in warning. "Yes, it is."

For a long moment, the two stared at each, but Grayson knew he wouldn't blink first. Sure enough, it was Dylan who turned and gave Cass something close to a polite smile. "Apologies on dropping in so late. I'll leave you two to it and see myself out." He turned and strode out.

Grayson stared after his father, the caustic feelings of old resentment and anger settling into worn grooves, and wondered when watching the man walk away would no longer matter. The door closed with a deafening snick that echoed through the tense quiet.

Cass turned to him. "What was that about?"

Unable to stand still, he let her go and started to pace. "Burton called him, told him I was hooked up with you, which is guaranteed to get his panties in a bunch. Then he saw the books, jumped to the wrong conclusions—which he's good at—and tried to reclaim a role he lost the rights to a long damn time ago." He dragged a hand through his hair then grabbed the back of his neck and squeezed. "Why did I open the damn door?" he muttered with his back to Cass.

"Because he's your dad?" Cass offered softly.

He laughed bitterly. "I buried my dad with my mom, Cass. That man, he's nothing to me."

"That may be, but you mean something to him."

He couldn't afford to believe her. "That's his problem, not mine."

"Okay, I'll give you that."

"That's gracious of you." The spiteful words escaped him before he could check his mouth. He winced and turned to face her. "Dammit, Cass, I'm sorry. That was uncalled-for."

"It was. However, you've met my family, right? So I get it." She then surprised him with a small grin. "But does it make me weird that you being mean makes me feel better?"

The riot of emotions his father's presence had evoked eased. "Uh, yeah?" he said, bemused.

Cass's giggle was quiet as she headed for the kitchen. "It's nice to know you're not perfect."

"Not even close," he murmured as he followed her. He took a seat at the counter.

She grabbed the kettle and started to pour. "So, what's his problem with me?"

"Apparently, he knows your family, and he's not a fan."

She raised a brow and set the kettle aside. "Did they do something to him?"

"Probably not." If he hadn't been watching her, he would have missed the slight tremble in her hand as she dropped the teabag into the mug. "It's more likely he's lumping them in with all the Families."

She opened a couple of cabinets until she found his plates and grabbed a saucer. "Ah, so more like a basic disdain of the OGs, then?" She set the saucer on top of the mug, holding the teabag in place as it steeped.

"It's a little deeper than that."

When she looked at him, he knew it was time to share, so he settled in. "Remember the story I promised?" He waited for her nod. "Well, once upon a time, my dad was a well-regarded Sentinel, and my mom was a highly respected Key. While my mom was happy working for the Guild, Dad preferred being able to pick and choose his own clients."

"As a Sentinel, going solo couldn't have been easy for him," she said, settling into a lean against the counter.

She wasn't wrong. When it came to personal security work, whether close cover or covert, most Families preferred a Guild-backed Sentinel. "It wasn't, but he had a solid reputation and, more importantly, an exclusive offer from one of the Families."

"That would do it," she said. "I'm guessing he didn't want to pay the Guild their cut."

Grayson shook his head. "I remember him and Mom discussing it one night, and he told her he'd already paid the

Guild back and then some. It was time to earn what he was worth."

"Did your mom not want him to take the job?"

"She wanted him happy. Things had been tough at the Guild. I'm not sure what was going on, if it was a shitty boss, or a midlife-crisis thing, but whatever it was, Dad wanted a change."

"And when the offer came, he took it."

Grayson nodded. "And for a couple of years, things were good. Then the Family he worked for decided to partner on a real estate development deal here in Vegas."

"Let me guess. A casino?" Cass set the saucer aside and removed the teabag. She took her mug and rounded the counter.

"A private one," he confirmed, picking up the books and setting them on the seat behind him. As she settled onto the barstool next to him, he angled so they could face each other. "Plans were underway, things were moving along, but then Dad's client discovered money was missing. An investigation was started, and then the client had a string of bad luck resulting in a couple of near misses. Dad started to hunt and narrowed in on a suspect fairly quickly, which was when things got messy."

"Your issues with Muses," Cass guessed—accurately—a slight frown marring her forehead. "Was that the suspect?"

"It was. She managed to get her hooks into Dad's memories and started to twist them. Her plan was to get him to protect her instead of his client, but she overreached."

Memories crowded in. His dad putting in longer and longer hours. His mom trying to share her concerns, only to have the conversation devolve into cold arguments that ended in colder silences. The way his father would sometimes look through him and his siblings, and eventually, Grayson's mother. Tension had seeped into their once happy, normal home, fracturing their family and Grayson's heart.

Horrified understanding flashed across Cass's face. "Oh my gods, she didn't!"

"She did," he said grimly. "She warped his memories until he barely acknowledged us, but my mom..." The pressure on his chest deepened, tightening his throat, and his eyes burned.

Cass covered his fisted hand with hers, watching him with concern.

He swallowed once, hard, and got the rest out. "Mom knew something was wrong. She followed my dad one night when he was meeting the Muse. There was a confrontation, and when the dust settled, both my mom and the Muse were dead, and my dad was nearly catatonic."

"Oh, Gray."

Her compassion eased the ache of memories, and under her warm touch, he forced his hand open. "Without Mom, it fell on me to keep Shep and Rae safe because after he finally woke up, Dad was useless. He buried himself in a bottle and eventually stopped coming home."

"Now I get what tonight was about," she murmured as she played with his fingers. "Did you ever find out where he went?"

"I don't know, and I never cared to find out. I had enough to worry about. I was fifteen going on twenty-five and had to figure out how to keep the three of us together."

"But you did it." There was no doubt in her voice.

"I did, but not without crossing the line."

"Your less-than-legit sources."

He inclined his head. "I'd been training with the Guild before things went to shit, but afterward, I needed money fast." He looked up, and it was hard to hold her gaze, especially since he was about to admit to things that might extinguish the soft light of something beautiful. "It started with a few off-the-book jobs. The pay was good, especially since I didn't have to hand over the Guild's cut. Word spread, and more jobs popped up, each one a little more slippery than the last, but the money kept going up. Pretty soon, I was doing risky jobs no sane Key would consider with clients that were more likely to take their cut literally."

There was no condemnation as she studied him, just tender empathy. "You went dark."

He'd never admit it out loud, but he'd played in the inky depths until he almost disappeared. "It's how I met my source."

Apprehension colored her eyes, and when she spoke, it was cautiously. "I've got to ask: Do you still work in that arena?"

He didn't take offense at her question, because he understood what drove it. He gave her fingers a gentle, reassuring squeeze. "No, but the contacts I made, the skills I earned, they're still useful."

"I bet." She brought his hand up and brushed a kiss over his knuckles in silent apology. "I'm grateful, then."

"Grateful?"

"Yeah." She cocked her head. "Did you think I'd judge you?"

In a moment of clarity, it hit him that yes, he had, which was why he'd held off sharing. "Most would if they found out someone was messing with dark magic."

"True, but you did what you had to do to survive."

He found it hard to accept her understanding. "It's dark magic, Cass."

She let him go but not for long. She cupped his jaw in her hands, her touch gentle but firm as she held his gaze. "And I break the rules and use less-than-legal resources on the regular to help those the law won't. Does that make me a bad person?"

"No."

She smiled at his quick answer. "I remember someone telling me that life is a series of choices, good, bad, and everything in between. Regardless of which way you went, in the end, what matters is whether you can live with the ones you made."

The last of his tension eased at what she was offering him. It was there in the warm light in her eyes, her soothing touch, and the sincerity of her voice.

He felt her slip deeper into his heart and dropped his forehead to rest against hers. "Is that your roundabout way of telling me the ends justify the means?"

Her hands slid around his neck as she angled her head to press a soft kiss to the corner of his mouth. "What do you think?"

"I think…" He pulled her closer, the slow burn of hunger that had simmered for days igniting under her teasing touch. "I've got another choice to make."

Her eyes darkened. "Yeah?" she asked huskily.

"Yeah." Then he captured her lips with his, utterly content to follow this woman into the flames.

chapter 17

Cass

CASS WOKE, wrapped in the heat of Grayson's body, his arm a welcome weight on her hip, his quiet snores tickling her ear. The unrelenting reality of the last few days was buffered by what they had shared the night before. It might not be the best timing, but she was falling for Grayson, and honestly, she didn't need her cards or her magic to be at peace with her choice. They both had their scars, but they weren't young kids running on hormones and drama. They were old enough to recognize how integral those life lessons were to who they chose to be, and she found she really liked who they were together. Too used to standing on her own, she'd never thought she'd like a protective partner, but with the way he handled her family and all that went with it, she found her mind changing. Then there was how honest he was in what he wanted. It was refreshing not to have to play the guessing games that so often came with new relationships. A bigger plus was that even knowing where she came from, he was still here, and more, wanted to be here.

Behind her, Grayson shifted in his sleep, his arm tightening, pulling her back deeper into him, and her body stirred in response. She couldn't help her instinctive wriggle and grinned as evidence rose that she wasn't the only one who really, really liked what they shared in bed.

Warm lips slid along her neck to her shoulder, and his voice held the rough edge of sleep when he said, "Morning, sweetheart."

She reached back, giving him room to explore, and managed a purring "Morning." Then she stopped thinking and just felt as he kept stroking her, slowly shifting their positions until she lay under him as he kissed her senseless and his hands drove her crazy.

Things were getting good when the doorbell rang.

Grayson lifted his head and aimed a dark look at the bedroom door. "What the hell?"

Cass caught her breath. "What time is it?"

Grayson check the clock on his nightstand. "It's not even seven."

The doorbell went again, and a whisper of anxiety crawled through Cass as reality intruded. Whoever was on the other side was not going away. Reluctantly, she let Grayson go. "We need to answer it."

She turned back to find Grayson watching her, his earlier irritation gone, replaced by understanding. "Call your parents —check on Sofia. I'll get the door."

He gave her a quick kiss then got up and dragged on a pair of loose cotton pants before heading out of the bedroom. Cass rolled to the other side, found her phone, and checked for messages. The edge of panic dulled when she didn't find anything new. She debated calling versus texting and went with the latter because she wasn't ready to field the unanswerable questions her mother would ask. Text sent, she got dressed. She took time to throw her hair up into a sloppy bun, brush her teeth, and wash her face. By the time she finished, she had a response from her mother that there was no change with Sofia and a demand to know when Cass was coming back with Grayson. Since Cass didn't have an answer, she ignored it. Instead, she opened the bedroom door and stepped into the living room to find a bare-chested Grayson talking with another man.

Their conversation stopped at her entrance, but Grayson held out a hand to her. "Cass, this is Zane. I asked him to look into Russ."

She took his hand, letting him bring her to his side. "Hello."

Behind the stranger, a faint flicker of a lone wolf bared its teeth in warning. *A Hunter, and one of Gray's shadier contacts.*

"Sorry to wake you."

Zane's voice was smooth and rich, perfectly matching the dark, piercing gaze under a heavy brow. His equally dark hair was slicked back from an angular face in shades of bronze, exposing an old scar that left a slash of white up near the left temple and an onyx stud in his left ear. A neat, closely cropped beard covered his chin, adding to his roguish appearance. His hands were tucked into the pockets of his black cargo pants. A sleeve of intricate tattoos covered one arm and disappeared under the short sleeve of his faded green T-shirt.

"But I thought you should hear what I've got so far," Zane continued.

Her stomach pitched at his grim tone. "That doesn't sound good."

There was a hint of sympathy in Zane's hard expression. "Let's just say if it was my sister hooking up with him, I'd have concerns."

She tightened her grip on Grayson's hand. "Tell me."

Zane's eyebrows rose, and amusement wiped away some of the shadows. "How about a trade? Details for coffee."

"Right, right, sorry." She was a little flustered, realizing how rude her demand had sounded. "I'll get a pot started." She let go of Grayson.

"No apologies needed." Zane headed to the living room.

Grayson ran a hand through his uncombed hair and turned to the bedroom. "I'm grabbing a shirt."

Cass went into the kitchen and got the coffee going. As it brewed, she tried to keep her mind from spiraling. She could hear Zane typing on his phone. It seemed to take forever for the coffee to finish, but when it finally did, she poured three mugs.

"Zane, how do you take yours?"

"Black, please."

She was pouring cream into Grayson's when he joined her in the kitchen, his chest covered by a wrinkled gray T-shirt. She held out a mug. "This is yours."

He took it from her with a murmured "Thanks." She finished doctoring hers, and before she could grab Zane's, Grayson had it. "I've got it."

She followed him to where Zane was sprawled in the easy chair, his legs stretched out and crossed at the ankles, his head tipped against the headrest, his eyes closed. At Grayson's approach, they snapped open with a disconcerting alertness.

"Here." Grayson held out the mug.

"Thanks." Zane took it and sipped.

Cass settled into the corner of the couch, her back to the armrest so she could see Zane, and crossed her legs tailor style. She waited until Grayson took a seat next to her, his thigh brushing her knee, before she spoke. "What did you find?"

"Russell Seagraves, a thirty-year-old Auctori mage, acquisition manager at Pythia Strategies, only son of Mira and Jared Seagraves of Huntington Beach, California. For the last seven years, he's worked his way through various companies as he climbed from procurement analyst into contract work until finally landing his job at Pythia." Zane set his coffee aside. "And for an Auctori mage, he's done a shit job with personal relationships."

"Not a surprise. He's an arrogant dick," Grayson said.

"Yeah, that's the picture I got," Zane confirmed. "His mother is a family therapist, and his father is a tenured faculty member at a local university. Both are well respected in their fields." He absently tapped a finger against the chair's armrest. "I managed to talk to the dad, who shared that they're not close to their son—haven't been in years. Their choice."

Grayson frowned. "Any particular reason why?"

"Seems Russell decided that the nice comfortable lifestyle his parents provided wasn't enough for him, nor did they appreciate how he could enhance that lifestyle if he just ignored a few ethical lines."

It didn't take a genius to understand the subtext, but Cass wanted to be sure. "He used his magic on innocents."

Zane nodded, his expression shifting to something darker, colder. "It started in high school. Initially, it was getting teachers to change grades or overlook attendance issues, but it didn't take long for it to spill over into his social life."

Disquiet crawled over her skin. "How bad?"

"Bad. It started with a couple of incidents with some guys that were giving him a hard time, but nothing could be proven." The darkness in the Hunter's eyes deepened. "Not until two girls came forward and claimed he'd forced their affection."

Her stomach rolled with the implication, and it was hard to get her question out. "Physically?"

"Emotionally," Zane countered. "Not that that's any better."

No. If anything, it was worse.

Zane continued his story. "One of the girls had a boyfriend, a popular guy, and they were fairly serious. The boyfriend clued in before she did, mainly because her behavior was so out of character, and he was smart enough to recognize Russell's influence."

"Oracle?" Grayson asked her, probably remembering their earlier conversation about why Cass had caught Russ's hex before he had.

"Maybe," she said. "But they're not the only type of mage that would recognize that kind of magic."

"Key, actually," Zane said. "He's now part of the Guild in California."

Which explained why Zane was able to get this kind of information so quickly. In her experience, most victims of manipulation mages tended to keep the details quiet. She remembered a timid, nearly broken man who'd been targeted by a powerful Auctori, a woman who didn't take no for an answer. By the time he'd reached out to Des for help, his life was in shambles. Once she, Isa, and Des were done, it was the Auctori scrambling to pick up the pieces, and her chosen prey was rebuilding his life somewhere far, far away.

"What about the other girl?" Cass asked.

"Shared her supposed 'feelings' with her best friend, who told her parents, who then went to his parents. They were horrified and sent him off to a therapist who specialized in behavior modification, hoping it would help."

She did not like where this was going. "It didn't."

Zane shook his head. "No, Russell just got better at hiding. He came back halfway through his senior year and spent the next few months toeing the line, but as soon as he hit eighteen, he left and hasn't been in touch with his parents since. My impression from his dad is they would like it to stay that way."

She couldn't blame them. "All right. So after high school and ditching his parents, where did he end up?"

"That's what I'm still trying to find out." Zane sat up

and leaned forward, his arms braced on his thighs. "I've got a two-year gap before he turns up at an overseas university. After graduation, he ended up working with a handful of companies scattered throughout Europe, each position lasting a few months here, a few months there, before he stuck with an Italian company for just over a year. Then he was back in the US, and he made steady progress until he reached Pythia."

As much as she would have liked to be able to use Russ's spotty employment to nudge her sister to break off her engagement, it wasn't enough. "Other than the gap, it sounds like any upwardly mobile young professional."

Zane's lips curled, not in amusement but with a feral kind of anticipation. "Sure, but if you scrape away the polish, you'll find that some of those European companies are just pretty shells."

Next to her, Grayson straightened as if catching the scent, but she was still nose blind. "What do you mean?" she asked.

"A couple only exist on paper, and the legit ones have been absorbed into larger corporations."

Her hands tightened around her mug. A whisper of warning drifted through her mind, and she gave it voice. "He targeted them."

Zane's attention on her sharpened. "That was my conclusion."

The whispers grew. "And now he's targeting Pythia." *And Sofia.* "Why?"

Zane looked at Grayson then back at her. "I don't know yet. And it's going to take me more time than I think you have to find out, but I will. I've already spoken to a couple of old coworkers. They didn't have much to add, but my takeaway is Russell's still playing mind games—he's just gotten better at it. He has no problem taking credit for others' work, and so long as it benefits him, he's game for anything."

Grayson stirred. "Did you run into anything that indicated Cabal involvement?"

"No, but you and I both know if it's there, that shit gets buried deep." The Hunter's attention narrowed on Grayson. "Why?"

Grayson raised his brow in silent question. Understanding he was asking permission to share, she dipped her chin, granting it.

He turned back to Zane. "I was able to confirm that the hex on Sofia is Cabal based."

Zane blinked once. "Well, shit." He sank back into the chair without breaking eye contact with Grayson. His fingers tapped out a slow rhythm on the armrest. "How much did our friend charge you for that?"

Grayson flicked a discomfited look at Cass, and she knew he'd left something out of their earlier conversation. "A favor."

That answer did not make Zane happy. "From...?"

"Me," Cass offered.

He looked from Cass to Grayson. "He'd want more than that."

"He did."

Zane's expression darkened. "Dammit, Grayson, you know—"

"Drop it." There was an edge to Grayson's voice. "I've got it, Zane."

The other man didn't look convinced.

"Grayson," Cass warned, not at all thrilled at being left in the dark.

He turned to her. "Not now, Cass. Later," he said with a hint of defensiveness.

She studied him, debating how hard to push this. His gaze didn't waver.

Give and take. The quiet voice in her mind sounded suspiciously like her yaya. She heeded it, reluctantly giving in. "Fine. Later." She set her coffee aside and started to rise.

Grayson put hand on her leg, stopping her. "Where are you going?"

"To get my phone and text my mother for Russ's address. I've got some questions for him."

Zane managed a disbelieving snort. "And you think he'll just decide to cough up the answers?"

She met the Hunter's amused gaze and felt hers harden. "I don't think he'll have a choice."

✦

An edgy quiet filled the ride to Russ's, and Cass spent it turning things over and over until her mind spun. She could align the pieces right up until she hit the why. Why had the Cabal chosen to target Sofia? Why not Pythia directly? The answer shimmered just out of reach, and her hands itched for her cards, but with the clock ticking, she wasn't interested in untangling the cryptic. Instead, she would get her answers directly from the source, willingly or unwillingly. After what Zane had shared, she wasn't much concerned about how it happened, only that it would.

Grayson turned into the parking lot of the three-story complex that made up the South Wind condominiums. Like many of the newer buildings popping up around Vegas, it looked like a high-end resort, the facade a mix of rust red, light sage, and earthy brown. Wrought-iron balconies festooned the top-level and corner condos, and reflective windows stared over the main visitors' lot and two gated entrances—one on either side—that led to the residents' parking.

"Over on the left," Zane directed from the passenger seat. "Third floor, back corner."

Grayson followed his directions past a large pool with

loungers and slid into an empty spot next to one marked for deliveries. The three of them got out of the car and headed toward the double glass doors that led inside. Cass tried to use the walk to calm her vengeful fantasies to an acceptable level because losing her shit on Russ wouldn't get her answers.

A keypad was embedded into the metal frame, but Zane still gave it an experimental tug. Locked. Cass stepped in front of him and input the four-digit code her mother had sent with the address.

There was a click, and then Zane was pulling it open. "After you."

She shook her head and stepped inside with Grayson on her heels. Quiet, melodic music greeted them as the cool air curled around her, erasing the morning's heat. Gray-washed floors stretched through the bright, open space where clean-lined, modular furniture with a Nordic vibe was arranged in cozy conversational groupings under elemental artwork. Unsurprisingly for a Sunday morning, the lobby was empty, but a sign directed guests to use the intercom system to the left to contact residents. By tacit agreement, the three of them didn't bother notifying Russ that they were headed up.

"Cameras are down," Zane murmured as they went toward the elevators. He hit the call button as he and Grayson stayed at her back.

The elevator slid open with a soft chime, and Cass stepped inside, moving to the side as Zane and Grayson followed. As she waited for them to enter, she snuck a glance at the lobby and noted the camera's dark eye aimed at the door, tucked discreetly in the corner. Next to the unmoving lens was a steady red light.

"You sure?" she asked as she hit the third-floor button.

Zane waited until the doors were shut. "That model is motion activated, and the recording light should be green."

Grayson moved a little closer to Cass. "Maybe it's just down."

Zane rolled his shoulders. "Maybe."

The elevator stopped, and the doors opened into a wide, well-lit hallway. There was no music here, just a disconcerting silence as they strode down the hall. Each apartment had an angled alcove for its front door, allowing a semblance of privacy. Cass kept expecting to hear something—the drone of a TV, the heavy beat of music, maybe a yappy pup or crying kid—but it was deathly quiet. Either the soundproofing was top notch, or this place was a freaking horror show waiting to happen.

She rubbed her arms as she followed Zane's broad back. "This is creepy," she murmured.

"What is?"

"The quiet."

He pointed to one of the tall potted palms that lined the hall. Each one was made of metal, their trunks etched in markings that resembled primitive lace. "See those?"

She nodded.

"Those are soundproofing runes."

Ahead of them, Zane halted, his arm going up, his hand in a fist, a universal sign to stop. They did, but Grayson pulled Cass behind him as Zane dropped his arm. She peered around him and caught the soft green glow that ignited along Zane's arms. The Hunter exchanged a look with Grayson, and they did the man-to-man silent-conversation thing.

Grayson gave Zane a nod then put his head near hers and whispered, "Stay here."

She swallowed hard and nodded.

The unearthly red of magic slipped over Grayson as he reached Zane. The two men each took a side of Russ's entryway. Cass crept a little closer, which earned her twin glares from the men, but she could now see what had set Zane off. Russ's door wasn't completely shut.

Well, shit.

Grayson and Zane moved in graceful tandem, pushing open the door and slipping inside.

Heart in her throat, Cass waited, fists clenched for sounds of a confrontation, but the seconds ticked by with nothing. Unable to handle the suspense, she muttered, "Fuck it," and followed the men inside.

chapter 18

Grayson

Grayson heard Cass's shocked gasp and knew she had ignored his request to stay out. He tamped down his flash of irritation and snapped, "Stop, Cass!"

He didn't have to ask twice. She froze just inside the door. "What is that?"

"That," Zane said from where he was edging his way along the kitchen counters toward the armored creature crouched inside a sickly orange circle, "is what we call a chimera."

The nightmare cross between a giant scorpion and a ghoulish canine matched Zane's movements, its body shifting from noncorporal to physical as it stalked along an unearthly reddish-gold magical net Grayson had thrown between the ransacked living room and the open kitchen. The front half was a massive hellhound with red eyes and a muzzle filled with bone-colored teeth stained by things best not imagined. The broad chest and heavy body were covered in plated armor as its muscled legs ended in the kind of thick claws found on a Komodo dragon. A segmented tail curled from the back half, complete with a barbed stinger that was swaying hypnotically.

It lunged with uncanny speed, its form solidifying as its arched tail struck. Grayson yanked on the magical net at the same time, thickening it. The stinger stabbed into the amber-tinged barrier and scored along the magical binding. The impact sang through the magical lines and up Grayson's arms, rattling his bones. He grunted, his muscles quivering as he sank deeper into the magic, reinforcing the barrier as the chimera darted back, once again going noncorporeal.

"Hurry the hell up, Zane. I won't be able to hold this long."

"Nag, nag, nag," the other man muttered as virulent green ribbons erupted from around him, coiling like a group of snakes preparing to strike. "Need an opening."

Grayson bore down, holding the shield as he adjusted his magic to allow Zane's to pass through. "Go."

The ribbons slid through the reddish-gold barrier like it wasn't there, surrounding the crouching chimera before splitting into multiple razor-thin threads that struck so fast they blurred. They swarmed the snarling creature, twisting and turning, searching for purchase—not easy to do when it kept shifting between dimensions.

"Come on, asshole. Come all the way in. You know you want to," Zane taunted.

As if it understood, the creature lunged, going solid as it closed in, barreling over the sofa, its thick claws tearing through cushions and leaving a wake of shredded stuffing. Barbs bloomed on the green threads and burrowed under the creature's protective plating. The chimera snarled and snapped, trying to dislodge them, its body slamming into furniture, sending the heavier pieces sliding across the tile as it tried to evade them. As more and more of the filaments took anchor, it roared, the noise shaking frames from the walls. It focused on Zane and raked its claws along the shield with a frenzied madness.

Under the onslaught, Grayson's arms began to shake, and then one particularly nasty hit sent him stumbling into the stainless-steel refrigerator. Yet somehow, he managed to keep the barrier up. Along the tail and heavy chest, faint columns of hazy gray rose where Zane's cords found anchor. Their green glow darkened as they wound tighter and tighter, the threads pulling in opposite directions. The creature ignored the ties, including the thin filament slowly winding around its neck, and increased its efforts to get to Zane. Bone-rattling snarls filled the air as it snapped its fang-filled mouth and tore at Grayson's barrier with its black-tipped claws.

Grayson felt his magic start to buckle. He set his feet and tightened his hold. "Zane."

Zane's hands swept through the air as he crafted the final part of his spell and sent it arrowing toward the hellish creation in a wash of green flame. In lethal tandem, the anchoring ties on the thrashing tail and thick neck burst into a blaze of white as they snapped tight and cut through the armor like hot wire through wax. The monster's pained shriek was abruptly silenced in a ghostly explosion of magic.

The crushing weight against Grayson's barrier winked out, and he fell forward, catching himself on his hands before his face met the floor. The sudden change in air pressure left his ears ringing.

"Grayson..." Zane's growl was muffled.

Grayson looked up to see an inky slash hanging in midair, the edge trembling as if a great wind was trying to pass through. *A dimensional rift.* "I see it."

He sat on his heels and patted his pockets. He needed... *there.* He scrambled across the floor and grabbed a piece of broken pottery. Staying on his hands and knees, he scratched out a series of sigils and began to cast.

Ab intus signati, signet ab extra, duque in sempiternum.

Power ran through the sigils, magical lines rising to where the rift still hung. He poured more power into the cast.

Ventus stricta, fortis, sigillum.

The lines began to weave faster and faster, forcing the edges of the rift together. Just before the edges touched, he caught a glimpse of an unusual signature. With a final magical shove, he forced the two edges together and welded the opening shut, his magic burning through the darker influence until only deep red remained. It burned silently in midair, slowly fading away and taking the rift with it. Grayson rolled to his back, closed his eyes, and tried to catch his breath. Something warm and soft brushed his hair off his forehead.

"Grayson, are you okay?" It was Cass, and there was a panicked edge to her voice.

"I'm good." *Well, goodish.* "Just need a minute." His head felt like it would float away, and his arms ached, but otherwise, yeah, he was fine. "Zane, you good?"

"Getting there."

Grayson decided it was safe to open his eyes. Cass was crouched next to him, her face pale and worried, her gorgeous eyes behind the lenses a little wild. He took another deep breath and, on the exhalation, held up his hand. "Help me up?"

She took his hand, and together, they got him to where he could rest his back against one of the kitchen cabinets. Zane was on his ass, arms braced on bent knees, head hanging as his shoulders heaved near what was left of the dining room table.

Well, that was fun.

Cass left Grayson and went back to the front door. She stuck her head out and then pulled it back in before closing the door. She stood with her back to it. "I think they undercharge for their soundproofing."

He choked out a laugh.

She picked her way through the kitchen and took a seat next to him, and they took in the scene. Not difficult with the open-concept floorplan. The kitchen spilled into the merged dining and living room, ending in a door that led to the outdoor balcony. Most of the chimera's damage was limited to the living room—the floor gouged, furniture smashed, cracks snaking through drywall. But the dining room told the real tale. A pub-sized table was shoved into a far wall, with a deep gash in the drywall where a corner had hit. On the floor was a scattered collection of mail, keys, change, charging cords, and broken pottery—most likely a wide bowl that had once resided on the table. Two of the four barstools were on their sides, and one would never be the same, its leg split. An over-sized picture on the wall hung at a crooked angle, and a plant had spilled its soil over the floor.

"This isn't all from the chimera," Grayson said, stating the obvious.

"Nope." Zane slowly got to his feet. He rolled his shoulder with a wince and used a hand to massage it out. "I'd say we weren't Russ's first visitors this morning."

Cass looked toward the shallow hall on the left, which had two doors. "Where is Russ?"

When she went to get up, he stopped her with a hand on her leg. She gave him a frown that he ignored. "Not you. Let Zane check it out." He had a feeling he knew what Zane would find.

She sank back down.

He looked to Zane, who snorted and headed over to check out the rest of the condo. He was back in moments. "Clear."

Thought so.

He eyed Grayson. "You catch any signatures?"

Grayson leaned back against the cabinet. "Slider. Unsanctioned."

Zane's expression darkened. "The lack of Guild backing means it had to be a hired gun."

Or worse. "Got any names that come to mind?"

"One or two."

"Could one of you elaborate?" Cass asked. When they

both turned to look at her, she added, "Maybe start with how that thing got in here and why no one is pounding on the door right now."

"Really good soundproofing." Based on Cass's unamused expression, his lame humor attempt fell flat.

Zane stepped in, pulling his phone out of his back pocket as he picked his way through the living room. "I need to make some calls, see if I can't get some eyes on the security here and then maybe take a dip in the darker waters, see what rises to the top."

"Maybe start with Candace at the Guild," Grayson suggested as his friend headed toward the sliding glass doors leading to the balcony. "She can probably get into the traffic cams. Not so sure about the interior ones."

Zane stopped with a hand on the door and gave him a look. "Pretty sure the interior cameras are a bust, but maybe we'll catch a break on the others." He muscled open the cracked sliding glass door and stepped out onto the balcony.

Cass waited until the door slid closed before asking, "Whoever took Russ, do you think they'll go after Sofia?"

"Not yet." Grayson got to his feet then helped her do the same. "They'll be busy with Russ."

"And who is 'they'?" A better question was why they'd gone after Russ.

Grayson only answered with a question of his own. "Do you know what a Slider is?"

She shook her head. "I don't think so."

"They're one of the more specialized mage classifications and tend to get recruited into Family or government infrastructures. They're one of the few who can use dimensional rifts to move from one place to another. Information about them isn't publicized, but years ago, I ran into one, which is why I recognized the signature type."

She frowned. "Okay, it's a little frightening to realize

someone could pop in anywhere at any time and just snatch you away."

"If it helps any, their magic has its limits." He shook out his arms, feeling the aches and pains release their grip on his muscles. "Sliders tend to go through rifts alone, but they can take a rider, although it makes the jump difficult. The one I met was attached to a Family, and he was basically the heir apparent's bodyguard. According to him, so long as he had access to what he called a lock, he could move his charge with him through the rifts. He never explained what the lock was, but my impression was it was unique to his charge."

Cass grimaced. "That makes me feel a little better." She looked over to where Zane was pacing on the balcony, phone in hand, face set in grim lines. "That also means they had to have a lock on Russ, which suggests they know him."

"Probably, or at least whoever the Slider works for knows him."

She turned back to him. "Just how far can these Sliders go? Like, can they jump from one city to another or..."

"Short distances. At least, that was my understanding. Say, from here to the parking lot or here to next door—that kind of thing. Anything farther is too risky, especially if they're bringing someone with them. I'm not exactly clear on why, but I know it has something to do with how deep they go into a rift."

"Kind of like how Oracles can only go forward so far without risking a spiral," she said almost to herself as she looked back into the living room. "And the chimera? Why leave that behind?"

He thought back to the hints of intent he'd caught while fighting the creature. He'd come in behind Zane and seen the chimera pacing back and forth in the living room. It hadn't had time to rampage through the condo.

"I think it was left to deter anyone seeking out Russ," Grayson said.

"So if someone selling cookies knocked, it would—what? Attack, take them out?"

Now that he wasn't worried about getting his face ripped off or making sure Zane didn't get a barb in the gut, he replayed his first glimpse of the hex. "No, it was more subtle than that." The hex had been linked to an existing cast that was tied to... he narrowed his eyes. "The security code."

Confused, Cass stared at him. "What?"

"The spell that triggered the chimera, it was tied to the security code." The picture rapidly fell into place. "You put in the code, right?"

She nodded.

"Do you remember what you were thinking when you entered it?"

Light color stained her cheeks as she folded her arms. "I was thinking of how to get Russ to answer my questions."

Based on the glint in her eyes, he took a guess. "Did those plans involve bloodshed?"

Her chin lifted defiantly. "I wasn't going to act on it."

He wouldn't have blamed her if she had. "No judgment, but that intent triggered the chimera." When her frown deepened into confusion, he explained, "You were pissed when you punched in the code, and you were pissed at Russ specifically. Those two factors flipped the trigger on the cast, which opened the rift and released the chimera. Until those two conditions were met, the hex lay dormant, keeping it locked on the other side. If I had time for a deeper examination of the spell, I'm betting there was a third condition that would trigger it to attack, one that was met when Zane and I busted in."

She rubbed her arms. "Was it really from hell?"

Remembering the oily slide of magic and the burn that lingered as he'd fought against it, he said, "No question."

"Is it dead, then?"

He shook his head. "Not really. Demonic casts are extremely difficult to kill."

She gave a delicate shudder. "So, that stuff Zane did at the end... what was that about?"

"Zane needed it to be far enough on our side so he could sever the magical bindings that allowed it to shift between its dimension and ours. Destroying those bindings basically locks it out of accessing our realm."

She angled her head and studied him. "What about that weird shadow thing at the end?"

He frowned. "You mean the portal?"

"Sure?"

The questioning lilt of her reply told him she was a little unnerved. Not that he blamed her. Wrangling monsters was bound to leave you a little rattled. Not to mention dimensional rifts were not run-of-the-mill occurrences.

He tugged her close, giving her something to hold on to. "It needed to be sealed before anything nastier found it and crawled through."

She eyed the empty living room. "You're sure nothing's coming back."

He rubbed a comforting hand along her spine. "I'm sure."

She rested her head against his shoulder. "As much as I want to get my hands on Russ, maybe we should head back to my parents so you can work on Sofia."

He rested his cheek against the top of her head and briefly considered not admitting what he was about to share. "I know you're worried about her, sweetheart, but honestly? Our chances of breaking her curse are higher if we can get to Russ."

She pulled back so she could see his face, panic in her beautiful eyes. "What do you mean?"

He opened his mouth to explain that his conversation with Walter and scanning through the books had only given him a general frame of reference. He needed to work smarter, not harder, and that meant determining how Russ had factored into setting the hex and, more specifically, what triggers were embedded within it. Otherwise, Grayson could spend days trying to undo the curse, and he didn't think Sofia had that much time.

He didn't get a chance to say any of that because Zane opened the sliding glass door and stalked inside, a keen light in his dark eyes. "Got lucky. Camera on a business behind the complex caught a shot of your guy being shoved into a cargo van." He turned his phone so they could see the screen, where a surprisingly clear video shot showed a dusty white cargo van awkwardly parked between one of the condo's back entrances and the cinderblock wall that separated the condos from the small business park. "Can't get much because that back wall is blocking the plates, but watch this." He hit Play.

The video started up with no sound. For a long moment, the van sat with its back doors open but blocking any view inside the vehicle. The windows were tinted, and the camera's angles kept the driver anonymous, but Grayson caught a shift of shadow from behind the wheel. There was a blip on the recording, and suddenly, two figures appeared at the van's rear door, one of whom was a disoriented, barefoot man dressed in a pair of plaid sleep pants and a white T-shirt.

Zane paused the video. "That's Russ, right?" He handed his phone to Grayson, who tilted it so Cass could see the screen.

"That's him," she said. "They must have woken him up."

"Probably grabbed him as he came out of his bedroom," Zane added.

Grayson studied the still. The kidnapper's pants, shirt, and ball cap were all a familiar shade of brown. "The Slider made sure to dress the part."

"Easy enough to do," Zane agreed.

Grayson zoomed in, trying to get a better shot of the Slider's face, but it was pointless. Under the cap, the lower half of the kidnapper's profile was obscured by an olive-green neck gaiter that was paired with black sunglasses. "Nothing."

"Yeah pretty much." Zane reclaimed his phone and hit Play for the rest of the recording.

Together they watched as the Slider shoved Russ into the back of the cargo van and slammed the door closed. Then he moved out of the camera's range as he went around to the passenger side. The edge of the passenger door came into view as it was opened and then disappeared as it closed. Seconds later, the van drove out of view.

"Is that all we got?" Grayson asked Zane.

The Hunter shook his head as he pulled up an image on his phone. "Your electro mage snagged a shot of the van on another camera about a half mile from here." He turned his phone around so Grayson and Cass could see what he was talking about. "Notice anything?"

The image wasn't the greatest, but it was definitely the same van. This time, the camera got a front-facing shot. The driver was in a similar getup as the Slider, but that wasn't what caught Grayson's attention.

"What is that hanging from the mirror?" he asked.

Zane's smile was all kinds of fierce and showed a lot of teeth. "That is a parking permit."

"For...?" Cass asked.

"The Incantanto."

chapter 19

Cass

"YOUR E-GEEK IS DAMN GOOD," Zane told Grayson, his attention on his phone as Grayson wove in and out of the traffic.

"What did she get?" Grayson didn't take his attention from the road.

Stuck in the back seat, Cass smothered a gasp and grabbed for the door handle as the yellow cab in front of them abruptly switched lanes and narrowly missed being rolled over by a truck decked out in billboards. Blaring horns filled the air as the cab blithely hit its brakes and took a sharp turn into one of the many resorts lining the Strip.

Zane, completely oblivious to the insanity, said, "She got into Incantanto's security."

"That was fast." Cass dared to let go of the handle and sat forward, pulling against her seat belt. "Are they there?"

"Looks like it." Zane shifted his phone so she could see the screen. "Candace says this is twenty minutes ago."

She watched the white van follow a trailer truck to the rear of the resort. A line of wide rolling doors with loading docks stretched along the rear, and at the far end was a ramp that led to a door that was currently propped open. More than half the docks were full. Forklifts zipped around workers, who shuffled handcarts as they loaded and unloaded the multitude of items needed to keep the tourists happy. The cargo van waited its turn as a trailer truck slowly made its way to an empty dock.

"How are they going to get him in without anyone noticing?" she wondered aloud.

"Not that hard," Zane said. "Watch."

The semi inched into its spot, and as soon as there was enough room to pass, the cargo van squeezed by and drove toward the far end. "We're going to lose them."

"Patience," Zane murmured as the image in his hand switched. It was a closer shot of the van as it pulled behind a utility truck and parked near the ramp. Both the driver- and passenger-side doors opened.

Cass's breath hitched in anticipation. *Come on, come on,* she silently urged.

The screen went black.

She jerked back. "What the hell?"

Zane cursed and touched the onyx stud, which blinked with a dark flash as he snarled, "Call back."

When ringing came from the phone in his hand, Cass realized the stud was a magical earbud.

There was a click, then a female voice snapped, "Don't give me shit. They used a jammer. I don't have time to unscramble it."

"We need to know where they are."

"Yeah, I'm aware," came the irate response. "I'm going through interior feeds now, but it's a bitch to stitch the videos together."

"We're five minutes out," Grayson warned.

"I'll have something when you arrive." The line went dead.

No one spoke as Grayson gave the cabbies a run for their

money. By the time he put the car in park at the valet station, he'd earned four flipped fingers, one red-faced rant, and three blaring horns, but the three of them had arrived in one piece. Grayson pulled in behind an SUV unloading a family and their luggage. They got out, and Grayson handed the keys to an attendant.

Zane demanded in a low voice, "Where are they?"

Cass glanced his way and realized he was back on the line with Candace.

As soon as Grayson joined them, they headed inside. The wide door swept open, releasing a wave of cool air with notes of sandalwood and spice. Ornate chandeliers lined the towering curve of the lobby, their light spilling over fresco-covered walls. Some sort of string music was playing under the low roar of voices, and every now and then, a blast of bells and rings from the casino floor that dominated the space beyond the check-in desks would cut through the din.

Zane led them across the tile floor and through the maze of luggage piles and the walking disasters of tourists too busy craning their heads to take in their surroundings.

"Why here?" Cass asked Grayson, who was keeping pace at her side.

"I don't know." He caught her arm, bringing her closer to him, as a bellhop swept by with a luggage cart piled too high to see around.

Zane cut through the casino floor, winding his way between the crowded tables and lines of clamoring machines. Despite how large the casino floor was, the air was warm, almost suffocating, as Cass did her best to keep up with Zane. There were people everywhere, which made it hard to stick close. She checked behind her and spotted a frowning Grayson about twenty feet back, stuck behind someone in a motorized scooter. She didn't want to lose him or Zane. She slowed, trying to stay between the two of them. Laughter and excitement gave the floor a carnival air. Hostesses decked out in ornate feathered masks and provocative uniforms loosely based on masquerade-ball designs just added to the atmosphere. The servers waltzed among the masses, smiles wide, eyes bright, their movements graceful despite their towering heels.

Zane's broad back made a sharp left. Cass was rushing to keep him in sight when a group of businessmen cut in front of her, their attention on a craps table. She pulled up short, and someone bumped into her with enough force to send her stumbling into a bank of slot machines. She caught herself with a hand on the machine's screen, which was filled with an artistic portrayal of a spinning wheel of fortune, as the toll of a sonorous chime rolled over her. In the screen's center, under her palm, was a vivid portrayal of Fortuna, the Roman goddess of luck. Cass's vision blurred.

Crimson a seeping stain across the profile of a black-armored, horned, helmeted Hades.

A lightning strike, then shifting shadows reveal a stern-faced Poseidon standing before a crumbling tower.

Another strike, and now blackened vines drag tower pieces together until it reforms into a crooked version of itself.

A trailing vine of poison ivy slowly writhes through a wheel of eight swords hovering over the haunting visage of Medusa before slowly wrapping itself around the raven-haired Hecate, the waning moon on her brow dimming.

Hecate's features shift into the haunting gold-eyed, white-haired Hera, her luminous skin cracking as vines force themselves through, leaving ashes in their wake.

"Cass, are you okay?"

Someone grabbed her arm, and the vision cut off like a switch had been thrown. Cass sucked in air as the present resettled around her. Her heart raced under the onslaught of adrenaline, and she couldn't shake the dread curling through her gut.

Still, she met Grayson's worried frown and managed a shaky "Yeah, I'm good."

He looked far from convinced. "You sure?"

There was no time to get into what she'd seen—not when she wasn't quite sure what it all meant. A warning, definitely, but about what, she didn't know. She straightened and rubbed where her upper arm had hit the machine. "Yeah." She looked around. "Where's Zane?"

"Up ahead."

Grayson led her over to where the Hunter waited for them impatiently, near a fake potted tree under a sign indicating that the restrooms were to his left. As soon as Cass and Grayson were in front of him, the Hunter said, "We need sublevel two."

"Access point?" Grayson asked.

"Just past the restrooms. It's an emergency exit to the stairwell."

Cass waited as a group of women wandered past then asked, "Won't that set off an alarm?"

"It's covered." Zane tapped the stud in his ear. "So are the cameras, but we'll have to move fast."

Electromage Candace. Right.

"Come on."

They headed down the hall, the noise of the casino floor fading the farther they walked. As they passed the openings for the restrooms, Zane murmured, "Start the clock."

They continued on to where a water-refill station sat next to a door labeled Authorized Personnel Only. As they got close, Cass heard a series of soft beeps as lights flickered on the electronic keypad set in the wall next to the door. Zane had his hand on the lever when it turned green. He pushed it opened then held it as first Cass, then Grayson slipped inside.

"Down the hall, first right," Zane directed as he shut the door and quickly outpaced Cass to again take the lead.

The hall was utilitarian beige, the overhead lights harsh and unforgiving. Cass spotted the cameras set in the ceiling, and the metallic taste of fear dried her mouth. She found herself sending up a litany of pleas that Candace had blinded those electronic eyes.

A set of stairs rose to the left, and one side of the hall was lined with industrial-sized laundry carts. They'd walked a few feet into the hall when a door from somewhere above opened. All three froze, and Cass held her breath as voices floated down. Someone was talking about needing more sheets. A warning hiss from Zane got Cass moving again. She did her best to keep her steps quiet as she followed Zane.

He got to the door, held it open, and waited for Cass and Grayson to pass through before he followed. Zane silently closed the door, not letting it go until the lock engaged with a quiet snick. They were in another stairwell, but this one led down.

"Go," Zane directed.

Cass rushed down, wincing as her footsteps echoed through the space. Two floors later, she was breathing hard and thinking she should probably up her nonexistent work-outs. She went to push open the door, only to have Grayson tug her back with one arm around her waist and the other blocking her reach.

He pulled her into him and, with his lips to her ear, whispered, "Not yet."

Swallowing, she dropped her arms and nodded.

Grayson let her go and nudged her to put her back to the wall, giving him space to take point. He slid past her. At the door, he looked at Zane. "Alarms?"

The Hunter listened to Candace. "Electronically clear, but you've got twenty seconds, tops, to verify."

A shimmer of red gold ran down Grayson's shoulders and enveloped his hands as he crouched and started to run them over the door's edges. He slowly straightened as Cass felt each second tick by. His hands paused near the top hinge. "Got a ward."

"Thirteen seconds and counting," Zane warned.

Grayson went to work, his hands and lips moving as he silently wove his magic. In the air, an intricate series of interconnected runes ignited then curled around the door's frame. Grayson's silent cast continued, and then he made a tearing motion with his hands. The red gold flashed then faded into a stunning fire of amber. The runes disintegrated into a glittering shower of sparks.

Before the last one winked out, Grayson had the door open. "Go!"

Zane went first, and Cass followed him into a space crowded with water tanks. The huge metal containers were connected by thick metal pipes that twisted and turned as they rose into the ceiling and back down the other side. It was a labyrinth of active machinery, filled with a dull hum that obliterated any chance of hearing someone approach.

She jumped when Grayson touched her arm.

He mouthed, "You okay?"

She nodded.

He grabbed her hand, and they followed Zane through the maze of equipment. Cass felt like she was ready to jump out of her skin. At any moment, she expected someone to spot them and tell them to leave. Or worse, make sure they couldn't.

Zane moved with uncanny self-assurance through the space, directed by the voice in his ear. When he lifted his fist and came to a stop, so did they. Grayson squeezed her hand and then motioned for her to slip behind the dubious concealment of the large mechanical cabinet. When she did, he caught up to Zane, and after a flurried exchange of hand motions, the two men split off in opposite directions, with Grayson disappearing to the left.

Cass crouched in her dubious hiding place, her heart pounding and nerves shaky. A pulse beat at her brain, urging her to run, but she forced herself to stay put. She wasn't about to jeopardize the two men by panicking. After what felt like an eternity but was more likely only minutes, Grayson was back.

He leaned in and spoke close to her ear to be heard over the constant drone of noise. "We found something. Come on."

He took her through the space to a back-corner office and stopped just outside the open door. Zane stood near the battered desk in the center of the office, an unearthly green glow simmering in his eyes as he slowly pivoted, his gaze distant as if searching for something, a frown lining his face.

"Where are you, you bastard?" Zane muttered.

Cass wanted to tell him to hurry up, but she kept her mouth shut and an eye back on the way they came. It wasn't long before Zane's "Gotcha" pulled her attention back around.

"Grayson," Zane called as he moved around the desk toward a large set of metal shelves overflowing with wires, notebooks, folders, and random pieces of metal. "There's a lock around here somewhere."

When Grayson joined him, Cass dared to leave the doorway and moved farther into the office. A few tense heartbeats swept by as the men continued their search.

Finally Grayson said, "Found it."

He touched a series of items on the bookcase. Each time his fingers made contact, a spark of amber erupted. When he grabbed the edge of the metal unit and pulled, the bookcase opened smoothly on nearly silent hinges.

Zane's grin was fierce, and little storms of green lightning rolled over his shoulders and down his arms until he was outlined in a faint luminescence. Without a word, he slipped through the opening.

"Come on, Cass," Grayson said.

She closed the office door, muting the mechanical drone from outside, then hurried over. She slid through the opening and into another stairwell. This one coiled around a thick pipe at the center of the tight space. The lighting—a couple of floor lights stuck under the risers—was dim, but peering down the pipe, she could see a brighter glow at the bottom. The stairs were contained within a concrete column with only one opening that led deeper inside. From where she stood, she couldn't make out much more than that. The top of Zane's dark head was just disappearing as she started down. There was a shift in the air above her. She looked up to see that Grayson had closed the hidden door and was coming down.

Why in the hell does the resort have a hidden room? It was a question for later, one she hoped she'd remember to ask.

They wound their way down. With each step, the noise above faded. She was halfway down when voices rose up. She couldn't make out the words, not with her ears still ringing. The only sign that Zane had picked up on the same thing was the way his movements went from a predatory stalk to a dangerous glide. A few feet from the bottom, he paused to look back and held up his hand for her to stop.

She froze.

He shot Grayson a glance, and whatever Grayson saw had him gently nudging her aside so he could move to the front. From behind Grayson, she caught a glimpse of Zane clearing the last of the steps. Without looking back, he disappeared into the space beyond. Grayson cleared the last stair and was moving toward the opening when a surprised yell was abruptly cut off.

"Stay here," Grayson ordered before he went to join Zane.

Heart in her throat, she ignored him, rushing to the entry

to discover a narrow entryway created between the long cement wall and a shorter interior wall. The opening only extended a few feet before widening into a larger space. The sounds of fighting drew her forward, then a burst of magic smashed into the cement wall. Cass jerked back with an undignified, terrified squeak and dropped into a defensive crouch, her back to the dubious protection of the shorter interior wall. Something heavy crashed into it, sending a vibration through both it and her back. More angry yells, accompanied by curses and pained grunts, came from the room she couldn't see. Staying low, she crab walked to the end of the opening, sucked in a deep breath, and dared to peek around the wall's edge.

Unlike the space above, the room was a cement box, maybe fifteen feet across in either direction. There was a worktable along the side, filled with things she couldn't make out. A rolling stool lay on its side, a bent leg impaling the wall next to the table. A few feet in front of her, a body was sprawled on the concrete, not moving. Beyond it, Zane was grappling with a muscle-bound behemoth. The green coils of Zane's magic snapped and stretched around him like a lethal tentacled nightmare as machinery tools whizzed through the air as if thrown by invisible hands. One of the coils snapped a sledgehammer aside, sending it careening through the air until it embedded itself in the concrete wall. Another sent a heavy pipe rolling across the cement, where it came to a stop a few feet away.

She darted out from her hiding spot, grabbed the pipe, and straightened just as a flash of movement in the far corner caught her attention. She looked over and locked gazes with a snarling scarecrow of a man standing behind another man strapped to a chair. She'd barely registered the fact that it was Russ in the chair when the other man abruptly winked out of sight.

The Slider.

A pained grunt came from her right. She spun in time to see Grayson suspended about ten feet in midair. A man, his back to her, stood below him. He spread his arms wider as if tearing something apart. Grayson's body jerked, his face paling, his eyes burning as he strained against the invisible restraints pulling his arms and legs out.

Without stopping to think, Cass rushed across the floor, clutching the pipe like a baseball bat. She was already swinging as the mage started to turn. The pipe sank into his ribs with an ugly sound. He stumbled back, one arm going to protect his torso, the other swiping out. Magic followed, picking her up and throwing her across the room. She lost the pipe and curled into a protective ball as she hit the ground with bruising force. The impact made her forget how to breathe for a few precious seconds. Panic started to inch in before her lungs came back online. She sucked in air, spots dancing in her vision, as the fighting filled her ears with the dull wash of noise.

She painfully rolled to her hands and knees and lifted her head to see Grayson had the air mage backed into a corner. She wasn't sure what was happening, but whatever it was, the air mage's face was slowly going from red to purple to white, his hands scrabbling at his throat, his mouth opening and closing like a fish on land. She shoved unsteadily to her feet, using the wall for balance, and realized she was now behind the man in the chair.

"Russ." She pushed off the wall and stumbled closer. When she saw the circle etched in the floor, she barely managed to pull up short. "Shit, shit, shit."

A couple of runes looked vaguely familiar, but the rest meant nothing to her. Magic ran through the symbols in a trickle of sickly-looking orange that warned her that crossing into it might not end well for her or for Russ. Stymied and desperate, she called out Russ's name, hoping he was among the living.

Nothing.

Her heart sank even as she skirted the circle, trying to get a better view of him. His head hung down, chin resting on his chest, his arms and legs chained to the chair, which happened to be bolted ominously to the cement floor. There were no telltale signs of violence—no blood or other nasty things—but she didn't like the look of the tendrils of orange slowly crawling up Russ's legs.

The sound of approaching footsteps was followed by Zane's voice. "Is he alive?"

"I don't know." She forced her gaze away from the magic and to Russ's chest. Nerves and dread tightened into a choking knot as she waited for it to move. It finally did with a shallow inhalation. "Yeah, I think he is, but I don't think this" —she motioned to the circle—"is helping."

"It's not." The grim confirmation came from Grayson, who was limping his way over. He got to Cass, and his gaze narrowed as he skimmed his fingertips along the pulsating ache in her face. "You okay?"

"Been better, but I'll live." She took in the red marks scoring his jaw, where someone had gotten in a couple of hits, and the lines of pain radiating from his mouth. "How about you?"

"Same."

"Me too, in case anyone's interested," drawled Zane. He sank into a crouch and studied the magic winding around Russ. "Looks like a Spanish Wringer."

Grayson worked his jaw, his attention on the circle, his face dark. "It is."

"What's a Spanish Wringer?" Cass asked.

"Remember history class and the whole Spanish Inquisition period, when Family turned on Family?"

It rang a bell. "Sure."

"This is what they used. A standard interrogation circle

filled with all sorts of nasty horrors designed to get you to confess to anything."

Zane pushed to his feet. "How fast can you take it down?"

A shimmer of gold lit the depths of Grayson's dark eyes. "Let's find out."

chapter 20

Grayson

As THE WRINGER's layers unfurled in his mind's eye, Grayson knew it was going to be a brutal race. The circle was a multilevel construct, twisting and turning from cursed-filled layer to curse-filled layer. Threads of interconnected triggers linked the layers and were an expected complication since the hex's intent was to tear through mental walls at all costs. Magic pulsed through the lines, seeping into triggers and dripping into the next layer as it continued its grim march. There were only a few more layers left before it would kill Russ. Stopping it would require finding the right rune at the right layer and reversing it.

He raced ahead of the magic powering the circle to the remaining untouched layers, then he started working his way back toward the encroaching threat. Time warped and stretched as he examined what lay before him. For a Key, magical skill went hand in hand with intuition, so he followed his gut and let his magic sweep along the lines. It brushed over the intent and will of the caster, felt the change as it approached a trigger, then spiraled off to the next line, continuing to search for that elusive difference that signaled he'd found what he was looking for. The faint worry he was too late hovered in his mind as he drew closer to the sickly-orange glow rolling toward him like molten lava.

Then he felt it—at the edge of a rune, a small, jagged snag that shouldn't exist. He zeroed in on it, taking precious time to unravel its original intent, and then moved to the one layered just beneath it. That one was the doozy.

Dammit, it's going to be tight. If he didn't time this right and flip both triggers in the right order at the right time, they'd lose more than Russ. For a second, he considered stepping back, but Cass needed answers.

Hell, so did he. He positioned his magic. "Zane, when I say go, grab Russ and get clear."

"Say when."

Grayson went to work on creating an opening for Zane to use.

"The chair," Cass warned.

"I've got it," Zane told her.

Grayson pried the circle open. "Go!"

There was a rush of movement as Zane followed his order, but Grayson was already shoring up the temporary path as he went to work on the triggers. Ugly flares of power surged forward, attacking Grayson's magic. Grayson ignited the first trigger just as a screech of metal sounded. There was a series of guttural grunts then the ear-splitting whine of a chair being dragged across the cement. He ignored it all, concentrating on the magic that beaded down toward the next layer. Just before the first drop hit, he flipped the second trigger. The glowing construct in his mind went dark, the lines and layers flaking away like ashes in the wind.

A heavy hand landed on his shoulder. "You good?"

Grit bit into his hands and knees, and he realized he was no longer standing. Zane was crouched next to him, his face concerned.

"Yeah," Grayson managed, shoving upward until he was sitting on his ass. "I'm good. Russ?"

Zane's expression turned grim as he shook his head, straightened, and held a hand out. "Come on."

Grayson took it and let the other man help him to his feet. They stepped around the now empty shackles and chair and joined Cass, who knelt next to the prone Russ.

"Come on, Russ, wake up." When Grayson crouched next to her, she asked, "Why isn't he waking up?"

"I don't know." He took in Russ's drawn gray features. There was a bruise along one side of his face, likely where he'd been clocked when kidnapped, but there were no other physical signs of harm. Releasing him from the circle should have ended whatever metaphysical and mental torture he'd been caught in. Instead, he was too still. He carefully shook the man. "Russ. Wake up."

When that only produced a faint groan, Grayson scanned him for any lingering spells. He found traces of a lethal hex that had been obscured by the Wringer and bit off a particularly nasty oath. They had mere minutes to get answers before Russ was a dead man.

He looked at Zane. "I need him conscious."

"How long do we have?"

"Minutes, so whatever you can get me."

Zane nodded then knelt on Russ's other side, put his hands at Russ's temple, and closed his eyes. A gold-tinted green glow ringed Russ's head like a crown. Zane's eyes remained shut, and his hands held tight as Russ's lashes started to flutter. When they finally lifted, the dark eyes were hazy and unfocused.

"Now, Cass," Grayson urged, knowing they wouldn't have long.

Cass leaned in so she would be all Russ would see. "Russ, who cursed Sofia? Who took you?"

The dying man stared up at her, his confusion clear. His lips moved, but no sound emerged.

Cass tried again. "Russ, who cursed Sofia? Was it you?"

Awareness sparked at Sofia's name, and Russ jerked, but the Zane's hold didn't budge.

Russ clutched Cass's arm. "Sofia. You have to save Sofia."

"I'm trying," Cass said. "Tell me who cursed her."

Russ grew agitated, yanking at her arm as he tried to escape Zane's grip. "Not cursed, loved her. Stop them. Going to hurt her."

Cass paled. "Who? Who's going to hurt her?" she asked sharply.

"Get to her, Cass! Don't let—"

Cass let out a pained hiss as Russ's fingers locked on to her arm and his body bent in an unnatural arc, his eyes widening and his mouth opening in a silent scream. When his body slammed into the ground, those wide eyes were empty.

Zane cursed, released his hold, and stated the obvious. "He's gone."

Cass scrambled to her feet, her face pale but determined, her eyes wild with panic when they met his. "We have to get to my parents!"

He rose with her, grabbing her hand, afraid if he didn't hold on, she'd be gone. He looked at Zane. "You've got this?"

Zane nodded. "Go. Keep me posted."

"Got it." Without letting go of Cass, he headed out, trusting the Hunter to clean up the mess. Cass was tugging against his hold when Zane called his name, and when he stopped to look back, she made a frustrated noise.

Zane's pitiless gaze met his and held it. "Make sure you take protection. You don't know who or what's lying in wait."

He thought of his kit and the gun locked in the trunk of his car and knew which he'd be carrying. "I'm covered."

Grayson had barely pulled up to the house before Cass had her door open and was halfway out of the car. He threw the car into park as she found her footing and took off.

"Gods dammit, Cass, hold up."

She totally ignored him.

He grabbed his compact, lightweight nine-millimeter from the console, shoved his way out of the car, and rushed after her. He managed to catch up with her as she fumbled with the keypad lock on the front door.

"Come on, come on, come on," she chanted under her breath as she lifted and reset her shaking finger against the keypad. The light turned from red to green, and she went to grab the knob, only Grayson got there first. She clawed at his hand. "Let go!"

With one hand on the door and one holding the gun, he went with the only option left to get her to take a breath—he crowded her up against the door, using his heavier weight to hold her in place. "Calm the fuck down, Cass."

It came out mean, but it did the job. She stopped trying to get away and fell still, the only movement the rise and fall of her chest as she sucked in air.

She matched his tone. "Let me go, Grayson."

Pressed as close as they were, he could feel the aggressive tension shimmering under her skin. If he did as she asked, he'd get a fist in his face, guaranteed. "You going to step back and let me go first?"

It wasn't really a question. He heard her teeth grind as she gave him an abrupt nod. Knowing that was the best he'd get, he kept his hold on the door but angled himself so she could slide away. She didn't look at him as she jerked away. Instead, she stood to his side, her hands fisted at her sides. He was fairly certain no one lay in wait, mainly because their arrival would be hard to miss especially since the front door was tinted glass. Still, it was better to be cautious than dead.

He held out the gun. "Do you know how to use this?"

She gave him a look hot enough to burn, snatched the gun from him, and repositioned her grip with an easy familiarity. Then she took up a position on the other side of the door. With his hands now free, he called to his magic and held it at the ready. A Key's offensive magic might be limited, but it could deflect a variety of magical attacks, which would give Cass the opening she'd need to level the field.

He gripped the handle, turned his body to present less of a target, looked at Cass, and mouthed, "Ready?"

She gave a short nod, her face grim, her hold on the gun steady.

He turned the knob, felt the latch slide clear, and shoved it gently open. Cool air was the only thing that rushed out. After a few breathless seconds, Grayson moved inside, Cass on his heels.

"Dad!" Cass shoved past him and rushed to the man sprawled face down on the floor just in front of the hall that led back to the bedroom and office.

Grayson didn't bother calling her back. Instead he reached out and found the protection spell he'd set around Sofia. A quick scan told him someone had tried to breach it but had been unsuccessful. Hoping that meant Sofia was safe for the time being, he scanned the open-floor-plan kitchen and living room for any lingering threats. There weren't any, but there were signs that Elias had been taken by surprise. Shards of glass, mixed with amber liquid, spilled across the tile by the stone coffee table. One of the couches had been shoved out of place, its cream-colored surface marred by smears of dirt and, more disturbing, blood. Based on the broken stoneware and crushed greenery, someone had either thrown a potted plant or tried to use it as a weapon. In front of the low shelves on the back wall was a mess of crushed art pieces that had once sat on display. Even though the heavy silence told him that whoever had been here was gone, he couldn't risk not checking the rest of the house. He crouched next to Cass, who had her fingers pressed to Elias's neck.

"He's alive." Her voice shook. "Help me turn him over?" Together, they got Elias onto his back, and Cass whispered, "Oh, Dad."

Elias had definitely been in a fight, and it hadn't gone his way. Bruised and battered, his right eye was swollen shut, his lips were cut and bleeding, and it looked as if his nose had been broken. More worrisome was the slow seep of blood low on his left side. A broken shard of bloodstained glass lay in the spreading pool of crimson.

Grayson ran to the kitchen, grabbed the hand towels hanging on the stove and dishwasher, and brought them back to Cass. He pressed them to Elias's side. "Call 911."

"Sofia and Mom," Cass said as she fumbled for her phone.

"Can you hold this and make the call?"

"Yeah, go." She took over for him as she tried to dial one-handed.

He grabbed the gun Cass had set aside and headed upstairs first, his magic sweeping before him. He was fairly certain they were alone, but if something had been left behind, he wanted to know. Cass's voice drifted up as she gave the address and told the operator to hurry the hell up. Then nothing.

It took him maybe two minutes to clear the top level. Whatever happened had been confined to downstairs. He came back down as Cass watched him, hands holding the towels in place. Seeing the question on her face, he shook his head.

"Is 911 coming?" he asked.

Worry darkened her face. "They're about ten minutes out."

He continued down the hall, feeling Cass watch him. The guest room door was closed, and the glass French doors to the office were open. He took a quick look inside the office. Files and papers were scattered across the floor, and one of the barrel chairs was overturned.

Same fight or different fight? Either way, there was no sign of Rhea.

His magic hit a snag just beyond the desk, and he made a mental note to come back for a closer look. Grayson started back down the hall, heading for the guest room. "Don't go in the office."

Cass's face grayed. "Why? Mom?"

Realizing where her mind had gone, he reassured her. "No sign of Rhea, but there's residual magic in there."

He moved to the closed door of the guest room, and with his hand hovering over the knob, checked for any lingering surprises. When he didn't find anything, he opened the door. Sofia lay on the bed, eyes closed, like a modern-day sleeping beauty. The protection spell had taken on an orange glow instead of the soft copper it should have had. A hint of unease ran through him.

"Grayson?" Cass called.

"Sofia's here." He tucked his gun into the waistband at the small of his back. Not the wisest place, but he wanted it close. He studied his spell, noting that someone had tried to recast the anchor runes. "Someone tried to get to her."

"Is she okay?"

He wanted to tell her yes, but he couldn't shake his growing unease. "I don't know."

Grayson didn't wait for her response but got to work. He focused on the damaged anchor runes. The magical weave had been warped, indicating a mage had tried to reshape the runes' intent, basically attempting to turn the spell from protective to harmful. Despite the battering it had taken, the spell appeared to have held, but the longer he studied it, the more certain he felt that something was wrong.

It wasn't until he went to restructure the second anchor that he triggered a subversion spell. Ugly, twisted ribbons of corrupted magic erupted around Sofia, searching for a way in. A thin tendril found a crack and went to work.

"Son of a bitch."

Frantic, he split his attention, bolstering the protective weave even as he swept the guest room with a magical scan. Somewhere had to be a focus—an inanimate object fueling the subversion spell. Something easily overlooked. His magic came up empty.

On the bed under the undulating magic, Sofia's body began to jerk. He caught another tendril making contact. Knowing he was running out of time, he tried again. Nothing pinged. Panic ran nasty claws over his spine as the subversion spell battered at the protective shield and bore down, searching for more cracks.

"Where are you, you little bastard?"

He switched gears, narrowing his search for any trace of Incarnate magic because this had to be connected to the initial cast. He scanned the space again, and this time, something scraped back. There, between the bed and the wall on the floor.

Grayson bent down and found a small, dull stone. *Got you, asshole.*

His magic slid over his hand in a protective glove as he picked up the innocuous-seeming object. It looked like a piece of gravel, easily dismissed if you couldn't feel the pulse of animosity at its heart. In his mind's eye, what sat in his hand wasn't rock but rather a nasty, tangled knot of magic with twisted tendrils that were currently boring their way through the protective spell. It was only a matter of time before those tendrils connected with the original spell. Once that happened, he'd lose Sofia. He blew out a breath, his pulse leveling into a steady beat that dropped him into that eerily calm headspace needed to ignore the silent ticking clock. Then he got to work.

chapter 21

Cass

CASS PRESSED the blood-soaked towels against her father's wound, her panic and fear held in check by a thin layer of glass. She could see it, knew it was there waiting to swallow her whole, but couldn't feel it—she couldn't feel anything. Instead, her mind was strangely clear as she stared into her father's battered face.

"What happened? Where's Mom?"

He didn't answer.

She listened for Grayson, who had disappeared into Sofia's room. It remained disturbingly quiet. Under her hands, her father's body gave a soft jerk followed by a faint groan.

A crack snaked through her protective emotional glass, leaking panic. "Dad? Can you hear me?"

His split lips moved, but no sound emerged. His hand rose and then slid off her arm.

She dared to lift one hand from the towels to catch it before it hit the floor. "Hold still. Help is on the way."

Elias tugged against her grasp and turned his head.

Worried that her grip was hurting him, she set his hand down. "Stay still, Dad."

"Cassandra?" he asked weakly, his body twitching.

"Yeah, Dad, I'm here." The stain on the towels under her hands grew. Heart pounding, she pressed down hard. "I need you to hold still for me, okay?" His fitful movements continued. "Stay still."

His one good eye fluttered then opened. It was bloodshot, but even more worrisome was how unfocused it appeared, as if he wasn't aware of what was happening around him. His blurry gaze swept over her. "What's going on?"

"You've been attacked."

"Attacked?" Some of the haziness cleared from his face, and this time, when he went to grab her arm, he made contact, his fingers digging into her wrists. "Rhea? Sofia?"

"Sofie's okay." She prayed she wasn't lying. "Mom's not here." Saying it out loud fractured the protective numbness, and her voice shook. "Can you tell me what happened?"

His eye fluttered closed, and she wondered if he'd lost consciousness, but then he started to speak. "I was with Sofia. Needed another drink. Went to the kitchen. Got to the living room." He grimaced and sucked in a breath as his fingers tightened, his eye opening again. "This man popped in out of nowhere. Right in front of me. Hit me. I went down." He let her go, and his hand drifted toward his head, where a raised knot was forming. "We fought. Then"—his hand drifted to where she was holding the towels—"he stabbed me with something sharp."

Reading his rising agitation, she pressed a little harder. "Don't move, okay?" When he resettled, she asked, "Did you recognize him—the guy who attacked you?"

Elias closed his eye, his face haggard and shiny with sweat. "No." His hand slid away from her arm and dropped to the floor.

Wanting to keep him conscious, Cass kept pushing. "And Mom? Where was she?"

"Office," he murmured. "Call came in from Cole. Had to take it. Urgent."

That was not a name she'd expected to hear. "Cole Burton?"

But her father didn't answer.

The well of fear crashed through the glass wall, breaking it into a thousand pieces. Panic turned her voice high and sharp. "Dad!" Her heart raced, and tears, hot and heavy, blurred her vision. "Dad! Come on, wake up! Please!"

It took everything she had not to let go of the towels and shake him. She had to hold the blood back, keep it from spilling across the floor. She focused on the shallow rise and fall of his chest, only vaguely aware that she was chanting, "Please, please."

Time warped, and she had no idea how much had passed when the shrill whine of a siren pierced her terror. "Just hold on, Dad. Help's almost here."

The noise drew closer and closer until it encompassed everything. Then it abruptly shut off, leaving a ringing silence that was broken by the heavy thump of a fist against the door.

"Come in!" she yelled.

There was a rush of movement, then someone was pulling her away. She fought them blindly, fearing if she let go, she would lose her dad. Eventually, the panic lifted enough for her to realize the EMTs had arrived and she was being held back by a female firefighter.

"Ma'am, I need you to calm down." From her calm tone, it was clear she'd been trying to talk Cass down for a few minutes.

Cass forced her body to still. "I'm good." A shudder wracked her, making her words a lie.

The arms around her didn't loosen. "Can you tell me what happened?"

One firefighter stood off to the side, talking into a radio

and watching the rest of the crew work. He was older, with an air of command. Two other firefighters worked in tandem with a two-man paramedic team, one of whom had his eyes closed and his hands on Elias's temples.

A healing mage.

Emergency kits were sprawled open as the men grabbed and discarded various items. They spoke in low, urgent tones cluttered with acronyms unique to their world. Mesmerized, she watched their well-rehearsed, synchronized dance. She didn't dare look away, afraid that if she did, the steady beep indicating that her dad was still here would turn into a flat keen of death.

Controlled chaos. The distant realization barely penetrated, just a strange observation, as if anything more would be too much to take in.

The arms around her fell away. "Ma'am, do you know what happened?"

"We came in and found him."

"We?"

The firefighters moved, blocking her dad from view. Cass blinked and turned to the female firefighter, her brain slowly playing catch-up. "Sorry?"

"You said, 'we.'" The firefighter's voice remained gentle, but her gaze was sharp.

"Grayson—he's with my sister." She started to fold her arms, only to stop when she caught sight of her bloodstained hands. Her mind blanked.

"Where are they? Are they injured?"

"No." The firefighter's questions buzzed around her like mosquitoes, and it wasn't until the woman caught her wrists and tugged on them that Cass realized shock was setting in.

"Let's sit over here." The woman guided her toward the couch. She made Cass sit, then she perched on the edge of the stone coffee table so they were facing each other. "What's your name?"

"Cassandra Alcmene."

"Hi, Cassandra. I'm Tracy."

Habit had her saying, "Hi."

Tracy managed a gentle smile. "The man on the floor—who is he?"

"My father, Elias Ambrose."

"And your sister?"

"Sofia Ambrose."

"Good. Okay, so who is Grayson?"

The series of questions steadied her, helped her claw free of the paralyzing shock. "He's my boyfriend." She stumbled a little over the description as her mind made up for lost time and spun, seeking traction.

"All right. Where are Sofia and Grayson, Cassandra?"

"In the guest room, down the hall." When Tracy turned toward the rest of her crew, Cass knew she was going to have one of the others head down the hall, so she touched the firefighter's knee. "Wait." Tracy looked at her, questioning. "They're not injured, but Grayson is a Key, and my sister was recently cursed." Scenarios flicked through her mind like fireflies, and she thought fast. "My family wanted to keep the situation private, so my parents asked Grayson to step in."

An expression of alarm bloomed under Tracy's professional demeanor. "Cursed?" She looked at Elias, her concern for her crew obvious. "Your father. Is he—"

"No." Cass knew she had to finesse the spin before it spiraled into a mess. "I think this, all of this"—she motioned to the room at large without taking her attention from Tracy —"has something to do with my parents' company."

"Are you saying this—your father, the curse—is some kind of business dispute?" There was hefty skepticism in Tracy's voice.

"Unfortunately, yes." Then Cass did what she'd never thought she would do—she played her mother's game, twisting and turning things to keep the authorities out of the loop. "Pythia Strategies works exclusively with the Arcane Families, and sometimes things can become volatile. Occasionally, our family will get caught between upset clients. And as you know, our particular clientele prefer to handle such situations themselves and don't appreciate outside interference."

A flash of something came and went in Tracy's face, but Cass couldn't pin it down. "Is that your polite way of asking us not to call in ACRT?"

"Please."

Involving the Arcane Criminal Response Team would only make things worse. The red tape alone would strangle any chance of finding her mom. Not to mention ACRT would pull Grayson off of Sofia, and Cass was not about to lose any of her family.

Before Tracy could respond, a rattle of wheels over tile announced the arrival of a gurney. Cass got to her feet and moved toward where they were loading up her father, Tracy right behind her. "Will he be okay?"

"We've got him stabilized," one of the EMTs told her, adjusting an IV before giving a nod to his partner. They began to wheel Elias out.

Cass stood frozen, watching as they disappeared through the open door. Behind her, she could hear Tracy talking to the older firefighter with the radio. Their voices were too low to make out what was being said. The two remaining firefighters continued to pack up their equipment.

"Where are they taking him?" Cass asked.

"Santos Medical," Tracy said as she came up to Cass's side. "You can meet them there."

"Thank you." She didn't dare explain that there was no

way she could sit in a waiting room with her mom missing and who knew what happening with Sofia.

Tracy touched her arm. "Cassandra, do you happen to have your father's insurance information?"

She blinked, turned to Tracy, and shook her head. "I don't. Sorry. I live out of state."

Tracy gave a nod as the firefighters started to clear out. "Okay, why don't you call your mother, have her meet you at the hospital. She can fill out the necessary paperwork there."

"I will. Thank you." Cass looked around for her phone and spotted it on the bottom stair, where someone must have put it out of the way. She went over, picked it up, and pulled up Eric Swanson's number. Someone needed to be there when her dad woke up.

It took a few more minutes to get everyone out. Just before Tracy left, she handed Cass a business card with the report number handwritten on the back. When Cass went to take it, Tracy held on to it for a moment, her gaze concerned. "Are you sure this is the best way to handle this?"

No. "I am," Cass lied.

"All right." She didn't sound convinced but let the card go. "Good luck, Cassandra."

As soon as the door closed behind her, Cass hit Eric's number, skirting the discarded towels and blood as she rushed toward the guest room. *Where the hell is Grayson?*

The phone rang twice, then Eric said, "Hello."

"It's Cassandra. I need you to get to Santos Medical. My dad's injured. Mom's missing." She got to the guest room and stopped just inside the door, her grip tightening on her phone. The room was awash in red-gold fire.

"Wait, what?" Eric asked sharply. "Why?"

"My dad was attacked. He's hurt." She didn't have time for this shit. "Mom is missing. Grayson's working on Sofia.

The EMTs took Dad to the hospital. They're going to need his insurance information and permission to do whatever they have to to save him. You're the family lawyer, and I'm assuming your power of attorney means you can handle all of that, yes?"

"Yes. What's been shared so far?"

She repeated the story she'd told Tracy then ended the call with "Go, do your job."

Cass pocketed her phone and inched her way into the room, keeping her back to the wall and staying clear of the symbols glowing around the bed where her sister lay. Grayson sat on the floor in a smaller, secondary circle connected to the larger one through an intricate chain of sigils. In an open palm, he held what appeared to be a piece of gravel wrapped in writhing shadows.

"Don't come in any farther." Grayson turned his head toward her. His normally brown eyes were eclipsed by a copper sheen. "I don't know if they've set any other traps."

"Traps?"

"I tripped one. It's trying to subvert my protection spell." He turned back to his previous position.

That did not sound good at all. "Sofia?"

Grayson's shoulders tightened. "Let me work, okay?"

Her gut pitched in a sickening dive. His gentle nonanswer was an answer. Sofia was in real trouble. Her mind whirling in useless chaos, Cass slid down the wall until her ass hit the floor. She pulled up her knees and wrapped her arms around them, holding herself together. She watched Grayson work as a grim determination wound through her fear and panic. She wasn't going to lose another sister.

Hasn't Fate taken enough? She doesn't get Sofia. Not if I have anything to say about it.

Cold fury blossomed until all that remained was the

merciless will of an Oracle determined to best Fate. In her mind's eye, Sofia's path began to unfold. Cass's heart stalled when only two roads appeared, the ending all but determined.

Sofia is wrapped in crimson fire while the malevolent strands of the curse tangle around her, layer after layer.

Grayson fights a bloated spider, their battle a never-ending storm of movement as they move along an elaborate web. That battle masks the stealthy scuttle of a smaller arachnid along one of the darker threads as it creeps steadily closer to Sofia.

Grayson kills the larger spider, but it's too late—the smaller one has reached its target and sunk its poison deep, and Sofia's life flickers, dims, then dies.

The second road.

This time, Grayson spots the smaller spider and aims a lance of crimson fire toward it.

There's a burst of magic as his weapon finds its target, and an inhuman scream tears through the air.

The larger threat rushes Grayson, its attack more focused.

The thread that the smaller one died on glistens in the flashes of power, beaded poison slowly sliding along the nearly invisible thread anchored in Sofia.

Grayson is tiring, his movements slowing, and he's caught unawares when lethal threads pierce his back, bowing his body, his mouth opening in a noiseless scream.

The true threat sinks into Sofia as Grayson's life drains away, and Sofia soon follows.

"No." Cass's denial echoed in her mind and in her ears.

Fuck that noise. This was her baby sister and the man she was coming to love. She would not lose either of them. Not like this. She called to her magic, and it answered with a roar, power pouring through her until she and it were one. She moved back along the path—not too far, just... there, where Grayson crafted his protection of Sofia. Her hands move steadily as she began to carve a third route, her mind clear as she forced Fate to her will.

Additional protection against the sly and unseen. Another thread to the shield, one that's barely discernible.

Then she moved forward toward the confrontation.

He turns to fight the larger spider, his movements fast and sure, as if guided by an invisible hand.

The smaller one rushes forward, only to disappear in a bright flash of magic as it trips Grayson's trap.

Crimson fire races along the threat's path, searing away the poison creeping along the thread, leaving ashes in its wake.

Grayson kills the larger spider then turns to unwind the curse, slowly at first, then faster and faster until Sofia is no longer bound.

The path under Cass's feet widened, pulling her forward.

You're not done. The whisper came from nowhere and everywhere.

She didn't want to walk this road, and she tried to stop, but the summons was relentless and sure. *Can't fight fate.*

This time, the voice sounded like Thena, and Cass knew she was in trouble. The path forward began to spiral, taking her into the inky void as her grip on the now slipped. Branches appeared and veered off, one after another in a relentless cascade, each one stretching further and further out, offering glimpses of endless possibilities.

To her left is an unknown figure, cloaked in shadows—her mother, broken and bleeding at their feet. A devil's bargain. "Will you take her place?"

"Yes!" She lunged toward her mother, but the road twisted, forcing her forward. "No, stop!"

Another bend. This time, vines erupt and slither around her mother, swallowing her. A cold laugh echoes. "Remember, this was your choice."

Desperate, she struggled to leave the path as horror and dread broke her heart. "Mom!"

Another curve, steeper, darker. "Someone has to pay for you interfering with our plans." The voice is a sibilant whip.

Heartsore and half mad with grief, Cass tried to step off the road, to go back, to change what was coming, but she couldn't—the pull was too strong, too fast. It dragged her deeper and deeper into the cold, unforgiving abyss as it spiraled down in a dizzying dance. Darkness closed in, like thick mud, creeping inexorably up her legs, her hips, her torso, until it dragged her under.

Then it will all stop. The thought was almost a relief.

"Cassandra! Dammit, wake up!"

Something wrapped around her wrists, burning through skin and bone, making the clinging darkness pause.

"Come on, Cassandra, come back to me!"

She knew that voice—recognized it, reached for it, wanted to hold it close, where it would chase away the ice in her veins. "Grayson?"

"That's right, Cass. It's me."

Blindly, she reached out, trying to find him. "Where are you?"

"I'm here. Right here," he said. Heat flared against her face, and the unforgiving grip of darkness loosened.

Her searching hands found purchase on warm flesh, and her fingers dug deep. "Don't let go."

"I won't."

She clung to his reassurance. "I can't see you." The choking fear that she would lose her grip and disappear into the spiral made it hard to breathe. "Where are you?"

"Here, I'm right here."

Frantic, she clawed at the arms she couldn't see, her breath coming out on a sob. "Grayson, don't let go."

"I won't."

She believed him. Believed the fierce determination she could hear in his voice. She strained against the cascade's hold, felt it give, and for a moment thought she would make it. Then a brutal tug yanked her back, and she lost what little ground she'd gained, the world around her spinning. She opened her mouth to scream but couldn't get air. Fear encompassed everything, and her body jerked.

Suddenly, there was Grayson, his eyes burning bright, his mouth hard, his hand gentle against her face. "Come on, Cass. Breathe. I've got you. Come on."

She held his gaze, fighting against the inexorable hold. "I'm here." She gasped, her grip on his wrists—now marred with raw scratch marks—tight. "I'm here." The relentless pull took a step back as she repeated the mantra. "I'm here."

Relief swept through his face, and he dropped his forehead to hers. "You scared the shit out of me."

"Scared me too," she admitted shakily as the present resettled around her, loosening Fate's brutal grip. "Sofia?"

"She'll be okay."

"You broke it?"

"Yeah, but I'm guessing that was due to your help." There was a hint of censure in his voice.

"Had to. Can't lose you or her," she said. He closed his eyes, but she didn't dare. "Thank you."

He pulled back, opened his eyes, and studied her for a long, uncomfortable minute. Finally, he said roughly, "You're welcome." He pressed a soft kiss to her lips and then held her close. "I want to make you promise that you won't pull that shit again."

Her heart ached, but she couldn't lie to him. "I wish I could."

His arms tightened as he sighed. "I know."

She burrowed in, relishing the way his warmth chased away the lingering chill. For a long moment, they just held each other. She tilted her head so she could see his face, then she reached up to brush her hand along his jaw.

She held his gaze when it met hers, and a slightly hysterical part of her bubbled up. "Still love me?"

Startled humor lightened his eyes and eased some of the worried lines in his face as his lips curved. "Yeah, I do."

chapter 22

Grayson

By the time Grayson pulled into his condo, the sun was doing a slow slide behind the Spring Mountains, leaving a colorful trail of reds, oranges, and purples in its wake. Although he was physically tired, his mind was anything but. He put the car in park and left it running so the AC could beat back the day's heat and then turned to Cass, who was curled up, asleep, in the passenger seat, her glasses at an awkward angle. She'd dropped off almost before they'd left the hospital parking lot.

Grayson couldn't blame her—it had been a hell of a day. He let his head drop back against the headrest and closed his eyes. He just needed a minute, maybe two, to get a grip on things. As soon as he was certain Cass wouldn't slide back into a cascade, they had rushed a groggy Sofia to Santos Medical. Swanson met them, briefly introduced the two-person private security team he'd brought in, and then informed them that Elias was already in surgery because the shard of glass that had pierced his side had caused serious internal bleeding. While Cass got Sofia checked in to a private room, Swanson shared with Grayson that the EMTs had lost Elias once on the ride in.

Fortunately, Cass missed that bit of news as she was busy with Sofia's doctor, who wanted the younger woman to be medically monitored as she drifted in and out of consciousness. The attending had grilled Grayson on the curse as she examined Sofia, eventually reassuring Cass that Sofia's reaction was well within expected norms. The younger woman simply needed rest, mentally and physically.

Once the doctor left, Cass asked Grayson to sit with Sofia while she took Swanson to the hall and caught him up. She was gone awhile, dealing with the family lawyer and the curious authorities, so Grayson called Zane. He updated the Hound on what they had walked in on and mentioned Rhea's disappearance, hoping Zane would find a usable trail. Zane promised to dig deep and fast but couldn't guarantee he would find anything. On Zane's end, he had the mess at Incantanto well in hand. He'd managed to identify the dead mages, who were known mercenaries, and set Candace on tracing their payments through a maze of ghost accounts. He was still tearing through Russell Seagraves's life, searching out any connections to the Cabal and the Ambroses. He told Grayson he had a faint scent he hoped would grow into something more substantial. It wasn't much, but it was something for Cass to hold on to when she returned to the room and paced the floor, worrying about her father, sister, and mother.

They spent the afternoon waiting for news on Elias. Waiting for Sofia to fully wake up. Waiting for Zane's updates.

Tense hours later, when the surgeon finally showed, it was to share that the team had stopped the bleeding and Elias was stable, his chances for recovery good. Once he was cleared from post-op, he would be moved to the adjoining room. That was followed by a call from Zane, informing them that Candace had managed to track the mercenaries' payment to an account buried deep within Burton Entertainment, the same group that held partial ownership of Incantanto. Adding that piece to the phone call Elias had told Cass about, Grayson knew a visit to Cole Burton was up next.

So did Cass, who had no intention of waiting to confront him. That led to an argument as Grayson wasn't keen on letting her get close to the man without knowing what they were walking into. Especially not after his close call with Sofia's curse. You could only tempt fate so far, and Grayson was pretty sure the odds were not in their favor. Not to mention that Cole Burton was not someone you accused—not without solid proof, and all they had were suspicions.

By the time they were ready to leave the hospital, he'd gotten Cass's reluctant agreement to follow his lead, but Grayson wasn't an idiot. Just because she'd given in didn't mean she wouldn't try going around him. He couldn't blame her. No matter how complicated her relationship with her mother was, there was no doubt in his mind that Cass would do whatever it took to save Rhea. Hell, she'd almost killed herself saving him and Sofia.

As he blinked his gritty eyes open and loosened his white-knuckle grip on the steering wheel, he realized he was still angry about that. *Gods, she scared the shit out of me.* That ugly fear still clung, and he needed to get over it.

He'd been working the curse, making his way through the layers and trying to keep Sofia from slipping further away, when his instincts whispered that he was missing something big. Urgency and caution collided and then things seemed to shift, like a lens slipping into place, crystalizing the details into an unmistakable path. He hadn't questioned his sudden insight, knowing, on some level, that this strange clarity was Cass's doing. He simply moved faster, quicker until Sofia was safe. Then he came back to find Cass sitting on the floor, her back against the wall, body twitching, and eyes an eerie ghostly white, and he knew with sickening surety that he was losing her to a cascade. He couldn't explain what had happened next, only that everything in him had reached for her and wrapped her tight, refusing to let her go as she was dragged further and further away. An echo of that panic beat at his temples even now. Maybe if she hadn't reached back, they both would have been lost, but he was just grateful she'd held on.

But if I hadn't caught her when I did... if I'd taken longer with Sofia...

That didn't bear thinking about. He scrubbed his face with his hands and turned to their more immediate problem. They needed a reason to see Cole and find out if he was involved. Grayson couldn't make the pieces fit. Yes, Burton was a client of Pythia, but he was heading toward a council seat. Why would he risk all of that to go after Cass's family? What were they missing? The answers were there, somewhere, and would take time to find. He just didn't think time was on their side.

Cass stirred, opened her eyes, and blearily looked around. "We're here?" She rubbed a finger under one eye, knocking her glasses to her lap.

He shook off his thoughts, grabbed his phone, and turned the car off. "Yeah, let's head upstairs."

She put her glasses back on, undid her seat belt, got out of the car, and met him on the sidewalk. Together, they went up to his condo. She was checking her phone as he powered down the security wards, opened the door, and nudged her inside.

"Anything?" He closed the door, threw the lock, and reactivated his wards.

"No. No ransom demands, no nothing." Frustration made her voice tight as she paced into his living room. "I can't wait for a call that may never come, Grayson."

"I know." He tossed his keys onto the counter.

She went to the glass doors that led to his balcony and stood there, staring out through the open blinds, her back stiff, her shoulders rigid. "I need to talk to Cole," she said with a hint of belligerence.

"I know," he repeated and started a text on his phone.

"What are you doing?"

He looked up to find her studying him with a little frown. "Getting Burton's address from my dad." He hit Send.

Her shoulders eased, and her expression lightened with relief. Then she was moving into him, wrapping her arms around his waist, and hugging him tight. "Thank you." It came out choked.

He set his phone aside and held her back. He wanted to demand she stay out of whatever this was, but that would never happen. Better that they deal with it together, even if he didn't like their odds.

Resigned to the inevitable, he said, "Something isn't making sense here."

"I know, but he's the only link we've got." Her voice was muffled as she kept her head on his chest.

Grayson ran a hand down her back, comforting them both. "And if that's the whole point?"

Her head lifted and tilted back. "At least it's another piece of the puzzle."

On the counter, his phone vibrated. Without letting her go, he reached back and grabbed it. On screen was a response from his dad—an address followed by a simple *Why?*

Cass turned his hand so she could see the phone's screen. Her fingers tightened on his wrist, and then she gave him a pointed look.

"He may not be home," he said.

"Okay, so we have Candace track his phone."

When he twisted his wrist gently, she let him go. He called Zane, putting him on speakerphone.

The Hunter picked up with an abrupt "What?"

"Need Candace to track Burton's location."

There was a pause. "Grayson, don't be a fucking idiot."

"Cass wants to talk to him."

"No, she wants to confront him," Zane snapped. "You two are going to get yourselves killed."

Cass frowned, temper coloring her face. She opened her mouth to speak, but Grayson quelled her response with a look. "Just get me a location."

"Fuck, fine!" Zane all but snarled then hung up.

Grayson set his phone aside, his gut churning as he held Cass's gaze. There were secrets in the green-gold depths and, even more concerning, a war between guilt and determination. His heart sank, but he managed to keep his voice level. "Are we walking into a trap?"

Her gaze slid away, and she started to pull back, but he tightened his hold, keeping her in place. Her hands went to his chest, her fingers curling into his shirt, but what she didn't do was answer.

Frustration made him sharp. "Cass."

"Yes."

Her quiet, reluctant admission lit the fuse on his simmering anger. He let her go and took a step back, worried he would resort to shaking her, as that rage burned through him, searing away his patience. Grayson locked his emotions down and refused to let her wince at his reaction penetrate his consciousness.

"When were you going to tell me?" he asked. Something flashed across her face, too fast for him to catch, and his anger went ice-cold. "Maybe the better question is, were you going to tell me?"

Color came and went in her face, but she held her ground. "Yes, I was going to tell you."

He wanted to believe her, but it was hard. He folded his

arms and continued to watch her, his doubt a silent accusation.

"I was, Grayson." She moved to him, her eyes on his, her hands coming up only to stop short of touching him. "I was," she repeated without looking away. "I wouldn't risk you like that, but I don't have much to go on. Just flashes." Her hands fisted at her sides as he continued to watch her. "They have my mom." She was pleading now. "They're hurting her. They want her to pay because she interfered with their plans. I know that much."

Questions whipped through him, but only one escaped. "Who's 'they'?"

A muscle jumped in her jaw. "I don't know."

His temples throbbed as his frustration and blood pressure rose. "But you're sure Burton's involved?"

"He's a connection." She started to pace, taking her glasses off to rub at her face. "Maybe? I don't know."

His hold on his temper crumbled more with each nonanswer. "What do you know, Cass?"

She spun around and glared at him. "That he's my only path to saving my mother."

"How?" he asked. When she put her glasses back on and continued to glare at him, he closed the distance between them in two angry steps. "Explain it to me so I can understand."

He watched her emotions chase across her face, and the fear that he would lose another woman he loved to useless self-sacrifice seared away the last of his self-control. He grabbed her arms and pulled her close as he got in her face.

"Tell me you aren't planning on sacrificing yourself for her," he snarled. "That you won't just hand yourself over to whoever these fucks are."

Cass's defiance dissolved. "She's my mother!" Fury, terror, guilt—it was all there in her voice and in the tears that pooled and then spilled from her eyes. She sagged against his hold. "She's my mom, Grayson. I can't leave her. Don't ask me to."

Her broken plea was a knife cutting through his resentment and fear. He gathered her close and dropped his head over hers. His rage eased back, replaced by a terrible understanding. His heart ached because he knew the forces tearing her apart.

"I won't, Cass, I won't." He rocked her, comforting them both. "But you can't keep me in the dark, no matter how bad it is, okay?"

"Okay," she choked out.

On the counter, his phone vibrated with an incoming text. Cass pulled back, and he let her go. She wiped the tears from her reddened eyes and shoved her glasses up.

He waited until she had regathered her composure before saying, "Tell me what you can so we can figure out how we're going to handle Burton."

She took a breath to steady herself. "It's not much, and some of it doesn't make sense, but I think whoever is behind all of this targeted Pythia specifically because of its connection to Burton. Something about him, or something he can do, is driving all of this." Her voice strengthened as she talked.

"And your family is Pythia."

She rubbed her arms as if chilled. "Right, so if you want to stop Pythia, you have to stop my family, specifically my mother as she's the lynchpin."

"And Sofia...?"

"Was the easiest way to gain access to my mother and, by extension, Pythia." Cass used the tail end of her shirt to clean her lenses.

These bits and pieces of information were linked by supposition, not the actionable evidence they needed to cover their asses, but it was a start. "Which made Russ a tool. And Burton? Is he another tool or the mastermind?"

Cass came up beside him and put her glasses back on. "That's the million-dollar question."

He grabbed his phone. The incoming text was from Candace, confirming Burton's location. He held it up so Cass could see it. "Then I guess we should go ask the one person who can answer it for us, then, huh?"

chapter 23

Cass

Cole Burton lived in the exclusive Mountain Ridge neighborhood that crawled up Spring Mountain and offered three-hundred-sixty-degree views of the Vegas Strip. Grayson and Cass were able to follow a low-slung two-seater, which looked like it carried a six-figure price tag, through the first set of gates. Had they not caught that bit of luck at the tall gates, they'd never have gotten inside.

Cass eyed the empty guardhouse as they drove past. "No night security?"

"Don't need it. You see those?" Grayson pointed to the statue of a sitting griffin to her right. Its twin crouched to his left.

"Yeah."

There was no way to miss them. At least fifteen feet tall, the pair towered over the road, their stone gazes fixed on those foolish enough to enter. Strategically placed accent lights cast eerie shadows across the fierce stone profiles.

"They're spelled." Grayson didn't appear too worried about it as he drove between the pair. "My guess, if you pass through with bad intentions, they don't let you get too far."

Cass shivered under the weight of the inhuman gazes and hoped he was right. "That's a hell of a security option."

"It's intimidating, and that tends to work better than anything else to keep the rabble out," Grayson said.

They continued through the neighborhood, and Cass couldn't help but gawk. Each home was like an architectural masterpiece. "Holy crap. These places must be worth a small fortune."

"And most are just Family summer homes," Grayson said drily.

Okay, there can't be that many wealthy Families in Vegas. "Not just local Families, I'm guessing."

"You'd guess right." He turned onto a road that curved along the mountain. "But a few of these are owned by various entertainment companies."

"I'm sure that goes over well with the neighbors."

They came around a curve and hit another gate paired with a call box. Grayson pulled up then turned to her. "Ready?"

She nodded.

He lowered his window and hit the button to announce their presence.

After a few moments, Burton asked, "Can I help you?"

"Cole, it's Grayson Beck and Cassandra Alcmene. We were hoping to have a few minutes of your time."

"Grayson, what a surprise. Please, come on up." There was a click, and the gates rolled back.

Grayson followed the long drive up the ridge, where a stunning multilevel home came into view. Lights lined each level of the house, whose stairs stepped down the side of the mountain as if the place had been grown from the rock. If the intent was to blend the structure into its surroundings, it worked. The drive ended in front of a multicar garage, where they parked and got out. Together, they climbed the stone stairs up to the first-level porch, where a barefoot Cole in linen pants and T-shirt stood waiting, haloed in warm light from the tall, narrow windows that sat on either side of the open, heavy wooden door. Behind him was a foyer, its chandelier doubling as an art piece as it spotlit a massive framed painting of a desert canyon on the foyer wall.

Cole greeted them with a smile. "Evening, you two. Come on in."

"We're sorry to just drop by." Grayson took the lead, shaking the older man's hand.

"Not a problem." Cole held the door and waved them inside.

Cass crossed the threshold then waited until Grayson came up behind her. He set his hand at the base of her spine as Cole closed the door. "We were hoping we could speak with you about a recent situation," Grayson said.

Cole's polite smile melted into a frown. "That sounds ominous."

"It's complicated," Grayson said.

"Well, then, let's chat." Cole moved past them. "We can grab a seat in here."

They followed him through an archway and into a living room done in muted earth tones and wood accents that managed to be both cozy and spacious. A cream-colored L-shaped couch angled around a low coffee table. To the right, Cass's attention was drawn to a wall of glass that could be opened to merge the living room with the patio, which offered a stunning view of the dancing lights of the Strip.

"Cole, is everything all right?"

The question came from Dana, who was curled up in the corner of a second L-shaped couch that mirrored the first. Both couches faced a large fireplace paired with a built-in bookcase, over which hung a wall-mounted TV, the screen frozen in mid-explosion. Behind the couches was another wide opening, this one leading into a kitchen. A waterfall counter with four pub-style chairs sat lengthwise, guarded on either side by nooks filled with appliances and lit spaces. Behind it all was another picture window that framed the shadowed outline of the mountain. Clearly, Grayson and Cass had interrupted an intimate evening in.

"Dana, you remember Grayson and Cassandra?" Cole skirted the coffee table, where a half-filled tumbler and bowl of popcorn sat, as Dana extracted herself from the couch. He arrived in time to take her wineglass as she got to her feet.

"From yesterday, yes." Upright, she brushed a hand down a feminine version of what Cole was wearing, as if smoothing out unsightly wrinkles. She gave them a polite, if puzzled, smile. "Hello again."

Cass did an awkward finger wave even as a rustle of feathers drowned out Grayson's murmured "Hello."

Cass's heart stalled as she fought not to react to the warning. Her skin chilled as she reached behind her to where Grayson's hand still rested and curled her cold fingers around his wrist. He gave a small jolt and shot her a puzzled look. For a moment, she wished she could talk to him mind to mind, but that was just wishful thinking. She gave the tiniest shake of her head before turning back to the other couple. Luckily, neither Dana nor Cole was watching their exchange.

Dana reclaimed her wineglass with a soft "Let me just take that, darling."

Cole handed her the glass then curled his arm around her, bringing her close. There was a pause, then with an ease that indicated she'd found herself in similar situations before, Dana waved her wineglass hand out. "Why don't I just—"

"No, please, stay," Cass cut in, hoping her smile didn't appear as fake as it felt. "We shouldn't be long. We just have a couple of questions for Mr. Burton."

"Cole," the man corrected as he motioned them to the

couch. "Please have a seat. Can we offer you something to drink? Water? Tea? Something stronger?"

"Water, please." Cass took a seat on the closest couch, leaving room for Grayson to take the spot next to her.

"Same for me, please." Grayson sat and rested his ankle on his knee.

"Why don't I grab those for us?" Without losing Cole's arm, Dana set her wineglass on the coffee table and picked up his half-filled tumbler. When she straightened, she turned in to Cole and brushed her free hand over his chest. "Did you want a refresh?"

"Please." He touched his lips to the top of her head and let her go. "Thank you."

She gave him a smile and made her way to the kitchen. Cass watched her move past the stove and to the nook near the back wall. Dana set the tumbler on the inset counter and opened the cabinet above, the door hiding her from view. When Grayson squeezed Cass's shoulder gently in warning, she turned back to the conversation.

Cole had taken a seat at the end of the second couch, facing them, his attention on Cass. "You had questions for me?"

She hoped her smile wasn't as shaky as she felt as she rubbed her hands down her thighs. Between the day's events and the auditory warning, she was feeling decidedly off-balance. That warning—had it been about Cole? Dana? Or a sign of something coming?

She set the questions aside and started to pick her way through the murky unknown. "I understand you talked to my mother earlier today."

He nodded. "I did."

When he didn't elaborate, she pushed. "May I ask what you spoke about?"

Cole cocked his head, his pleasant demeanor replaced by a

steady, considering gaze. "For the last week, Burton Entertainment has been in the midst of some complex negotiations on a new venture."

Considering who Cole was, Cass wasn't surprised her mother would be the one to act as his negotiation strategist. "I'm assuming Pythia was providing advice on how to maneuver successfully through these negotiations."

"Yes." His fingers began to tap on his knee. "Early this morning, Dana was informed our potential partners were grappling with some concerns. In order to mitigate those concerns, I required Pythia's input. Hence my call to Rhea."

It sounded legit, but it didn't fit. There had to be more than simple business involved. She took a chance and pressed harder. "And that was all you spoke about? The contract negotiation?"

Cole's gaze sharpened. "Yes."

Frustration bloomed, so she switched gears. "During your conversation with my mother, did anything happen?"

Cole's fingers stilled, and he frowned. "Like what?"

"Did she cut the call short? Was she interrupted?" Grayson covered her hand, and only then did she realize she'd been nervously plucking at her pants.

"No." Cole's eyes flickered to Grayson's hand on her thigh then came back to her. Whatever he saw on her face had him leaning forward, his forearms braced on his knees. "Why? What's going on?"

She searched his face, hoping to spot a sign that she was being played. When all that stared back was genuine concern, she looked at Grayson. He, too, was studying Cole intently. When he turned to her, he squeezed her hand, dipped his chin, then let her go.

Okay, so I'm not missing anything.

Reassured, she took a steadying breath. "At some point

this afternoon, my father was attacked, and my mother is now missing."

There was a gasp from Dana, who had paused halfway into the living room, holding a tray with two tall smoked glasses and one whiskey tumbler, her mouth opened in a small *o* of shock.

Cole's back went straight, and his face turned hard. "Attacked? By whom?"

"We don't know," Grayson answered.

"Oh my gods, is your father okay?" Dana came the rest of the way in, set down the tray on the table, and handed out the drinks.

"He's stable for now," Cass said, taking one of the tall glasses.

Dana turned to hand the second glass to Grayson. "That's a relief." She straightened, shot Cass a look, and turned away.

Cass, who had her glass halfway to her mouth, paused and narrowed her eyes. *What was that?*

Before she could figure it out, Cole got to his feet and started to pace. "And Rhea? You said she's missing."

"Yes." Cass set aside her water and wiped her damp fingers on her pants. "Your potential partners—would they resort to violence like this to gain an edge in the negotiations?"

Cole spun to face her, absently taking the tumbler Dana handed him. "No, that's not their style." He took a sip of his drink as she picked up the tray and took it back to the kitchen. "Why do you think that mess is related to me?"

"You are aware of the depth of services Pythia offers, right?" Cass watched Cole's gaze turn guarded. "I may not be part of the company now, but that hasn't always been the case."

"Is that so?" He studied her carefully. "And what was your role?"

"Oracle."

His eyebrows rose as he looked at Grayson then back at her. "I see." He paced a few steps away, came back, then shook his head. "No, actually I don't see. At all." He set his drink down and folded his arms as he faced them. "You think I'm behind whatever happened."

Dana came back to the living room, rounded the edge of the couch, and rubbed a comforting hand along Cole's spine. "That's ridiculous. We've been here together all day. We're sorry about your parents, but it has nothing to do with us."

The arrogant edge to Dana's words set Cass's back up and escalated the tension in the room. Cass started to stand, but Grayson stopped her with a simple touch and pinned a hard look on the other couple. "That's not quite true. The mages hired to attack the Ambroses were paid from an account in Burton Entertainment."

Indignation colored Cole's face. "That's bullshit."

"It's not." Grayson's unruffled denial stopped Cole's temper in its tracks. "The account belonged to Tetra Pictures."

"Tetra?" Cole repeated, rubbing at his chest. "That account's been closed for a couple of years."

"Then someone reopened it," Cass pointed out unnecessarily, keeping her attention on Dana, who was watching the conversation with a strange detachment.

"Why?" Cole shot back. "What's the point of going after Rhea and Elias?"

"Was the contract your only business with Pythia?" Cass asked.

Cole stilled, his eyes darkening, and his face paled. "No," he admitted. "There's another opportunity I was exploring with Rhea."

"The council seat," Grayson said.

Cole frowned. "That's not exactly common knowledge."

"No, but word gets around."

Cole didn't dispute him.

Unable to sit any longer, Cass got to her feet and felt Grayson do the same beside her. "Mr. Burton, Cole, what did my mother share about the council seat that would put a target on her and you?"

Cole cleared his throat and rubbed his chest. "There were signs that—" He gave a choking cough that bent him in half. It was followed by a series of harsher coughs that had him catching his balance with a hand on the coffee table as Dana took a step back.

Worried, Cass moved toward Cole. "Are you—"

Before she could finish, Cole groaned and collapsed. There was a rush of movement from Grayson, but Cass was frozen in place as thick black vines erupted from the floor and wrapped around Cole. As they tightened their grip, the older man's face grayed, and he began to seize.

"Cass! Help me."

Grayson's barked order snapped her free of the apparition. The vines were gone, but Cole was on the floor, his limbs spasming as if pulled by invisible strings. She got to Cole, grabbed his ankles and held his legs still.

Grayson forced his leather wallet between Cole's teeth. "What the hell?"

Cass tore her attention from Cole, and her gaze landed on the whiskey glass on the coffee table. The amber liquid inside shifted to a putrid yellow then back to a warm burnt gold.

"Poison." The word slipped from her.

"What?" Grayson asked sharply, shattering the vision.

"He's been poisoned."

As Cole fell ominously still, her breath stalled. An unearthly amber fire erupted and swept over Cole as Grayson released a series of muttered oaths. "This is going to be a bitch."

Cass cautiously let go of Cole's legs as the wave of magic worked its way toward her. Movement caught her attention.

She looked up and found Dana standing on the far side of the couch, her gaze riveted on Cole, a small curve playing around her lips.

When her gaze lifted to Cass, that curve turned into a mocking smile. "You're too late. For him and your mother."

It took a second for her taunt to penetrate, but when it landed, it hit its target. With a snarl, Cass popped to her feet and lunged for the couch, the shortest path to the other woman. There was a shift in the room, like a change in air pressure, and a portal ripped through the air behind Dana, the inky edges tearing apart reality and creating a void in Cole's living room. The shadows writhed and came together into an indistinct figure walking toward the unearthly opening.

Cass scrambled over the cushions and used the back of the couch to launch herself toward Dana. The woman's laugh was dark and mocking as she reached back and took the figure's hand. Cass used the back of the couch to launch herself over it.

No. Gods dammit.

Dana stepped inside the portal as its edges seared closed. The last thing Cass saw was the insulting wiggle of Dana's fingers.

chapter 24

Grayson

Grayson's ears popped, but he didn't dare look away from where he was working on Cole. *Portal.* Partially deaf from the resulting tinnitus, he tried not to panic that Cass might have chased Dana through it.

"Cass? Are you still here?"

Her muffled "I'm here" sent relief sweeping through him.

"I need a protection spell." His Mystic-based magic found Cole's Elemental power and forged a connection, giving him an anchor for his counterspell. "Can you cast one?"

"Yeah," she said, sounding edgy.

In Grayson's mind's eye, Cole's magical fabric rippled under the invading web of the poison-based hex. It didn't take long for Grayson to recognize that Dana's hex was also Elemental in nature, meaning she had a natural bent with pathogens. Even worse, his chances of stopping it were slim to none. A Key's best chance at halting such a hex lay in the precious moments before the magical virus naturalized and went active.

As he watched the hex work, his gut clenched. Tiny cuts spiraled out from the center of Cole's body, leaving a tattered trail, which continued to unravel but at an incrementally slower pace. Pulses of sickly green heralded another tear. Then it flitted, like an ember, to another spot, where it pulsed, and another cut appeared. Nearby, other flickers followed the same pattern.

He was too late. Dana's spell was very fucking active. Even worse, it had one goal—to kill Cole.

"She's a damn Venenarius."

He heard a drawer slam closed, then Cass said, "What?"

Grayson realized his ears had stopped ringing. He raised his voice. "Dana. She's a Venenarius."

"Great, so we're dealing with a bougie Poison Ivy."

A powerful one, based on how fast the spell was moving. It was making its way through Cole's abdomen, and sickly green tendrils were inching down his hips. Even more concerning were the ones creeping toward his chest.

There was no way to neutralize the threat. Instead, Grayson would have to buy Cole time, and for that, he needed a way to slow the hex's progress. There were a few options that might work.

"If you find a moldavite crystal, bring it," he said.

"Moldavite?" Her voice was closer.

He sent his magic through Cole until it surrounded the invading spell. "Looks like green glass." If he was lucky, Cole would have it around somewhere. "Amethyst or quartz will work too."

"Got it."

Leaving her to it, he held his magic just outside of where the hex was wreaking havoc. Then he sought the spell's initial entry point. Since Dana hadn't had time to be clever, he found it fairly quickly. The seeds had been in Cole's drink and were now rooted in his stomach, spreading like demented kudzu. With the target acquired, Grayson's magic surged forward, the red-gold power colliding with the venomous green in a fury of magic, the resulting impact tearing at Grayson's mind. He endured the barrage of acidic bites, driving it to the edge of his awareness, as he reinforced his counterspell. The reddish-gold magic continued to press mercilessly forward, forcing the poisoned magic to retreat. It was a slow, hard slog, but he gained a little bit of ground.

Suddenly, another power joined the battle, adding its weight to Grayson's fight. Cass had completed the protection spell. Using the reinforcing energy, he quickly wove the protective layer into his counterspell, tightening the cage around the main pool of poison. Once certain it would hold, he went after the insidious flickers that had escaped his initial roundup. With lethal focus, he hunted and snuffed out each loose ember until what remained of the hex writhed in the burning confines of his counterspell.

He opened his eyes to find Cass crouched on Cole's other side. "Did you stop it?"

"It's contained for now." He started to shift but stopped when he saw the salt line and series of interlocked chalked runes that encircled him and Cole. There was athame at Cole's feet, a flickering candle to Grayson's left, and a wooden bowl with burning herbs at Cole's head.

But it was the softly glowing palm-sized green crystal resting on Cole's chest that eased some of Grayson's worry. "You found one."

"And an amethyst." Cass motioned to the chunky purple crystal near her. "Is he going to be okay?"

"If we can get him to a healer."

"You can't reverse it?"

He shook his head.

"I called Zane and filled him in," Cass said. "He's about fifteen minutes out."

"Good."

She looked at Cole. "Once Zane is here, you can get Cole help."

A hot edge of alarm rushed through him. "You're not going after Dana on your own."

She shot him a look and, with studied patience, said, "No, that's why I called Zane."

He started to argue, but Cole let out a groan as his lashes lifted. It took a second for awareness to replace the haze, but he reached out and covered Grayson's hand on his chest.

"What the hell happened?" His voice was rough.

Grayson didn't sugarcoat it. "Dana poisoned you."

Shock slackened Cole's face, but the furious edge of betrayal wasn't far behind. There were a million questions in his eyes, but he didn't ask any of them. He let Grayson go and tried to sit up.

Grayson stopped him. "No, lie still. I've got a counterspell in place, but it's barely keeping this shit in check."

Cole resettled, his jaw clenched as a grim darkness hardened his face. "Where is she?"

"Gone," Cass said. "There was a Slider. He took her through a portal."

Cole looked between Cass and Grayson. His reaction wasn't long in coming. He grabbed Grayson's hand. "I need you two to go after her," he said coldly. "I want to know—" He started again. "Her engagement ring. So long as she's wearing it, she can be tracked. She doesn't know it's spelled."

Cass's eyebrows rose. Grayson couldn't miss the flare of excitement in her eyes.

"The council's consideration was enough to put a target on me and anyone close to me," Cole continued. Emotional pain burned through the icy fury in his eyes. "I wanted to keep her safe—wanted to know, no matter what, I had a way to get to her." He squeezed Grayson's hand then let go to fumble at his watch, whose wide face was inset with four stones. "This is keyed to her ring." He removed it and handed it to Grayson. "You know how to use it?"

"A tracking spell? Sure." Grayson took the watch. The metal links were still warm from Cole's wrist. "We'll need a paper map."

"In my office."

On the outside of the circle, Cass got to her feet and made her way to Grayson, careful not to smudge any of the lines.

Cole continued with his directions. "Down the hall, take the elevator to the second floor, third door on the left. It's in —" A harsh cough interrupted him.

Grayson handed Cole's watch to Cass then helped the man roll to his side as he continued to cough. Cole curled over, his legs drawing up, his arms clutching his stomach. Grayson shifted his attention back to the magic, checking his counterspell. The poisoned hex had redoubled its efforts and was chipping away at the barrier. He reinforced his counter-spell and seared through another onslaught of twisted vines. They retreated, protecting their roots. He didn't dare push forward, afraid that if he did so, he'd leave an opening for the hex to slip through. For the moment, the temporary fix would have to do.

He came back to the sound of Cole's harsh breathing and had a moment to be grateful the older man wasn't coughing. "We need to get you to a healer."

Cole's face was pale and sweaty. "This Zane person—you trust him?"

"He's a Hunter," Grayson said. "So yes."

"I'll have him take me to someone I trust." Cole slowly uncurled, his attention going to Cass. "The map, it's in my desk, left bottom drawer."

She clutched the watch to her chest, her voice soft with gratitude. "Thank you."

Cole's smile was more of a grimace. "Go find her, and find Rhea."

By the time Zane arrived, Cole was nearly gray with exhaustion and his coughing fits were coming faster and harder with each wave. Grayson had managed to battle back another surge and was worried the next time he wouldn't be so lucky. Cass returned with a paper map of Vegas and Cole's phone. Grayson got the name of a healer from Cole and had Cass use Cole's phone to call him. Once the healer had been brought up-to-date, he agreed that time was of the essence and suggested meeting at a private clinic nearby, as it would be the fastest option.

Cass was disconnecting the call when Zane rushed into the house. The next few minutes swept by in controlled chaos as Zane and Grayson got the barely conscious Cole upright and then, as each took a side, got him moving. As they carefully navigated the stone entry steps, Grayson filled Zane in.

Zane connected a few more dots. "Found out that Russ and Dana were both employed by the same company over in Europe at the same time. Not sure, but I'm thinking that's when the two met. And according to Candace, once you scrape away the initial layer, that Tetra account has Dana's prints all over it."

"If Russ was working with Dana, why would they take and kill him?" Cass asked from where she followed behind them.

"I'll be sure to ask when we pin that bitch down," Zane said.

"Not you," Grayson said. "You're getting Cole to a healer. Cass and I are going after Dana." When Zane looked as if he wanted to argue, Grayson explained, "Cole's got a tracking spell on Dana."

"Fine," Zane shot back as they got Cole to Zane's car, where Grayson buckled him into the passenger seat.

Cass handed Cole's phone to Zane, who was settling in behind the wheel. "I pulled the clinic address up. The healer should be right behind you."

He took the phone and shot Grayson a look. "Send me your coordinates."

"Will do." Grayson snapped the seat belt in place and moved back to close the door.

"Gray," Zane said, stopping him.

He met the Hunter's gaze.

"Be careful."

"Always." Grayson closed the door and stepped back as Zane put the car in reverse. He and Cass watched Zane do a three-point turn and race down the drive.

"What are his chances?" she asked softly as she leaned into him.

He wrapped an arm around her shoulders, bringing her in close. "He's tough, and if that healer is as good as Cole thinks, there's a chance." Or at least, he hoped so. "Come on—let's check the map. See what we're dealing with."

She nodded, and they went back inside. They skirted the remnants of the circle and went to the coffee table, where she had spread out the map. She handed him Cole's watch. "Here."

Holding the watch face down over the map, Grayson let his magic unfurl. The tracking spell was straightforward, expertly crafted by Cole, who happened to be an Air mage. Grayson murmured, "*Anulum sequere*," and a glowing blue dot appeared on the map. It glided along Clark County Road 215, heading north at a steady pace.

Cass frowned down at the moving marker. "Where are they going?"

"I don't know, but they're about twenty minutes ahead of us."

"Will the map stay active, or do we have to keep the watch and the map paired?"

"Let's find out." He pulled the watch away. The light faded. "Dammit. They have to stay paired."

"Fine." She folded the map over and under, keeping the portion where the light moved face up. When it was manageable, she handed it to him. "You take this, and I'll drive."

chapter 25

Cass

CASS IGNORED the speed limits as the county road turned into a divided four-lane interstate, leaving the more populated areas behind. Night covered the desert, and since the only hints of civilization were the overhead freeway signs, she figured there wasn't much out here.

"Take the next exit," Grayson said. "Looks like they're turning off."

"Got it."

Tense quiet settled back in as the minutes ticked by and asphalt unspooled under the tires. She was doing her damnedest not to get lost in her mind, but it was hard. The feeling of time slipping through her fingers beat at her. She tried to console herself by remembering that her mother was a force to be reckoned with, but it wasn't helping. Rhea had been gone hours, and images of her father, beaten and bloody, mocked her.

How hurt is she? Is she even alive?

That last question shredded her heart. Despite their contentious relationship, losing her mom would damage her in a way she wasn't sure she'd recover from. How many times could you fail to save those you loved before the losses destroyed you? She didn't want to learn the answer.

"They stopped," Grayson said.

She flexed her fingers on the wheel, feeling the blood rush back in. "Where?"

Light flicked against the windshield as he activated his phone and checked the paper location against the real-time map. "Looks like one of those new-construction home developments."

"In the middle of nowhere?"

"Maybe that's why they chose it."

Her headlights swept over the green sign spanning the road. "Exit's in three miles." She pressed her foot down on the accelerator, watching the speedometer tick past ninety-five.

"We need to get there in one piece," Grayson reminded her gently.

"I know." She leveled off at ninety-eight and only started to slow as the exit approached.

"Go right, follow it down, then take the fourth left."

When they hit the surface streets, she dropped her speed to a more respectable forty-something and continued to follow Grayson's directions. They drove along a wide road split by a median filled with shrubs and the occasional overgrown tree. Every now and then, they saw a battered, overflowing dumpster squatting off to the side. More than half the streetlights were dark, and those that worked were dim, barely illuminating the area around them. For a long time, that was all there was. Eventually, cracked sidewalks appeared, edging the road. An occasional street sign would interrupt them. Then a cement wall appeared, the gray rock decorated in graffiti.

"Go down another block and make a left." Grayson picked up the paper map and checked the tracking spell. "They haven't moved in the last few minutes."

"So wherever they are in here, they've holed up?"

"That's my guess." He leaned forward, peering through the windshield. "When you hit the stop sign, turn off your lights."

She got to the four-way stop, hit the lights, and made the left, slowing even more. Without her headlights, she could only see a few feet ahead of her. "There's no way they're not going to hear us coming."

"Got an idea on that," Grayson said. "Just need a spot to pull over."

On the other side of the cement walls, the pale wood of partially built homes took shape. They continued down the unmarked road of what looked like an abandoned planned community. The tattered Now Selling banner hanging from one of the working lights was one clue. The fact there had been no lights, cars, or signs of life since they'd turned in added to that impression.

"There." He pointed to her left. "Pull in there."

She turned into what was meant to be the entrance to one of the smaller neighborhoods. They passed darkened homes that looked finished, but when they rolled under a streetlight, Cass realized the houses had been left at that near-completion stage. Some were missing stonework facades, while others sported broken windows and missing doors. One house had a garage door that looked as if it had been rammed with a truck, and another wore an elaborate piece of graffiti with an anatomically incorrect suggestion. She drove by a long orange dumpster and rolled to a stop next to an empty lot.

Grayson was on his phone, his fingers flying over the screen, then came the swoosh of a text being sent.

"Zane?" she asked.

"Sending him our location." Grayson slipped his phone into his pocket. "We can leave the car here." He rechecked the tracking spell. "The map has Dana one street over and down."

She undid her seat belt and watched him pull his gun out of the glove compartment. "Do you have one for me?"

"No, but pop the trunk. I've got some things we can use in the back."

They met at the trunk, where Grayson put the gun in his waistband at his back and then lifted the liner. "Hold this for me..." he muttered.

She held the liner up as he brushed his fingers over a small rune etched in the metal near the wheel well. There was a flash of crimson followed by the soft thud of a lock releasing, then a portion of the trunk popped up, revealing a compartment with multiple filled cubbies. Grayson picked up a stoppered bottle from one and a stone threaded with a cord from another.

"Put this on." He handed her the corded stone.

She slipped it over her head, and the stone came to rest against her breastbone. "What is it?"

Grayson caught the stone in his hand and made a fist. A burst of reddish gold seeped through his fingers as he activated it. "Protection amulet. It won't stop bullets, but it'll help." He popped the top of the bottle and handed it to her. "Drink this."

She brought it to her nose and caught a sharp, earthy, slightly musty odor. She grimaced. "Does it taste like it smells?"

"Just drink it, Cass." He had another opened bottle in hand and shot it down.

She did the same. It wasn't good, but it wasn't bad. The flavor of nuts offset the pungent bite. She coughed a bit with the aftertaste. "It's like some weird radish."

"It's an antitoxin potion. The base element is burdock root, hence the radish thing." He took the now empty bottle from her and put it back in the box. "It won't completely stop

Dana's magic from taking hold, but it will give me enough time to counter whatever she throws at us."

"Okay, so we've got Dana covered. What about the Slider?"

Grayson touched the butt of the gun at his back. "This will keep him from going anywhere."

"And whoever else is with them...?"

He went back to the compartment and pulled out what looked like silvery eggs. "These are flash-bangs." He handed her one and put the other in his pocket. "All you have to do is break them, preferably near whoever you want to distract. They'll leave a person blind and deaf for a few moments. Hopefully, that's long enough to even the odds."

She rolled the flash-bang over her palm. It was cool and surprisingly heavy. "How close does it have to get?"

"Just aim for the ground near them." Grayson closed the compartment, replaced the liner, and lowered the trunk lid until he could press it closed.

He turned to her, and under the faint orange glow of the streetlight, he searched her face. She didn't know what he was looking for, but she knew what she wanted and needed. She closed the few inches between them, caught his face, and brought it to hers for a long, sweet kiss. It steadied her, that touch. When she felt like she was holding herself together with a wish and a prayer, his presence—his taste—gave her an anchor. He let her have it for a moment, then he took over, his hands going to her hips and pulling her in until she could feel him, hot and solid against her, as she rose on her toes to meet his hunger with hers. When she finally pulled back, she was breathing hard, and her pulse was pounding.

"Promise me you'll be careful," she whispered fiercely.

He dropped his forehead against hers. "I promise, so long as you do the same."

"I will."

His grip on her hips tightened as he drew back and pressed his lips to her forehead. "Okay, let's do this."

He stepped back and, with a murmur, ignited a ball of soft illumination. It hung in the air at waist level, providing enough light for them to see where they were going. The light stayed with Grayson as he started out at a near jog that Cass was able to easily match. Halfway down the block, they cut through a series of empty lots, the dirt muffling their footsteps. They hit the street where the spell told them Dana would be, which was lined with half-finished homes. They made their way past dumpsters—some empty, some overflowing—and skirted more debris piles as they stepped over a low line of bricks delineating the lots, which sported hooked rebar like rusted antennas.

As Cass followed Grayson, she kept an eye out for anything she could use as a weapon. Charms and potions were great and all, but she would feel better with something that could make someone think twice. She was starting to worry she was out of luck when Grayson cut through the open framing of a house on a corner. They went in through the garage and down what was probably a hall. Wire cables hung from the open ceiling, and stubby pipes poked up from a floor littered with nails and staples and other things that rolled underfoot. They were passing a room that could have been a bedroom, or maybe an office, when something glinted under the ball of light. Cass touched Grayson's back. He stopped and turned, the light following his movement. She inched into the room and found a piece of cut pipe about two feet long, which she picked up. It was almost too big to hold in one hand, but with two... she took a couple of experimental swings, feeling the rough metal bite into her palms. Doable. Definitely doable.

When she rejoined him, Grayson whispered, "Feel better?"

"Much."

He shook his head, and they stepped out of the hall and into the wide-open space that stretched along the rear of the house. Unlike the front half, the rest of the back half was dubiously enclosed in plywood, except for a wide gap filled with strips of heavy plastic that rustled in the breeze. Thick posts were shoved under the joist that ran along what was supposed to be the living room. The cracked cement floor was littered with nails, staples, bits and pieces of tubing, and splintered wood. The space spilled into what had to be the kitchen, based on the pipes jutting up in front of the half-finished lower cabinet on the back wall.

Grayson doused his ball of light and stuck to the shadows as he picked his way into the bumped-out space off the kitchen. Cass followed him to a large framed window with a straight view into the house behind it, and when he dropped to a crouch, she did the same. As she peered through the empty window, she could make out the shadowed exterior of the house behind them. It was further along in its construction than the one they hid in. The exterior plywood walls were wrapped in chicken wire, and sheets of wood on the roof held scattered piles of tiles. The waning moonlight glinted off the broken glass in two large windows on the far side, both of which were blocked by something paler than plywood—most likely sections of drywall. A sliver of light leaked from the edges, yet no light spilled over on the opposite interior side, where a dark gaping hole stood in place of the intended patio door.

Huddled next to Grayson, Cass murmured, "Is she in there?"

"According to the tracking spell, yeah." Grayson continued to study the house behind them.

Cass's pulse beat heavily in her ears, and the urgency to rush in to confirm that her mom was still alive beat at her. The only thing holding her back was the annoying voice of logic pointing out that she had no idea what she would be facing, and getting killed wouldn't do a damn bit of good for anyone.

Grayson cocked his head, his eyes narrowing. "Do you hear that?"

She shook her head even as she evened out her breathing, searching, and finally finding, a bit of calm. As the rush of adrenaline faded, she strained her ears and kept her eyes on the thin line of light. The breeze shifted, bringing with it murmurs, and a shadow interrupted the seeping line of light. She tightened her sweaty hold on the pipe.

"Head's killing me..." a woman whined.

Dana.

There was an indistinct response with a sharper edge in a lower register, but the breeze took the words away. When it came back, it carried another male voice. "Up. You were supposed to wait. You didn't, and..." The rest disappeared into the night as someone moved behind the blocked windows.

An angry feminine response followed. It was drowned out by the rustle of plastic, but Cass caught the last word— "Fault!"

She shared a look with Grayson. Dana, the Slider, and one unknown. "Can you make out what they're saying?"

He shook his head. "We need to be closer."

She looked over the torn-up dirt that spread between the two houses. "If we cross that, they'll know we're coming."

Grayson studied the other house for a long moment then stood decisively. "Come on."

He headed back toward the front of the house, and Cass rushed to keep up. As soon as he got to where the framing opened back up, he slipped between the two-by-fours, hopped the retaining wall, and started to jog down the dark sidewalk. A broken streetlight sat at the corner, and as they got closer, Cass could make out the hood of a parked car. She followed Grayson as he darted toward the far side of the car, keeping it between them and the house. Together they crouched down, staying out of sight.

Grayson angled up to look through the windows, and when he dropped back down, he pulled out his phone and started thumbing the screen.

Confused and frustrated, Cass hissed, "What the hell?"

He shot her a look. "Give me a second." He went back to his phone, and minutes passed before he tilted it so she could see what he was looking at. A floor plan filled the screen. "They've set up at the back, here." He zoomed in on the rear of the house, which was laid out like the one they had just been in. "You go in through the garage and head down this hall here."

The hall had bedrooms and a laundry room branching off of it. Just beyond the laundry room, it opened into the living room, which spilled into the kitchen.

Cass eyed the alcove under Grayson's finger. "Where will you be?"

"I'll go in through the front." He shifted the floor plan to show the front porch that led to a foyer with a den off to the side, with the kitchen just beyond it. "I'll be here. Once you get into position, count to ten, throw your flash-bang, but stay back until I've taken my shot. Wait for the second flash-bang before you go in. Understood?"

Heart in her throat, she nodded. She switched the pipe to her other hand, wiped her sweaty palm on her pants, and then repositioned her grip on the weapon. With a grim expression, Grayson shoved his phone back into his pocket and pulled out his gun.

He gave her a long look. "Ready?"

"Ready."

They split up, Cass going through the doorless two-car garage and Grayson heading toward the front entryway. Cass tried to keep her footsteps light as she rushed across the cement and into the darkened interior. As she moved down the hall, the voices got clearer.

"Just leave her." That was Dana, her voice cold and snide.

"No," a harder, male voice answered. "We can still use her. I just need to break her."

"Good luck with that, asshole."

Her mother's familiar voice, although slurred, sent relief careening through Cass and weakened her knees. She leaned a shoulder against the wall until the weakness passed. There was a pained gasp that got Cass moving again. She crept toward the opening, careful to stay out of sight. She dared to sneak a quick look around the corner.

A slender male stood with his back to Cass. Dana was to his right, her arms crossed and a defiant pout on her face. In front of them, bound to a chair and looking worse for wear, was her mother. Just behind her and to the left was a second man, his chest and shoulders thick and broad, his feet braced apart.

Cass ducked back into the hall and carefully set the pipe against the wall so she could pull out the flash-bang. Holding it in her palm, she counted to ten then angled herself just enough to toss it toward the man closest to her. She ducked back and grabbed the pipe as the flash-bang hit the floor. A concussive boom and blinding burst of light erupted.

The gun shot that followed was dull by comparison. Then came a second explosion. The ground rattled under her feet, and her ears rang as she rushed from the hall, her makeshift bat at the ready. Through the cloud of hanging dust, she could barely make out her mom, who was struggling in her tipped-over chair. Cass was so focused on reaching her that she missed the body crumpled on the ground until she tripped over it. She lost her hold on the pipe as she simultaneously tried to keep her footing and sucked down a lungful of dust. Coughing, hunched over, eyes starting to water, she stumbled forward until a dull shout brought her head up just in time to see a shadow tinged with a sickly green glow charging toward her.

Dana's snarling face came into view, and Cass had one paralyzing moment to think, *Fuck*.

A sharp crack split the air, and the ground rose up as if some giant creature was sliding under it, then it slammed down, the wave throwing her one way and Dana another. Cass's back slammed into something with bruising force, and a bright burst of pain radiated from shoulder to hip as her ass hit the floor. A crack split the cement in front of her, and she watched in stunned amazement as it snaked its way across the floor with unnatural speed, arrowing for the two men locked in a struggle. She scrambled back, ignoring the pained protest of her body, and shoved herself to her feet with a vague thought of warning Grayson. She never got a chance.

"You bitch!"

A flash of green whipped through the dust-clogged air, and against her chest, the protection amulet flared in response. The spell hit Cass and knocked her back a step, but Grayson's protection held. Cass started to turn, but something crashed into her, slamming her to the ground. For the second time, her lungs forgot how to work. She didn't have time to panic as fingers closed around her neck in a brutal hold.

"You fucking interfering bitch!" Dana hissed, looming above her, hair dull with dust, eyes wild with fury, and face smeared with blood.

Shoving at the ground with her feet, Cass clawed at Dana's arms, leaving behind bloodied rake marks and torn skin as her lungs started to burn. She bucked and twisted but couldn't unseat Dana. The other woman's lips curled back in a feral snarl as she leaned in deeper. Desperate, Cass reached out, searching for something, anything. All she found was debris-ridden dirt.

Good enough.

Using both hands, she closed her eyes and shoved fistfuls of dirt into Dana's face, grinding it brutally in. Dana let go as she reared back with a shriek and tried to knock Cass's hands away. Cass bucked hard, throwing Dana off of her. Sucking air into her aching lungs, she rolled to her hands and knees then her pushed herself to her feet. Unsteady, coughing, she started toward Dana, who was standing, wiping at her face. Cass made it a couple of steps before the ground rolled again, and a panicked shout turned her attention behind her.

A slab of broken concrete hurtled in her direction. Instinctively, Cass dropped flat, arms over her head, as she waited for it to hit. There was a rush of air then a sickening thud.

She lowered her arms and turned to see where it had gone. Her stomach pitched. The concrete lay in pieces around the still, bloodied form of Dana. There was no time to process what had happened because the floor continued to roll, cracks spreading and widening, turning the once flat cement floor into a shifting pit of unnatural quicksand.

"Cassandra!"

She heard her name and saw her mother still bound to the damn chair and surrounded by broken concrete and boiling earth. "Mom!"

"Help!"

Cass scrambled up and ran toward her. The ground kept shifting, the noise ominous, and portions rose up like cement waves, so she had to dodge and weave. She could see Grayson fighting with the earth mage, magic heavy in the air, but had no way to help him. She jumped a widening gap where cement sank into the dirt and disappeared. She reached her mom, who lay on her side, still strapped to the chair. Around them, the ground kept crumbling, forming a pit. Cass started in on the rope at Rhea's ankles, but when the strands remained suspiciously solid instead of fraying, she realized they had been reinforced with magic. Her heart pounded, and panic clawed at her. She studied the way the wooden legs were screwed into the chair's base and knew the only way to get her mom free was to destroy it.

"The chair, Mom!"

Her mother's dirt-streaked, bruised face turned to her. "What?"

"The chair," Cass repeated, standing up and searching for something she could use to help. "I have to break the chair." She found a fist-sized chunk of concrete and grabbed it.

Comprehension replaced Rhea's dazed expression, and she stopped moving. "Okay, okay. Do it."

With the pit closing in, Cass pounded at the chair. The wood cracked and split and finally gave way. She and her mom got Rhea's hands free. They were working on her legs when an unearthly howl screamed through the room. A whirlwind of dirt erupted into violent life, picking up debris and adding it to the rock, dirt, and choking dust. The nightmarish twister tore through the open space, creeping closer and closer to Cass and her mom as the walls of the house shuddered and groaned.

Cass tried to ignore the twister and the pit as she lifted her concrete and, with a hoarse yell, slammed it down on the chair. With a crack, the last piece gave way. She was helping her mom claw free of broken wood and rope when something sharp sliced across her shoulders. With a pained hiss she looked up and realized they were out of time. The leading edge of the twister filled with lethal debris swirled through the air, and the pit around them had widened, eating the floor and trapping them in the path of the screaming dirt storm. Cass dove for her mom and curled awkwardly around her. She closed her eyes as the edge of the whirlwind hit, and her back and arms lit up with stinging bites. Behind her closed lids, an amber light danced while the storm intensified, filling the air with angry shrieks, turning those bites into gnawing agony. Unable to do anything else, Cass buried her face in her mom's hair and prayed.

Someone must have been listening, because after a few terrifying moments, the storm shut off as if a switch had been thrown. Her death grip on her mom loosened, and she lifted her head to see Grayson sink a vicious kick into the earth mage's gut. She barely registered her mom pulling away.

Then Rhea's face filled her vision. "Cassandra, get up!"

Snapped out of her strange daze, Cass shoved herself to her feet and then helped Rhea up. Her mom leaned heavily into her as they stared at the widening pit. The ring of violently churning earth was about three feet wide and growing.

"Can you jump that?" Cass asked her mother.

"Yes."

"Then go!"

Her mom took a stumbling jump, and Cass held her breath until Rhea landed on her hands and knees on the other side. Then it was Cass's turn. She pushed off, cleared the ring, and felt the jarring impact as her feet hit the uneven ground on the other side. She'd barely caught her balance when the air shifted and another dirt storm burst into life. Cass grabbed for her mom, found her hand, and pulled her in until she could wrap an arm around Rhea's waist. They stumbled forward as the symphony of creaks and groans intensified, and Cass wondered if they were about to be buried in this damn house from hell.

With eyes narrowed against the whirling dust and grit, she could barely see. Her foot hit something heavy, sending it skittering across the floor. The storm paused, and she caught a glimpse of Grayson's gun and, just beyond it, the hall that led to the front door. Without letting go of her mom, she grabbed the gun and turned to search for Grayson.

She found him just as he took a nasty hit that had him

reeling back and tripping over the Slider's body. Off-balance, Grayson fell back. His head hit the ground with a thud. With an enraged roar, the earth mage raised the two-by-four over his head, his intent clear.

Cass didn't think, just reacted. She brought the gun up, aimed at the earth mage, and pulled the trigger in a quick one-two shot. For a breathless moment, she thought she'd missed. The earth mage stumbled back, dropping the two-by-four, a hand raised his shoulder. He turned, his face a mask of fury, and took a step toward her. A burst of dark amber wrapped around his legs. There was a sickening crunch followed by the earth mage's agonized howl, and he dropped like a tree.

Grayson pushed himself to his feet. "Cass, you good?"

"I think so." She lowered the gun, the muscles in her arms quivering. "You?"

"I'm good." He looked at her mom. "Rhea?"

"I'm breathing," the older woman said as she leaned against Cass.

The ground rolled under their feet. Grayson spun to the earth mage, and the amber bindings flared. Another crunch sounded, followed by a thin scream. "Keep it up, and I won't stop at your legs, asshole."

"Fuck you." What was supposed to be a curse emerged as a whimper.

A car door slammed, then heavy footsteps rushed in. Cass had the gun pointed at the hall when Zane burst into the room.

He took in the destruction and drawled, "Am I late?"

epilogue

Two Days Later

GRAYSON HELD Cass's hand as they stood in Elias's hospital room. She seemed steadier, likely because she had spent most of yesterday and this morning talking to her family. He wasn't sure what all had been said, but the earlier tensions were replaced by the beginnings of something healthier. He figured she'd catch him up that night, which was good as they were headed back to Phoenix the next day. There was no room for Grayson to sit. Rhea sat on the edge of Elias's bed, while Sofia and Cole took the two visitors' chairs.

Nearby, Zane leaned against the wall, arms over his chest, as he filled them in. "Samson's still not talking."

"Not a surprise," Grayson said, thinking of the earth mage, who hadn't stopped fucking around until Grayson had shattered both his legs and his hips. That kind of defiance was fueled by stupidity or fanaticism, and since Samson was the brains behind this entire mess, he was far from stupid.

"No, but that will change." Zane sounded certain. "We're still trying to pin down the Slider's identity, but with Burton's additional resources, it's only a matter of time before we have that. As for Dana Marr, we had to dig deep to find her real name." He shot Cole a sympathetic look. "Daniella Novak."

Cole's skin still held a pallor, but his eyes were dark and hard. "She's related to Jude?"

"He's her uncle," Zane confirmed. "Her targeting you was twofold—taking revenge on the council for killing her uncle and using you for the Cabal."

"And Russ?" Elias asked.

"He and Daniella worked for the same company, and while we don't have solid proof, the assumption is she managed to convince him to work for the Cabal."

"And targeting us got them what?" Rhea asked as she held Elias's hand.

"A coup," Cole answered. "Pythia is a crucial component in many pivotal decisions."

"Including tracking a potential council member's nomination," Zane added.

According to what Cass had shared with Grayson the previous night, that potential would most likely turn into an actual council seat. When he'd asked if she was planning on sharing that information with Cole, she had shaken her head and told him she wasn't interested in tempting Fate anytime soon.

Next to him, Cass stirred and spoke up. "Not to mention that if the Cabal could embed an agent in Pythia, they could find a way to stop or change prediction outcomes."

"And if he was to marry into our family, even better." Sofia's tone was disillusioned. "Especially if he married the naive youngest daughter."

"Not so naive," Cass corrected gently. "You weren't going to go through with it."

Sofia gave her a small, grateful smile. "There is that."

Zane cleared his throat and appeared to be a little uncomfortable. "If it helps any, Russ had real feelings for you, which is why Dana turned on him."

Color rode under Sofia's cheeks, and sorrow shadowed her face for a moment before she looked away.

Feeling for her, Grayson decided to switch topics. "So, what happens now?"

Cole carefully got to his feet and straightened his shirt. "Now I have the lovely Candace verify that no more rats have infested my businesses, while Zane hunts the one pulling Samson's strings. In the meantime..." He walked over to Rhea and took her free hand. "I owe you and your family my sincerest apologies. I'm sorry for all of this ugly business. I would understand if you prefer to no longer continue our professional relationship."

"Don't, Cole." She pulled her hand free and shared a look with Elias, shadows flitting across her face. When she turned back to Cole, her expression was clear. "We've always been aware of the risks involved. Pythia has no reason to dissolve your contract, and my mother would have read me the riot act if I even suggested it."

A faint flash of humor lit Cole's eyes as he inclined his head. "Thank you." He turned and shook Elias's hand. "Elias."

"Cole."

Cole turned to Zane. "We have a meeting tomorrow, I believe?"

"I'll be there."

"Grayson, Cassandra, I appreciate all you've done," Cole said. "If you should ever need anything, please don't hesitate to ask." With that, the soon-to-be-councilman took his leave.

"I'm heading out too," Zane said as he straightened. "Mr. and Mrs. Ambrose. Sofia." He went to Cass and gave her a careful hug, mindful of the abrasion on her back. "Got to say, Cass, it's been interesting getting to know you."

She gave a small laugh as he let her go. "It's been something, that's for sure."

"You going to give Grayson a run for his money?" he teased.

She leaned into Grayson. "That's the hope."

"Good luck, then." The Hunter turned to Grayson, and they clasped hands. "You give me a call when you get back from Phoenix."

"Will do, man, and you keep me posted."

"Deal."

As the door closed behind Zane, Cass squeezed Grayson's waist then let him go. He uncurled his arm so she could go to her parents. She walked to the other side of Elias's bed and touched her father's arm. "We're going to say goodbye now, Dad, since we head out early in the morning."

Elias's hand turned and grasped Cass's as she bent down to press her lips against his head. She whispered something, and the older man closed his eyes. "Love you too, Cass."

She straightened, her eyes shiny with unshed tears. Her glasses were long gone, lost at some point when they were trying to save Cole. She came around the bed as Rhea rose, and the two women hugged. Then it was Sofia's turn.

"Don't get up," Cass chided, bending down to hug her sister. "You call me for anything, understand?"

Sofia nodded against her and pulled back. "I will."

Grayson did his round of farewells, and then they were leaving. They stepped out of the hospital into the bright afternoon sun, and when they got to his car, he pulled her to a stop, looping his arms around her hips and holding her close. "You good?"

She brushed her hands over his chest as if smoothing out his shirt. "Yeah, I am." She looked up at him. "You sure you want to do this?" *This* being finding out just what kind of opportunities a Key like him could find in Phoenix.

"Wouldn't have offered if I wasn't."

"It's a lot, and it's sudden."

It was, but he was willing to take the risk with her and for her. "I like my odds."

Her eyes sparked, and her lips curved in a mysterious, sexy, knowing smile as she rose on tiptoe to kiss him. "Me too."

Not ready to close your tab at Wonderland?
*Then let me pour you another round of intrigue as Isa and Locke join the party in **BITTER SPIRITS**, wherever books are sold.*

If you don't want to miss out on exclusives and new release information, sign up for Jami's monthly newsletter at
https://www.subscribepage.com/jami-gray-books

Share the love and leave a review at your favorite book dealer!

Not ready to leave the world of the Arcane? Then go back to the starting line with the Arcane Transporter series, available at all retailers.

about the author

"This story is an emotional roller coaster, from betrayal, anger, fear, love..." —InD'tale Magazine

Jami Gray is the coffee addicted, music junkie, Queen Nerd of her personal Geek Squad, Alpha Mom of the Fur Minxes, who writes to soothe the voices crammed in her head. Her series combine high-stakes urban fantasy and edgy paranormal romantic suspense into books you don't want to put down. Buckle up and get ready for a wild ride through the fascinating worlds of the Arcane, the Kyn, the PSY-IV Teams, and the Collapse.

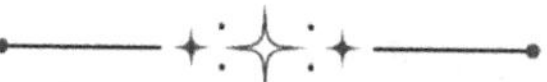

Come visit Jami's website at **https://www.jamigray.com** and stay up to date on what kind of trouble she's getting into and when you can expect to join in.

amazon.com/author/jamigray

instagram.com/jamigrayauthor

facebook.com/JamiGrayWriter

threads.com/@jamigrayauthor

goodreads.com/JamiGray

bookbub.com/authors/jami-gray